# SNOW HALL

*Recent Titles by Elizabeth Gill from Severn House*

DREAM BREAKERS
THE FOXGLOVE TREE
THE HOMECOMING
HOME TO THE HIGH FELLS
PARADISE LANE
THE PREACHER'S SON
THE SECRET
SILVER STREET
SNOW HALL
SWAN ISLAND
SWEET WELLS
WHEN DAY IS DONE
WHERE CURLEWS CRY

# SNOW HALL

## Elizabeth Gill, *1950 -*

This first world edition published 2010
in Great Britain and in the USA by
SEVERN HOUSE PUBLISHERS LTD of
9–15 High Street, Sutton, Surrey, England, SM1 1DF.

British Library Cataloguing in Publication Data

Gill, Elizabeth, 1950-
  Snow Hall.
  1. Inheritance and succession–Fiction. 2. Durham (England
  : County)–Social conditions–20th century–Fiction.
  I. Title
  823.9'14-dc22


ISBN-13: 978-0-7278-6942-5    (cased)

*All Severn House titles are printed on acid-free paper.*

Severn House Publishers support The Forest Stewardship Council [FSC],
the leading international forest certification organisation. All our titles that
are printed on Greenpeace-approved FSC-certified paper carry the FSC logo.

**Mixed Sources**
Product group from well-managed
forests and other controlled sources
www.fsc.org  Cert no. SA-COC-1565
© 1996 Forest Stewardship Council

Typeset by Palimpsest Book Production Ltd.,
Falkirk, Stirlingshire, Scotland.
Printed and bound in Great Britain by
MPG Books Ltd., Bodmin, Cornwall.

*For Carol Robinson*
*Thank you*

# Author's Note

I have used the name Snow Hall for the main house in my story simply because I liked it. The original Snow Hall was built in 1622 on the River Tees and has nothing to do with my book. The other house, Black Well Tower, I simply made up. Lots of houses in the north-east have similar names.

# One

*1907 Castle Bank Colliery, County Durham*

It was almost summer but for weeks and weeks it had hardly stopped raining and there in the back room of the shop it was as cold as November and almost as dark. Lorna Robson could barely see beyond her finger ends and it was not nearly time to stop work for the day. The lamps could not be lit, her aunt would be in the back of the shop in seconds if she saw such a thing, yet at the front, beyond the closed door, Lorna could see a line of light and knew that, with the neat and discreet windows such as benefited what her aunt called 'an exclusive ladies' millinery salon', it would be ablaze with lights so as to attempt to attract 'passing trade'.

That was another of her aunt's sayings. As far as Lorna could tell there never had been passing trade and why would there be? They lived in a small pit village and of course there was custom because both men and women wore hats. They needed to buy them somewhere and they needed them mending but no fine lady had ever walked through the door of 51 High Street.

Lorna doubted whether her aunt's dream would come true and sometimes she had noticed her aunt looking out through the rain at the long wide straight street, dreaming that someone would come past in a shiny carriage with matching horses or that down at the bottom of the High Street even now some well-dressed man would step from a cloud of steam by a soon to be departing train and would, in his long coat and trilby hat and gold-topped cane, make his way with neat soldier-like steps and would pause outside the shop and open the door and step inside and the bell would tinkle and he would order a hat to be made for a special occasion – a top hat for a society event in London.

Her aunt would sit him down and measure his head with polite dexterity meanwhile keeping up a flow of conversation about events of the day to amuse him. Perhaps he would order several hats over a period of time because he was moving into the area and he had a wife who would want hats for going to church and to parties and for visiting friends. Maybe she would even notice some of the hats which were already on display in the shop. Her aunt had made them years ago when she first began the business and her hopes were high.

There were close-fitting hats to follow the shape of the wearer's head and wide-brimmed ones to keep off the June sunshine and bonnets in pink and blue for babies and round-brimmed hats for little girls and special hats trimmed with pheasant feathers glistening blue, green, black and brown, and some with tiny black veils for mourning and hats with cherries – not real, of course – and hats with long ribbons for gala days and winter wool hats to keep out the freezing north wind which cut across the high fells and hats with strings to tie neatly under old ladies' chins and hats so wide and yet dipping that lovers could kiss in secret beneath their shadow.

As it was, the customers her aunt would have wanted, such as the doctor's wife, the wives of the pit owners and the steel foundry and even the tradesmen like the butcher's and the hardware store, went into Bishop Auckland or even further to Durham City, stepping on to the train early in the morning and coming back after tea, laden with parcels.

The pitmen wore cloth caps and her aunt said with some bitterness that she was glad of it, they were good customers, only because she sold men's hats she had to employ a man to serve them and there were two sides to the shop for slight discretion in such matters and it was expensive to hire Mr Humble who came in every day though Lorna thought privately that Mr Humble was either miserly or was paid very badly for he was a shabby man of indeterminate age.

She thought he must be old because he complained that all the standing around played havoc with his varicose veins. Her aunt would not allow either Mr Humble or herself to sit down. She thought it made them look as though they were not busy even though Lorna suspected they might stand for hours before anyone entered the shop, she could hear the bell from where she sat.

Lorna was able to sit down as she sewed but then she was out of sight. Her aunt always sighed when she said that as though Lorna's lot was a much easier one than her own, which Lorna thought was not the case. She saw nobody all day and did nothing other than repairs most of the time of which there were a great many. Men's caps and hats were brought in by their wives and were often greasy with the odd hair attached and they smelled stalely of tobacco and sweat and felt sticky to the hands.

New hats for the local women never seemed to need a satin rose – which her aunt had taught her to make very early on in her career – or a neatly placed piece of good material to enhance the brim. A hat could be transformed by a band of colour. Among the matrons of the church and chapel the colours were always serviceable, black, navy or brown, and did not require ornament of any kind. It made for dull work. Lorna knew that had she had to keep the front of the shop as her aunt did she too would soon have been gazing into the distance, eyes searching the disappearing road for a carriage or the pavement opposite for a tall dark figure with a gold-topped cane.

She always went in by the back way so she had no opportunity to look for such things but she knew as well as her aunt that the sights on the front street were of pit wives in headscarves – the worst head covering of all, it made her aunt sigh to see such things – carrying their heavy shopping bags filled with flour and sugar and potatoes, the pitmen black from a long shift on the way home or small boys bareheaded and shouting their way towards broth over the kitchen fire.

All she could see was the darkness of the room around her and all she could hear was the sound of somebody calling across the back lane or the goods train puffing away from the little town.

It was well into the evening when Lorna finished. The lamps had been lit for three hours by then but the fire had been allowed to die down – her aunt was always afraid that she would daydream and set the building on fire and also, unlike the pit families, they had to buy their coal, so the fire had seen no new coal for at least two hours. Her fingers were numb with cold and because she had not moved since mid-afternoon when her aunt made tea, her body was stiff and unyielding when her aunt locked the outside door and came through and said, as she always did, 'I think that's enough for today, Lorna, don't you?' as though Lorna might protest and say with a flourish that she was not quite finished the creation she was working on, there was just a bow here and an ostrich feather there in pink and white to be tweaked.

She put down the last of the repairs, Mrs Tweddle's Sunday best hat, which had been sadly torn when it blew into a gorse bush the previous Sunday on the way back from the Presbyterian church on the edge of the town where the High Street converged on the two roads, Bridge Street which led away to Bishop Auckland and Wolsingham Road which led down into Weardale.

Lorna's aunt had tried to sell Mrs Tweddle a very good hatpin which would have made the repair unnecessary as she pointed out had Mrs Tweddle owned such a useful item in the first instance but Mrs Tweddle said she had two at home and had just mislaid them. The repair could barely be detected, Lorna thought with some pride, but her aunt merely looked at it, sniffed and said she felt sure Mrs Tweddle would have been a great deal better off to have bought something new as it must be ten years old, it certainly looked it.

They trod together up the chilly narrow stairs to their living quarters and Lorna wished as she did at about this time each evening that it could be fine and she might go out for a few breaths of air because it was still light. Her aunt rarely entertained it even in summer because she was convinced that the young miners stood outside the public house, drinking beer and making rude remarks in the light nights as 'ladies' passed by. Her aunt always called women 'ladies', even the least of them, as though calling them so would enable them overnight to become valued customers, the kind of women who could 'carry a hat'. Her aunt longed for even one person who could 'carry a hat well', someone with a long neck and aristocratic bearing.

Lorna had never heard the young pitmen shouting remarks across the street but even if they had she would barely have understood it because they had a language which was all their own and she had never mixed with them and her aunt said that was not the point, that no decent woman should understand what they said but they must not be given the opportunity.

Unfortunately there were public houses in almost every direction except at the back, sometimes three or four to a street with names like the Victoria, the Colliery Inn and the Pit Laddie, and then Lorna had to walk past three or four streets to get clear of the town and her aunt was not convinced that the people who lived in Railway Street and Station Road were the kind of people you would want to encounter so Lorna's walks were very often cut short unless she escaped beyond the shrillness of her aunt's voice.

There was no chance of any of this now and as they reached the top of the house her aunt said, as she always said, that it was not too cold because heat rose from below and became trapped beneath the roof. They had three rooms up here, a small kitchen, a bedroom and a dining room cum sitting room where they sat to eat their supper. Tonight it was pie and peas and then they sat over the fire, drinking their tea before bed.

They slept in one bed in the room next door. Lorna sometimes lay awake thinking that if she should ever have enough money she would sleep in a bed by herself, perhaps even in a room by herself, so that she would not have to endure the somehow over-familiarity of her aunt's warm and unpleasant breath, or the way that her mouth fell open as she snored or her freezing bare feet which were always on Lorna's side of the bed since she contrived to sleep sideways.

If it had been warm Lorna might have got up and opened the window – her aunt didn't believe in night air so Lorna would wait until she fell asleep – and then she could lie awake and listen to the silence or even an owl hooting away down past the station and along the lane in the vicarage garden. Sometimes there were two owls, calling to one another across the lawns while the town slept and out on the fells the pit wheels turned as the miners laboured.

# Two

Aidan Hedley had ended up going to the old man's funeral. He told himself that he ought to go but the real reason was out of respect for his own father, and standing outside St Oswald's Church in Durham City in the pouring rain he found that but for the Carlyles, a few old women who Aidan was convinced made it their hobby to attend funerals and a tramp who had come in to keep out of the rain, it was an empty church.

The Carlyles were a very old northern family and something like seven hundred years ago had been cattle-rustlers and sheep-stealers along the border and since then had risen to riches and prosperity. They owned a wonderful house, Snow Hall, in five hundred acres on a piece of land where they had lived for as far back as anyone could remember though they had not lived there for fifteen years since the old man had been taken ill and moved in with his son's family to a much more modest house, Black Well Tower.

Snow Hall was the prettiest place that Aidan had ever seen. It sat amongst a wealth of fields which in the summertime were blue and orange with wildflowers waving in the warm wind. It had been there since thirteen hundred as far as he knew and had been lost by the family during the Rising of the North when many of the nobles of Durham, Northumberland, Yorkshire and Cumberland had thought to replace Elizabeth with Mary, Queen of Scots. They had been Catholics and wished to remain Catholic. Those of them who were not hanged, drawn and quartered did not go back to their inheritance for many a year but after that they had prospered somehow, as adventurers often did, he thought.

The house had a great hall at one side and a chapel at the other, outside staircases to extend the romantic idea. The staircases had crumbled, the family had done the same but you could not keep a Carlyle down, so the saying went, and they had risen. For a long time after the foiled attempt at altering history it had been a farmhouse but was won back and restored at least two hundred years ago and had been the envy of their many neighbours ever since.

There were people who gloried in the way that the grandfather would allow no one of his family to live there these last fifteen years and Aidan could not help but be curious as to what would happen now and also he had a vested interest because he was the Carlyles' solicitor.

He had inherited this from his father and his father before him. The Carlyles and the Hedleys had history back so far that Aidan would not have hesitated to call it a thousand years though he thought it was only the romantic in him which allowed his usually accurate solicitor's reasoning to waver that far.

The Carlyle family had had half a dozen paper mills on the River Wear and it was commonly known that the mills had been losing money for years. Foreign imports had been the downfall of a dozen local mills and the ones that were left were struggling. The mills had long since been sold for what Aidan didn't imagine was a vast profit in a falling market.

The Carlyles didn't look as if they were in a bad way if expensive clothes were anything to go by. The women wore furs against the cold rain and the kind of ridiculous hats which Aidan did not doubt had been handmade by Newcastle milliners. Leather gloves encased slender hands which he was sure had never worked.

Ralph Carlyle was still in his twenties but was already widowed. His wife had died two years ago after giving him a son. The child had been dead within the week, the mother soon after, falling from a second-storey balcony in midwinter. Some said grief had carried her there, others that it was an accident.

Ralph was tall and black-haired and dark-eyed and looked as though he had just come screaming down a glen, Aidan thought, kilt and hair flying, brandishing some sort of old-fashioned weapon in both fists, scaring seven kinds of shit out of the enemy. He was a border man and in this region you were often Scottish fighting English, Scot and Scot or English and English, for reiving had gone on sideways as well as across the border and nobody was free from it and many a woman bore the enemy's child.

The other Carlyles were Henry, the older brother, who was fat and perspiring in his dark suit and tight collar, his wife, Camille, and older people, uncles and aunts, Aidan guessed, and other minor members of the family. Ralph's father, Stephen, had died, supposedly of drink and excess, some years earlier.

St Oswald's was a big church and with so few people in attendance it looked even bigger and emptier. Aidan could not help comparing the scene with his father's funeral a year ago, his mother tight-lipped, his sister, Beatrice, singing hymns and how she had afterwards hidden in the hall cupboard when her emotions bettered her. He had stood outside, saying, in a soft voice, 'Bea, will you please come out of there?' so that the mourners in the drawing room would not hear.

Eventually she had emerged, blowing her nose with gusto and brushing him off.

St Cuth's, as it was affectionately known, the local saint Cuthbert being of such importance that his name was always shortened, at the top of North Road, had been packed with family and friends and everybody who had known Aidan's father whether he was their solicitor or not was there, his father had been so well liked.

It was unfortunate that his father's partner, Cyril Jameson, had died almost two months afterwards, leaving Aidan in sole charge of the firm. Cyril Jameson had had neither wife, children nor relatives to inherit, had lived with Aidan's family since a young man when he first came to Durham and then at the County Hotel and had left his share of the business to Aidan.

Having inherited everything with the proviso from his father that his mother and Bea should be allowed to stay in the house either until they married or died, Aidan was lost for words. His sister, however, was not.

'What a wonderful prospect,' she had said bitterly.

'I'll make half of it over to you,' he offered.

'Don't be ridiculous,' she said, 'you need money to run the offices and the house and I wouldn't insult you even though I feel insulted myself.'

It was the more galling for her, he thought, because she was older than him.

'You could study.'

'At thirty-three?' She looked scornfully at him. She did not say, 'Besides, Mother needs me,' but it was true. His sister ran the house. After his father died his mother had gone into what was popularly known as 'a decline'. His parents had had the kind of marriage which had put off himself and Bea, that was the truth of it, his mother was never happy with anything and made her feelings felt daily, his father would hide at the office or go out without her and she would complain of neglect. His father had been a gentle, scholarly man who would fight like a lion for the people who came to him but was too tired to do so at home and they had all suffered for it.

Aidan had made both his mother and Bea allowances which Bea called 'obscenely generous'.

'Please, Bea,' he said, 'don't make me feel any worse.'

His mother merely sniffed and said things had come to a pretty pass when her son dictated her income.

'You could have a house of your own if you would like,' he told his sister.

'What, leave you here with Mother? You would strangle her within a week or do you suggest that we should both go and leave her alone?'

'It's a nice idea,' he admitted, knowing that neither of them would do it.

'Besides,' she said, 'people would gossip if I lived alone and whatever would I do?'

There was however one thing which he thought his sister might like.

'We could move. We could afford a much better house.'

His mother would not be swayed.

'Why ever would we move? It's close to the church.'

His mother's only consideration, he thought, was the church and it was true. St Cuth's was just across the road and a little way up past the Garden House Hotel. His mother abhorred drink and every time she went to church she looked beyond the hotel as though it did not exist.

The only thing she cared for about the house was that there should be no alcohol in it and he and Bea had taken to hiding wine, whisky and brandy in various places which his mother did not visit, as though they were drunkards, and all these things, instead of being something which could be taken moderately at table and when they liked, had taken on the delicious air of illicitness.

Bea, of course, could not sneak off to the Garden House and various other places in the town which Aidan frequented but

Aidan went to pubs quite often in the evenings with his friend, Ned Fleming, who ran the local newspaper, the *Durham County Chronicle*, which was the weekly and of late the *Guardian*, which was the new daily.

The past year had therefore been a huge burden both at home and at the office. Now Aidan was almost afraid to sing among so few voices, he did not trust himself to manage the song or the words because of his memories but he did because it would be noticed if he did not.

Since his father and Mr Jameson had died Aidan had had nothing but female company at home so he liked to linger at the office, to say nothing of the fact that there was far too much work.

'You might say when you're not coming home to dinner,' Bea told him as he arrived just as the grandfather clock in the hall struck nine. 'Mother had the meal put back twice and the beef was kizened.'

He made no explanation and ventured into the study, only to find that she followed him there.

'Old Carlyle's funeral bad, was it?' she asked.

He sighed with relief at her understanding.

'Only the Carlyles, half a dozen women with nothing better to do and a gentleman of the road.'

There was a knock on the door and the maid brought in a tray. 'Thank you, Heather, my brother is extremely grateful for your forbearance and tell Mrs Donald to try not to spit curses over the kitchen fire because of him.'

Heather laughed and went out. Aidan looked over at the tray.

'Kizened beef sandwiches just for you,' Bea said and she went over and put several, cut neatly into triangles, on to a plate and poured tea for him.

He had already seen the wrinkled frown on her brow and he knew that she was worried about the situation of the Carlyle inheritance.

'The trouble is now that I have to find the granddaughter, since he left her everything. I doubt she's called Carlyle any more.'

Bea handed him cup, saucer and plate and then she sat down, facing away from the window. It was a lovely summer's evening and the sunshine was casting great shadows across the lawn but he was too tired to care or ask to have the windows opened.

'And how do you think Ralph is going to react to that?' Bea said. 'He must think he's finally going to get his hands on the house.'

'I've no doubt he thinks so but he won't. I will have her found and I've seen the birth certificate and her first name is Lorna.'

Bea frowned.

'Don't you think you should start with any servants they used to have?'

'I don't know of any.'

'Don't you remember old Mrs Storey?'

'She died in the winter.'

'What about that woman he used to . . .' she stopped there and said with mock refinement, 'what on earth is the term – bounce?'

Aidan choked over his sandwich.

'No?' she said, pressing her lips together so that she wouldn't laugh. 'Roger?'

Aidan put down the rest of the sandwich.

'Robson,' his sister said.

'I never heard it called that—'

She saw the glee in his eyes. 'Idiot,' she said.

'I think you're right, you know, Bea. Wasn't it something silly like Fenella? Felicity!'

'That's right,' Bea said, getting excited, 'but why on earth would she get involved?'

'When the son's wife died and the son disappeared perhaps old man Carlyle paid her to take the child away.'

'Why would he do that? You can say what you like about the Carlyles but they stick together. They wouldn't throw out a child of their name.'

'There must have been a good reason,' Aidan said.

Aidan was not so very surprised therefore several days later when his secretary, Mrs Manners, came into his office, looking rather flustered, to tell him that Mr Carlyle would like to see him.

'He has no appointment and you have Mr Finch in less than thirty minutes and I told him—'

Ralph Carlyle appeared in the doorway at that point and Aidan was obliged to tell her that it was all right and she went away after giving Ralph the kind of look which most would-be intruders gained. He flashed her a smile that would have made Eskimos homeless and waited until she closed the door before standing in the middle of Aidan's rather worn carpet, dominating the room in a way which made you feel as though you ought to get to your feet and defend your territory or he would end up making off with your cattle and your wife. Aidan didn't move.

'Mr Carlyle. Good morning.'

Ralph reached for the nearest chair and put it down heavily at the other side of the desk.

'I saw you at the funeral. Why haven't you been in touch?' and he sat down in the chair which was two hundred years old and not used to being hauled away from its nesting place near the window like that. Aidan made a mental note to have it taken out of the room before it suffered any more damage. 'Isn't it usual to read the will to the family?'

'Only when it concerns them.'

That made Ralph pause.

'Didn't the old bastard leave me everything, then?' Ralph sat back in his chair and put one expensively shod foot on the other knee in a way which was no doubt supposed to imply that he was relaxed. 'I had a feeling he wouldn't somehow. He had no friends, no servants, he damned well lived on us, I looked after him. The ungrateful old sod. You might have told me, instead of leaving me to find out like this. Damn it all, I need the money.'

Aidan said nothing. He wished he had had time to prepare for this, he had known Ralph would do it.

'Snow Hall must be worth a fortune and as for the property, it's in a good site right next to the newspaper office. I'm sure Fleming would buy it from me, he wants to expand. So who gets it?'

'You know very well I can't discuss it with you.'

'I'm going under, like a lot more people. I was depending on that. I have a lot of family to consider.'

Aidan wished that just for once he could say what he thought, that Ralph might have bought fewer diamonds and fur coats for his women friends and horses and carriages for himself and spent less time at the races losing money, that he could have given fewer lavish parties, spent more time at the mills instead of leaving the managers to get by themselves.

He had not been a good owner, he had spent nothing on
the kind of new machinery which might have got him out of the
financial hole he was now very firmly in, he had not been a good
employer, he hadn't looked after the people who had worked for
him. His neglect, coupled with the times, Aidan allowed, had
meant they had lost the mills some time since. Ralph was not
even a good man and yet it was difficult having him here in the
office not just because Aidan was his solicitor but because Ralph
obviously thought of him as a friend.

'You never come to my parties. Do you think you're above me?'

'Of course I don't,' Aidan said quickly.

'Well, that's how it comes across. You don't want to be asso-
ciated with me—'

'I'm your solicitor first.'

'You're obviously my grandfather's solicitor first.'

'You know very well there's nothing I can do.'

Ralph got to his feet. Aidan made himself stay where he was
for a few moments, allowing Ralph to tower over him and then
he got up and their eyes were on a level once more.

'Mr Gray is in the general office. He'll show you out,' he said.

'You'll regret this, you sanctimonious bastard,' Ralph said softly
and he turned around and swung out of the room, banging the
door so hard that it shook. Aidan waited for the slamming of
the outside door and after that there was silence.

There were thousands of people called Robson in Durham, Aidan
had discovered. There was no way he could send letters to them
all and what if the girl had not changed her name. He could not
also send letters to people called Carlyle though at least there
were not many of those. Robson seemed to him a much better
idea but he could not think what he should do next. When he
went to look at the Carlyle records none of it was any help.
There was no mention of Shaun Carlyle's marriage or of the
child's birth.

He toyed with the idea that names had been changed even
further so that they would not be found but that made him so
depressed that he gave up on it and tried to think positively. If
the Robson woman had taken the child why should she worry
about being found, after all what had been done had most likely

been done in a legitimate perhaps even friendly manner? She had no need to hide, she had done nothing wrong as far as he knew except give a child a home when nobody else seemed to want her or her grandfather trusted nobody with her.

It took Bea to do the intelligent thing. She came to the office one morning about a week after the funeral and sat across the desk from him and said, 'It occurs to me that you have not thought very carefully about this.' She sat forward in her enthusiasm. 'If the woman was called Robson and she took the child away and she was not married the rest is obvious, isn't it?'

'Don't let's play guessing games, just tell me.'

'She must be in business of some kind.'

Aidan cursed himself inwardly for his stupidity. Bea was right.

'Unless she married?' he said.

'With a small child? Not very likely around here. Middle-class women have no one to marry in the pit villages and unless she moved a long way from here – and it would depend on her resources – she does something.'

'Like what?'

'Housekeeping.'

'Or?'

'What about a shop,' Bea said. 'She could still be here in Durham though I think it most unlikely. If it were me I would go but not too far. Let me see if I can locate her.' Aidan began to protest and then stopped. His sister had little enough to do and she fretted, being at home all day with his mother.

Bea had a friend called Imelda Watson who owned a shop at the end of Elvet Bridge. Bea loved the shop. Imelda prided herself on the fact that she had London fashions and Bea and her mother and most of their friends met there not just to buy but to talk. Imelda's shop was no small affair and the back of it had windows which overlooked the river with a straight drop since there was nothing but falling ground thick with vegetation beneath it.

The shop was one of Bea's favourite haunts. Imelda was a clever woman and managed to blend business and socializing to such an extent that the prosperous women of the area spent their money painlessly, knowing that they did not have to buy to be there.

Imelda said privately to Bea that she considered her shop as a women's club. There was no name on the door or above the premises on the hoarding. All it said was '11 Elvet' in silver over black and the windows were a source of interest to people passing by, so classy that they would stop to gaze on their way from one main thoroughfare to another so almost everybody passed the shop at least once a week. They would point and sometimes laugh, depending upon what Imelda put in the window.

Sometimes, like this month, there was a single figure in the left-hand side window, wearing the kind of thing a woman would be wearing to go to a seaside town and around her the back-drop was a painting of the sea, the sky, a pier and on the floor by her feet, which were clad in gold sandals with improbable-looking jewels, were exquisite large and fine shells in wonderful intricate shapes, pink within and amber and pale pearl and white without.

In the other window was another figure, in the sort of outfit one might wear for a wedding since June was a favourite month for brides. The church was painted on to the background, hand-fuls of confetti lay on the ground. Imelda did the windows herself, labouring in the evenings, and many a time Bea went in and helped and other friends would drop in to assist with the painting or the placing of various objects so that they felt that they had a part in the whole thing and they would drink tea and congrat-ulate themselves on their taste and bring their friends to the shop to see what they had done.

On the particular morning that Bea went in several of her mother's friends were already sipping coffee at small cream tables and eating pastries which were provided daily by the Silver Street cafe across the Market Place and down towards the other bridge. It was a narrow street and in the early mornings the smell of cinnamon and apricots baking in sweet pastry wafted up and down the cobbled street so that people could not resist going in and buying the glistening brown and amber delicacies.

Others had strawberry jam swirling through the pastry which was golden with egg yolk and others had almonds and honey and Imelda bought these and warmed them as though they were ready baked and the smell of freshly ground coffee would seep its way through the shop.

She had two assistants, one was her sister, Chloe, who was older than she was and brought in the newly married set, and then there was her mother, Phyllis, who brought in older custom, so when Bea indicated she wished to speak privately Imelda ushered her through into the office at the back.

A tiny window looked out at the river. The university students were mostly gone now but there was someone sculling on the river below. For the past two weeks it was common to see the students in evening dress on the streets, singing merrily when the almost darkness fell before midnight and playing violins at the parties in the various houses' back gardens.

Bea had only heard music played so freely when she and her father and mother and Aidan had spent their holiday in Venice and from the balcony of their hired house there was the sweet smell of baking and the sharp wistfulness of violins. Bea was always sorry when the students left for the long summer break. It was comforting, she thought, that however old one grew the students remained the same age.

The office at the back of the shop was cluttered with boxes, papers, clothes on rails and Imelda had to find a chair for Bea before they could talk. Bea explained the problem and was met with silence.

'Of course she could have married or she could have moved so far away that we won't find her or she might not be in business or—'

She stopped there because Imelda held up a hand.

'I have heard something. I wish I could remember. Robson. Robson. Yes.' She looked triumphantly at Bea. 'Henrietta Callan bought two hats from me last week and I remember she spoke to me and said that there was a draper – no, it wasn't, it was a milliner – because she was going to go there, it being not that far away but you know they live in the middle of nowhere. But she didn't want to take a chance on somebody she wasn't sure of. Hats are of such importance, being the first thing that people notice about what one wears.'

Bea waited impatiently.

'Where was this?' she asked after what seemed to her like an interminable pause.

'I wish I could recall. My mother might know.'

'Could you ask her discreetly?'

'I could try.'

She left Bea and was gone but a few minutes though it seemed like a short forever. She came back triumphant.

'She remembered,' Imelda said.

# Three

Felicity Robson had taken to getting up earlier than she had done before and even though it was by now midsummer the early mornings were cold, the little town thick with mist. Up there on the hilltops it had snowed only the week before and had lingered where it could be seen for several hours before the wan sunshine finally melted it into the rapid streams which had run down the hillsides for thousands of years, causing narrow gullies and in places sparkling waterfalls, alongside the farms which were set grey into the more sheltered places.

She had begun getting up earlier after the first letter had arrived. She was unused to having such post, a thick cream envelope and formal educated writing on the front and they were addressed to 'Miss Lorna Carlyle'. It had been so long since she had seen the name written down that it made her hands shake when she picked it up from the tiny mat which stood behind the front door of the shop.

She had not wanted to open it, she had taken it upstairs and put it into the little table drawer where she did her accounts and she had tried to pretend that it had not arrived but she could not sleep, she lay awake long after Lorna was breathing quietly and evenly in the little room above the workshop and after several hours she got up and found it in the darkness and then she went softly downstairs where she lit a lamp and she opened it with trembling fingers.

It was from a Durham solicitor. The years rolled back when she saw it. They had found her. Her first instinct was to leave but she could not. She had no money, she had nowhere to go, she could not pick up Lorna as she might have done when Lorna was a child. All the letter said was that they wished her to contact them, there was no information at all. She quickly folded up the letter and put it into the pocket of her dressing gown and then she went back to bed. She tried to calm herself, she would burn the letter in the morning and then she would decide what to do and she would have some time before anything else happened.

When the second letter came Felicity burned the first and kept the second in the same place. Somehow if there was only one it didn't seem too bad. There was an interval of more than four weeks before the second arrived but after that she could not sleep and lay there, dry-eyed and guilty, as the long summer wore past.

She couldn't eat and would stand by the window day after day, thinking that there might be another letter or that even worse someone would arrive to make enquiries. It was August and the summer had turned to rain after a hot July.

At first people were glad of it for their gardens and allotments but gradually they began to complain about it, that it was just like early summer had been and could they never have two days together when it was sunshiny, that the vegetables were rotting in their beds because they were standing in water. People went out only when they had to in such weather and in the shop some days it was no pleasure to be there.

The rain had stopped on the day that the young man came to the shop. It was midday and September and Mr Humble had gone home for his dinner. Sometimes she envied him that. There was no one ever to do such things for her. She was so alone. In other circumstances she would have been pleased to see the young man.

He was just the kind of person she had hoped to see there and she wished that there had been a lot of people on the broad pavement outside her windows to observe his entrance and then she changed her mind. He had an air of business about him, not somebody who had nothing more to do on a Tuesday morning than make his way up the High Street. He moved with a kind of dedicated patience, as though, being so young, he could have walked the length of the long street in moments but because of his trade he did not. He was used, she thought, to dealing with difficult problems.

He was about thirty and had a prosperous look about him. His suit was expensive, his hands had never seen any kind of physical work and there was an intelligent look in his shrewd blue eyes. He walked in with resolution. Felicity had to stop herself from fleeing, either into the back or away down the street. She could do neither.

'Good morning,' he said, as he closed the door and doffed his hat. 'I am Aidan Hedley. I am a solicitor. Are you Miss Felicity Robson?'

She wanted to deny it, to say that she was the shop assistant, but there was no point. When she didn't answer him he went on.

'You have a Miss Carlyle living here with you. I need to speak to her.'

'There is no one here of that name,' she said.

'I have written twice over a number of weeks and have received no reply. I would like to speak to her.'

He looked about the shop as though his quarry would materialize and seeing no one, his gaze was drawn to the closed door which led to the back of the shop.

'Could you please tell her that I am here?'

She didn't speak or move.

'Perhaps you would prefer it if I went for the constable?'

Still she made no reply.

'Is she Miss Robson, perhaps? I have business with her. I've expended time, energy, paper and ink. Please don't let us waste any more of these.'

'You have no right on my premises.'

At that moment, possibly because they had raised their voices, the door to the back of the shop opened and Lorna stood there. Felicity tried to see her as he would. She was like an animal emerging from a cage, blinking because the rain was not darkening the sky now, it was almost the end of the storm and the pavements were silver, the light rose from them almost as harshly as sunshine.

Felicity did not delude herself. Lorna was pale because she only went out on Sundays. She wore cheap ill-fitting clothes. Her brown hair was pushed into a bun like she was much older and had half come down since early morning when it was hastily contained and her clothes were so blue that they were almost black.

She was thin, her wrists were bony rather than slender and her hands were red from constant work. Her eyes had no particular light and no special colour, Felicity had not thought before.

Aidan was undeceived. The girl before him might have been

any poor seamstress, ruining her sight in a back room for more prosperous women's vanity, but she had one distinguishing feature which made her unmistakable. She had the same eyes as Ralph Carlyle and on a woman of such pale face they were even more noticeable. Her white cheeks accentuated the huge dark brown of them as she stared across the room. Aidan made no mistake.

'Miss Carlyle,' he said, 'how do you do? I'm Aidan Hedley, your family's solicitor. I've come here to speak to you.'

It seemed to Aidan a good long time before Miss Robson moved in front of the girl so he looked at her as best he could. 'I have written to you twice. Did you receive my letters?'

'No letters came and there is no one here they should have come to,' Miss Robson said.

The girl spoke and it was for the first time and her voice was soft as though she had no need of it most of the time and it had a tinge of the local accent.

'I'm Lorna Robson. I don't understand.'

'Then I must speak with you in regard to an inheritance which has been left to you. I have reason to believe that you are the granddaughter of Ramsden Carlyle.'

'But how do you know that I am this person?'

Aidan took a chance.

'What is your full name?'

'Olivia Lorna.'

'The inheritance is left to Olivia Lorna Carlyle. Do you suppose there is more than one Olivia Lorna in such circumstances?'

She looked at the other woman, waiting for her to speak, and he saw the emotions which passed over her face, disbelief and then puzzlement and finally frustration because Miss Robson said nothing.

'Aunt? Do you have the letters?'

Felicity Robson moved so that he could see the girl better and the girl was so thin that her cheekbones were accentuated and she had an air about her as though she was always tired. The dress she wore must have been made for somebody bigger and nobody had had time or thought to alter it, it hung off her small frame making her look almost like a child.

'They were correctly addressed?' Miss Robson said.

'They were,' he said.

'Then they should have come here.'

Aidan stepped forward and handed the girl his card and she read it and she said, 'I've heard of you.'

'I spent some weeks trying to find you and then—'

'Don't listen to him,' Miss Robson said. 'It's all lies and you will come to regret it.'

The girl raised her strained face.

'We have a good life here—' Miss Robson said.

The girl looked uncomprehending and then she indicated the door.

'Please come through,' she said.

How desperate she must be, he thought, to ignore the way that the other woman began to rant and rave, begging her to take no notice, that none of it was true and even when she began to follow them the girl went on.


Ushering him through the back room and up the stairs Lorna realized for the first time how shabby it was. She ignored her aunt protesting again and again, saying, 'You can't take him up there,' as she preceded him into the sitting room.

She was amazed at herself. She had just met this man, why on earth should she trust him rather than the woman who had brought her up? She didn't know why, just that there was something about the way he spoke which sounded like the truth and she had already seen in her aunt's eyes that there was a problem here and it was something she did not know about. She could not send him away without hearing what he had to say, every instinct was screaming this at her so she carried on.

Were solicitors rich? They must be. She had not seen anybody who looked like him before. The young miners were either too shy to look at her or so cocky that she didn't dare to meet their mocking eyes. He was well dressed, confident and well spoken and her mind was in turmoil. She asked him to sit down. Her aunt came up the stairs and into the room and he said, 'I would like to speak to Miss Robson alone.'

'You have no right to ask that.'

Lorna had never seen her aunt so flustered. Her cheeks were bright red, her eyes were narrowed and hard.

'You could have stolen that card and sent those letters—'

She stopped short there, realizing her mistake, Lorna saw with dismay.

'So we did get the letters,' Lorna said.

'He said he sent them, that's all. They're nothing to do with us and he has no right to come here like this.'

There was a note of panic in her voice which Lorna did not remember having heard before.

'Please leave us, aunt.'

She couldn't remember having challenged her aunt before and maybe it was the shock of this that made her aunt leave or maybe she heard the firm note in Lorna's voice or maybe she was ashamed that she had not shown Lorna the letters. Whatever, she went clattering back down the stairs and Lorna long remembered the set of her shoulders as though she was physically shrinking somehow.

Lorna invited Mr Hedley to sit down and noticed how he waited until she did so. She thought she should have offered him tea but that was complicated. The fire in the kitchen was banked down for the day, it would take time and some delay to the interview so she offered him nothing.

'What makes you think I'm the person you're looking for?'

'Your aunt was a – very great friend of your grandfather, he was very fond of her and when your mother died and your father disappeared he asked her to take you.'

'Don't the Carlyle family own things, don't they have a lot of money?'

'They used to have mills. Now they have debts.'

'I thought they were rich powerful people. If I'd been one of them why wouldn't they take me?'

It was a question Aidan had no answer to.

'Do you possess anything which might give us a clue as to your childhood, a piece of jewellery which was your mother's or a letter or a keepsake of some kind?'

Lorna shook her head.

'Will you wait here for me just a little while?' he asked.

She nodded.

Aidan went back down the stairs. Miss Robson was in the front of the shop and an old man had joined her.

'I would like to speak to you privately,' he said.

He thought at first that she was going to refuse and he was not certain what he would do after that but she merely nodded, told the old man to come for her should there be a customer he couldn't deal with and they went into the gloom at the back of the shop where Aidan had no doubt the girl had spent years, sewing and mending and earning her keep, though it did not seem to him that Miss Robson had a successful business and why would she have in such a place?

'I am right, aren't I? This is Lorna Carlyle.'

'Yes, of course,' she said faintly.

'Then why did you not give her the letters?'

'I knew no good could come of it. The Carlyles – you must know the kind of people they are. She cannot go back, there is no life for her with them. I was trying to save her—'

'That was not your decision to make.'

'I didn't even know he had died,' she said and went further away from Aidan into the shadows as though it would hide her feelings as well as her face.

'I'm sorry.'

He gave her a few moments and then, as he had thought she might, she told him.

'He never really cared for me. I wanted a child but nothing happened and this child was left with nobody to care for her and when Ramsden knew it was a girl he didn't want her either.' She looked at him across the room through the silence and she said, 'You have to be born a son to be a Carlyle. Daughters aren't allowed.'

'Then why did he leave her everything?'

'Who was he meant to leave it to, Ralph? Henry? They've practically ruined the business, they've spent everything, that's what I heard. He gave them the mills and they lost them. I had nothing so he gave her to me and enough money to start the shop. She's all I've ever had of my own. I taught her the only thing I knew.'

'Do you have proof of who she is?'

'I have the letters which her grandfather wrote to me with regard to her welfare and even a likeness of her grandfather holding her and she is wearing the locket which her father bought for her mother. Ramsden was so disappointed in his sons.'

'Will you find the necessary proof while I go upstairs to talk to Miss Carlyle?' and he left her there with her head down, cheeks burning.

Lorna was astonished and did not regard her fortune as good. The way that Mr Hedley described the place made it sound big and a responsibility. There was also a premises, it had been a book-shop, a stationer's in times past and a printer's, but in the last few years it had been closed. She enquired where it was and he told her that it was in Durham and the street where it was and she could do with it what she liked because it would be hers. She did not know the streets of Durham, her aunt had never taken her there.

Lorna had never been to school, her aunt had taught her at home at the same time as she taught her to sew, she had been to Bishop Auckland, they had had picnics in the park there beside the bishop's palace beyond the Market Place in the town and so few times that she remembered well the deer enclosure and how she had longed to go inside the palace itself.

She had been to Crook to the shops and enjoyed that and she had been to Weardale to the country shows and had been on the roundabouts and had gone to see the various animals in enclosures, sheep and cattle and hens and rabbits in cages in the tents and vegetables, leeks and potatoes and cabbages and there were other categories like jam and cakes and paintings and needlework and she liked to go and see who had won prizes. Sometimes they went to Wolsingham, the first village after the road descended into the dale, and had tea but these occasions were few.

The shop was open except for Wednesday afternoons and on Sundays, and Sundays were for cleaning the house and the shop and on Wednesdays there was still always work to be done. She had not complained because she had known no other life and because it was what her aunt had expected and also what her aunt did herself. They had to work hard to make so little money. If they didn't work they would starve, that had been made clear.

When Mr Hedley had gone she went back into the shop. There were no customers and her aunt was upstairs. Mr Humble had never seen her leave the shop on a Tuesday before but he had had his dinner and would stand there until the shop closed and if there was a customer he could go into the back and call up the stairs. Lorna followed Felicity and found that she had made the fire blaze and put the kettle on and she was kneeling by the kitchen fire as though she could not think to get up.

'I suppose you think that I have been very harsh and deceitful. I didn't mean to be,' she said. 'I thought there was no other life for us. It did not occur to me that Ramsden – that your grandfather would leave you anything.'

'He didn't want me there?'

'No.'

'And did nobody else want me?'

'I don't think they were given the chance. I don't think he told anybody about you.'

'And my mother and father?'

'I know nothing about them.'

'What business did the Carlyles have?'

'They had paper mills. Your cousin Ralph tried to run them after his father died but he was young and there was no money. Ralph is a wastrel as far as I can gather though I haven't been to Durham in years and Ralph is very young. I suspect the mills were doing badly before he got his hands on them.'

Her aunt sat down on the little stool before the fire. The kettle was not boiling yet.

'Mr Hedley is going to write to me,' Lorna said.

'Don't worry, I shan't burn or hide the letter.'

Lorna went over and got down and hugged her.

'You must come to Durham with me and see the house. The premises in Saddler Street are also large and were a bookshop and even a printer's once.'

'I can't come with you, Lorna.' She spoke softly and turned a little and looked sadly at her.

'I don't want you to stay here without me or do you love it so much?'

'It's never been what I wanted but I cannot go back to Durham, people know me there. I think if you go back there you will be sorry for it and everything I have done for you will count for nothing. I shall stay here and I think there will come a day when you will come back and wish that you had never left. There are worse things than this.'

# Four

There was another letter from Mr Hedley about three weeks later and this time Felicity gave it to Lorna but left her there with it in the back room and went into the front of the shop to open up. Lorna had thought that the tedium of her life would not matter now that she could see past it but it was not so.

She had become impatient to be gone since the opportunity had arisen and before she had always thought of Felicity as her aunt and had respected if not loved her. Now it seemed that Felicity had run away.

Lorna could see that there were good reasons for doing it but she resented having been hidden in such a place and the youth in her was desperate to get out. Her work became careless for the first time and Felicity complained. They no longer had any bond. Lorna redid the work that she was asked but she lay in bed at night and ached for the city and the excitement of a new life.

The letter said that if she was able to come to his office in Durham the following Tuesday he would be happy to show her the house and the premises and they could talk about what she might do with her newly acquired property.

It had obviously not occurred to him that she had no money at all. She was obliged to ask Felicity if she might have enough for her train fare and for pen, paper, ink and a stamp to reply.

It astonished her to think that she had never had any money in her hands before. As it was Felicity sniffed over the cleaning of the shelves in the shop and said she didn't have any money, there had been no sales that week and only a few repairs and she had spent that on food and coal, and she refused to discuss the matter further.

'But how am I to get to Durham?' Lorna said, watching the turned back as Felicity concentrated on the cleaning more vigorously than before.

'I'm sure you will think of something now that you're so well off,' Felicity said.

Afraid and trembling, Lorna left the shop without permission for the first time in her life and went across the road and down the opposite street until she reached the bottom of the hill and then she walked into Lloyds Bank and since there was nobody in she went to the counter and asked if she could make an appointment to see Mr. Mortimer, the bank manager.

The cashier looked slightly surprised but asked for her name, asked her to wait and disappeared into the back, returning a few moments later to say that she could see him now if she would like.

This made Lorna feel quite sick, she had expected it to be difficult to see the bank manager, she knew that people were afraid of him and of his power to refuse them loans and that he was thought pompous but when ushered through the darkness into a surprisingly large room at the back of the establishment she found a smiling Mr Mortimer, who greeted her by name, sat her down across his big oak and leather topped desk and offered her tea.

She said yes to the tea because she was too surprised to say no to anything and it came in fluted china cups with neat little chocolate biscuits which at any other time she would have been happy to devour because she rarely had such treats but which she knew she would choke over now.

She showed him the letter, explained her problem and Mr Mortimer read the letter, listened with more than polite interest and then said, 'I had heard a little about your good fortune and I know of your solicitors so in spite of the fact that you do not have an account with us I think in the circumstances we should open one for you and that we will be able to oblige you with a small loan.'

The relief was such that Lorna immediately felt much better and she promptly ate a biscuit, only wishing she had enough appetite to manage another.

She said nothing more to Felicity, they scarcely spoke all that week but she told Felicity on the Monday that she would not be working on the Tuesday.

'You must work.'

'You said there was nothing more to do and I have done the repair work which came in. I'm sure you can manage without me for a day.'

'If I can manage without you for a day I can do without you altogether,' Felicity said.

It was evening. Lorna had been dreading telling Felicity that she was going but could see no way round it. Felicity went off to the kitchen to check on the potatoes which she was boiling for their dinner. Lorna had thought of putting this off until they had eaten but she didn't think she could eat anything until it was sorted out. The smell of meat pie wafted through to her.

'What do you mean?' she said, going to stand behind the other woman as she prodded the potatoes hard with a knife as though they had done something.

'I mean that you needn't come back.'

'But—'

'This is not a hotel, you cannot come and go as you please. You can't go, you have no money.'

Lorna was going to tell her about Mr Mortimer and then didn't.

'I have written and told Mr Hedley.'

'You have no idea what you are taking on and Aidan Hedley has no right to give you illusions like this. You will get there and find that this is false and that you are entitled to nothing and then you will have nowhere to go. Don't come crying here when that happens,' Felicity said.

She had turned around and her face was white, her mouth thin and her eyes glistening with tears.

'Mr Mortimer told me I should go and he loaned me the money,' Lorna said and then half wished she hadn't.

'Well then, I dare say you could borrow some more so that you can support yourself when you get there because you won't be coming back here,' and Felicity brushed past her and left the potatoes boiling so hard that Lorna was convinced they would fall to pieces in the pan and turn to mush.

When Felicity slept Lorna got up and put the few clothes that she possessed into brown paper and tied it up with a piece of string, both of which she took from the shop. When it was light she left, making little noise, and then she walked down the main street to the station and she sat in the cool wind which rushed in from the fell. She didn't have a coat, she went out so little that it hadn't seemed to matter but it did now as the air seemed to find its way through the thin layers of clothing which had been all that Felicity could apparently afford.

Lorna wondered now whether Felicity had kept money back, possibly thinking of harder times or old age. Whatever, as other people gathered on the station platform, Lorna looked enviously at their warmer clothes and wished the time away until the train finally arrived.

She had no regrets about leaving, she didn't care if she never saw the place again, but watched through the window eagerly as the miles slowly put distance between her and the woman she had worked so hard for, thinking that Felicity was all the family she had and that there was love between them. It had been a small kind of affection, she thought now.

The little pit towns they went through looked very much the same, grimy streets and terraces of back-to-back houses and the nearby countryside full of pit heaps and pit wheels but the countryside around it was pretty too with neat houses and little stone farms.

Durham looked bigger than any place she had seen before, at first the train rushed past the streets of houses on the outskirts and then above them and above the fields and trees beyond where the leaves had begun to turn autumn colours and above the River Wear running grey and deep and the churches and then she saw the castle and the cathedral. She had not seen such buildings before and had she not had to get off the train would have gone on gazing at them, the height and splendour, the grey stone, the towers, the intricacy and beauty of the buildings.

She asked the way to Mr Hedley's office and was directed down the long winding hill and into the town, over Framwellgate Bridge where the view of the cathedral and castle, the river and its banks were best of all and then up Silver Street winding with cobbles and shops and cafes on either side and beyond the Market Place and then down on the right towards Elvet Bridge and beyond.

There lay the smart premises of her solicitor, the only give-away the brass plaque beside the door where it read, Hedley, Jameson & Hedley. She didn't give herself time to be afraid, she went in and found a gentleman and a lady, both of whom seemed eager to help. Minutes later she was shown into Mr Hedley's office and he got up and shook her hand and said how pleased he was to see her and agreed to take the brown-paper parcel from her before she sat down.

The middle-aged woman came in with coffee and cake. Lorna had eaten nothing that day but she was nervous. She accepted the coffee and when the woman went out Mr Hedley cut cake she had denied she wanted. He even cut the slice of cake into finger-sized portions in case that would encourage her to eat and he put it on a little table to her side and not on his desk as though that might make her more comfortable.

He asked after Felicity and Lorna could not tell him anything without saying, 'I cannot go back there. She doesn't want me any more. Is it possible that I can move straight into the house?'

He looked taken aback.

'I hadn't considered it,' he said, 'I don't think it's habitable. It wants a great deal of money spending on it and you couldn't live there alone.'

'Why not?'

'It's huge and it stands in grounds though it isn't far outside the city. I will take you there to see it—'

'Then I must find a hotel or a boarding house—'

She had known before she stopped speaking that she had reduced Mr Hedley to silence and for a few moments she wished she had never received the letter and never met him, she felt as though she was stepping over a cliff edge and she remembered what Felicity had said, that she would wish herself in the back room sewing in the poor light, but she only wished it for a few moments, it was just that this was new and she was afraid because she didn't know what was going to happen but there was no need to be cowardly about it, surely nothing could be as bad as what she had left.

'Perhaps you would like to come and stay with my family until something is sorted out,' he said.

She panicked again. To stay with people she didn't know?

'I don't think they would like that,' she said.

'It would only be until you sell either the business premises or the house and then you will have sufficient money to buy a small house and — and do whatever it is you wish to do.'

And that, she thought, was the whole problem because she had no idea what she wanted to do next.

Snow Hall made Lorna wonder what falling in love was like. She had never felt for a man — and thought she never would — half the feeling she had for the house when she beheld it for the first time and it was not all pleasure. Her eyes filled with tears and blurred the exquisite view.

It was all built in the same grey stone so although it might have been built at different times it had a completeness about it which she liked very much. The autumn sun was shining through the trees. The grass was long, the whole appearance of the house was neglect. Ivy overclung, leafy fingers around the windowpanes, which reached from floor to ceiling by the looks of things. The steps outside the front door had broken and fallen into an untidy heap and best of all was the lake at the front and even now there were ducks upon the water and that made it so friendly, so personal somehow and she loved the look of it instantly, its turrets square at the top of one part, the lower buildings and the whole completeness of it with a courtyard and various living places.

He led the way carefully down the rutted road which twisted around the lake and came to the front door and he unlocked the door and he even stepped inside first and she knew it was not from impoliteness. If Aidan Hedley had faults they were not of this kind, he was not certain what he would see inside, she was sure, and he moved into the hallway and then turned and said, 'Do come in, it appears to be sound.'

The hall was huge and smelled of damp and mould. A big dog-leg staircase jutted up from there and on every side there were rooms with big double oak doors. It had once been a magnificent house, she thought, and it had been left here without warmth or any kind of care for all these years. She could not understand how anyone could do such a thing, unless there was no money and there was none. Mr Hedley had told her that.

They moved forward and Lorna wanted to weep for the house. The first room on the left was a dining room. The autumn sun made its way as best it could through windows which were covered in cobwebs inside and dull with ivy outside. There was a big fireplace and the light gave the room a welcome glow even though it was dimmed.

The house was the kind of place which cast a spell, even as neglected as this – or because it was and because if she had had money she would have spent it lavishly here.

She could sense that people had lived here on this land for

longer than anybody could imagine and they had been her family. She was so pleased to think that she belonged anywhere, she had never felt like that before, Felicity had always shielded her or made her feel so apart. She had never played with other children when she was little, never felt like a child, she had always been in that dull dark place sewing, mending.

She already loved this place with a savage desire to save it and when she saw the old square part with the turrets she could not help but think of fairy tales and that however solidly built it had been at one time now it was falling down and could not be accessed.

They went on to the next room and she thought it was the most lovely room that she had ever seen. It was a library, the bookshelves stretched across the walls and somebody had laboured long and industriously and there were two fireplaces and the sun poured in through its floor-to-ceiling windows.

She loved the little room next door which was at the back of the house, or at least the side, and had pretty tiles around the fireplace. He told her they were Dutch and she believed him, blue and white and small as though the room was meant for soft talk and whispers and the fire slowly dying in the grate and lovers unable to tell their parents what they felt and the maid bringing in tea and wondering whether the lad along the lane was still waiting.

'I like this room best, Aidan,' she said and then blushed pink at the use of his name and she apologized and he said it didn't matter though of course it did and she must never do it again.

The kitchens were big and down a long corridor so that meals in former times must have come cold to the table and there were little rooms beyond which made her think of the back room at the shop, cold with cracked windowpanes and untouched shrubs which knocked their overlong branches against the glass and she thought of it intricate with frost and the maids with red fingers, left there to peel potatoes in the almost darkness and the icy blasts along the corridors and the arched ceilings beyond which more prosperous girls than they were danced and laughed and showed off the best sides to men who had money and influence and could rule their lives, lift them up to the dubious joys of marriage and children or cast them into spinsterhood and the kind of poverty which she had known or the neglect of being a maiden aunt.

What was it like to be stuck here in a uniform somebody else had decided you should wear when there was music and wonderful food for other girls to enjoy?

At the front again was another great big room which she decided had been the drawing room, with marble fireplaces, and windows which overlooked what had once been terraces and flowerbeds and there was a huge conservatory where plants had died from lack of water and too much cold and too much heat and then she went upstairs and there was bedroom after bedroom, all empty except for dust and they were all dark because the shutters had been closed for so long.

Mr Hedley said, 'I was going to suggest that if you don't wish to sell at present that you should let the house and the land surrounding the house. I'm sure the local farmers would be glad to take it on. You have no money; it would be the sensible thing to do.'

'I've been sensible all my life. I would like to wait just a little.'

He drove her back to town and took her to see the business premises. This had been the place which the family once owned and she thought she could still smell the paper.

Lorna liked this place as much as she had liked the house and wondered if that meant that she was more of a Carlyle than she had thought. She liked the street where they were, Saddler Street, which led up the cobbled road towards the cathedral and it was next to the newspaper offices which were also large.

The moment she walked inside the sunlight fell through the door and she was at home here as she had not felt at home in the back room of the millinery shop.

It did not frighten her as that had. She remembered the dark nights, the back streets, the black faces of the pitmen as they gazed at her but she turned around and was so taken with the place that she wanted to run from room to room, throwing open the doors to see what lay beyond and as Mr Hedley escorted her politely from one to another she loved the little fireplaces in the small rooms and the big windows in the larger ones and the neat wooden floors and the desks which had been left there. She liked the front of the shop which had huge windows on both sides, lots of shelves and a long wooden counter. She could almost imagine the pens and notebooks and journals and—

'I could sell books and I could have a lending library and give people the books they most want to read, popular books.' She glanced at him, as she knew that he wanted to suggest she should let these premises too because he didn't say anything to her enthusiasm, but he just shook his head.

He insisted on taking her home with him and she was too nervous to protest, though going to stay with people she didn't know seemed worse than a hotel but he said she could not possibly stay in a hotel by herself. He seemed to have very set ideas about what people should do, women in particular, perhaps it was just because he was a solicitor or it was the way that he had been taught, she didn't know but she thought he knew more than she did about the social rules of the town so reluctantly she went with him.

It was not that his house was very grand, in fact it was something of a disappointment, being in town and not the fine affair of her imagination. It was in fact very ordinary, part of a terrace on a steep hill in the North End of the city.

It had a narrow garden which would have gone down on to the road but for a wall at the bottom. Inside the walls were dark brown, the floors were brown linoleum, the main rooms went off the hall and the rooms seemed tiny after the rooms at her house and they were full of chairs and tables and ornaments and dark corners filled with more ornaments and there were sideboards with glass fronts and these too were full to bursting with cups and saucers and plates which were obviously never used.

The house really did not matter after she met first his sister and then his mother and she could feel the hostility coming off them. His mother was so thin that she was scrawny and his sister was exactly the same as his mother only several times larger so that Lorna could not help thinking one had jumped out of the other a generation older. His mother wore black which made her seem even thinner and older and she looked Lorna up and down in a way which made her want to shiver. She did not welcome Lorna to the house but only sniffed when Mr Hedley introduced them.

Lorna was shown up to her bedroom by his sister and her manner was frosty so that Lorna's hands shook. It was a horrid dull little room without a fire and freezing cold. Lorna put this down to the fact that her hostesses had not known she was coming there. The room was very clean and as she looked around there was a hasty knock on the door and when she didn't answer a small maid dashed in, begged her pardon and put a match to the fire so the room didn't seem quite so bad after that with its friendly lamp burning and the sticks and coal beginning to catch in the grate.

When they went in to dinner which was ready instantly she saw how formally they dined with lots of cutlery which she had never seen before, snow-white napkins and plates which matched. She didn't recognize the food, which came in small portions.

First was soup, which she saw she was eating wrongly. The others did not scoop it up into their mouths but pushed the spoon away from them and as the soup grew less they tipped the bowl away so that presumably if they spilled it it did not end up in their laps. It was very odd and she was immediately full and couldn't eat anything and chased the second course of some fish with lots of bones around her plate before it was taken away by a neatly uniformed maid who didn't speak and didn't look at anybody.

There was meat which came in thin slices so that it tasted of nothing and then there were boiled vegetables, limp. Eventually the pudding was brought in and it was some slippery kind of pale cream blancmange which shivered on its plate and again had no taste.

After dinner Mrs Hedley went upstairs to her room and did not come back and Lorna was only glad when the night finally cut in because there was nothing to do. Mr Hedley apologized briefly and went off to his study to work and his sister read a book.

The house was not uncomfortable, Mrs Hedley had fires in every room and the maids kept the house very clean. The meals were dull but she didn't think they were any worse than in any other house and for the first time in her life she had nothing to do. She took to going for a walk every day – by herself, Miss Hedley didn't offer to go with her but she didn't like to spend any money and shops where you could make no purchase soon lost their appeal.

The back of the house was interesting only in that it over-looked and across at other similar houses which Mr Hedley's sister assured her were filled with respectable people, teachers and university lecturers and people who had the bigger shops in town. There was also the railway line and she could see and hear trains taking people away to Edinburgh and to London and sometimes she would stand at the window and wonder whether she should do as Mr Hedley had suggested and sell everything and move away completely but she couldn't imagine where to since she had nobody to go to and no purpose.

There was a cook, a housemaid and a parlourmaid, and someone came in to do the garden, sweeping up the leaves which fell from the trees, soggy and brown into the grass below. Mr Hedley was at the office all day and Lorna missed him. She felt that without Aidan at her side she was vulnerable and when she went out she thought that people were staring. She had never had leisure and was astonished at how soon it palled and to her amused horror she thought back with affection to the little shop and the rooms upstairs. Now she felt adrift and unsettled.

Nobody came to dinner, and they did not go out to visit friends or family so there was no amusement of any kind. Her walks along the riverbanks past the cathedral and to the very ends of the city grew longer and longer.

The city itself was better than she had imagined but it fright-ened her too because it seemed so alien. Sometimes Bea went out during the day or in the evenings but she never asked Lorna to go with her and Mrs Hedley would sit and drink tea and not speak and Lorna could not think what to do and waited for Aidan coming home. She was obliged to stop herself from running downstairs to greet him when he finally did come back.

She had to learn how to behave and to remember to call him 'Mr Hedley' and to maintain the form which was expected but she longed for him to tell her to use his first name and for Miss Hedley to be friendly and do the same. Their mother seemed not very well and stayed upstairs in her room a good deal but when she enquired of Miss Hedley as to the condition of her ailments Miss Hedley dismissed it.

'My father died last year and she doesn't care to have company or go out,' was all the reply she gained.

Lorna felt like a fire waiting to be lit and nothing happening. She had very little money left though she bought nothing other than necessities and wasn't sure how long she would be there and was ashamed of her dull shabby clothes.

Lorna waited for Aidan coming home one evening when she had been living at his house for three weeks. He was difficult to catch, he left early, he came back late, he worked every day in spite of his mother grumbling that he should not do so on Sundays and it was only when he told her that everything was sorted out legally and she could move into her house since she chose to do so that they had private conversation.

'I can go and live in my house?' she said, when he shut the study door and assured her that everything was settled legally.

'Yes, but I wish you wouldn't.'

'Why not?' and when he didn't answer her she said, 'I can hardly stay here forever, I have nothing to do and no money and although your mother and sister have been kind to me I have no place here. I feel at home at the big house.' She stopped there and reminded herself that he had taken her there which was possibly why she had felt comfortable. Without another person she had no idea how she would feel.

It was a great relief to her the day when she was able to leave, look her hostesses in the face and thank them for their hospitality. Mrs Hedley said she had never heard of a young girl going off to live in a great house like that alone, it was not respectable but then the Carlyles never had been. This was not meant to be said in Lorna's hearing but Mrs Hedley had a loud voice and Lorna had sharp ears.

She could not but think that if Aidan should choose ever to marry, a prospective girl might look askance at his domestic arrangements but perhaps Mrs Hedley would think differently of a girl from the right background. Lorna was beginning to realize that the name Carlyle did not do her any kind of service in the city and being considered rich because of her property would not open local society's doors to her in the same way a solid middle-class name would have.

She did say to Miss Hedley when she left that Miss Hedley

must come to visit and bring her mother but all Miss Hedley said was, 'I hope you'll be happy there,' in a tone which showed that she very much doubted it.

She moved in on a wet winter day and the house did not look nearly as welcoming as the first time that she had seen it. The winding drive which led to it was dark with wet leaves and a good many lay rotting in the road. The lake was dark and empty. The windows looked blackly out across the lawns and the stone of the house was soaked with driving rain. The front door had swollen and was difficult to budge and when she got inside there was a dank empty smell. Lorna listened to the echoing sound of her feet through the huge front hall and wanted to turn around and run away.

The house seemed much larger than it had before and she walked from room to room wondering whether Miss Hedley was right and how she would ever find any degree of comfort in such a place. There was very little furniture and since the house had not been lived in for more than fifteen years and had seen a great many cold winters, some of what there was had suffered.

She pulled off the covers and they were heavy and damp and the wood of what had been an elegant dining-room table had splintered and split, the shine was gone. It was the same with the long mahogany sideboard and the ten chairs but nothing could diminish Lorna's joy at being in her own house.

The day before she and Miss Hedley had gone into town and bought what she thought of as necessities, food and household cleaning materials, sheets and towels. Lorna had had to stop before her money ran out. She had intended visiting the bank because there was a branch there too but she didn't want to try explaining to the manager that she intended selling neither of her properties and had no idea how she was going to survive financially, let alone pay them back the money they had advanced her.

Mr Hedley, having driven her there, was so obviously reluctant to leave her alone that when he did leave Lorna felt like running down the drive after him and shouting that she had changed her mind so she stayed inside, having thanked him for all he had done for her.

The first week was possibly the longest loneliest of her life. She saw no one, it was almost Christmas and the house was bitterly cold. It was also much bigger when the sounds were of your own footsteps and very little else and the windows did not fit in the rooms and although she intended going upstairs to bed she did not do so and took to huddling beside the kitchen fire because the idea of going into the hall and up the arctic stairs was too cruel to contemplate. During the day she brought in wood for the fire and attempted to clean and put right some of the rooms and twice she walked into the city and brought back food but she met no one she knew at all.

On the eighth day, when she was just beginning to wonder whether she might find the courage to go and visit Mrs Hedley because she couldn't think what else to do, the snow began to fall so heavily that she abandoned the idea. She needed money, she knew that she must find the courage to go to the bank and ask for a loan so that she could start the business.

She had spent enough time here to make it as homely as she could and she was not convinced that it was any better than when she had started so she thought she would wait until the snow melted in a day or two and then go to the business premises and see what was to be done. She would have to be brave.

In the meanwhile she read and in the afternoon she ventured upstairs only because she was tired of the kitchen and then she heard a noise. She took the lamp she had with her and started down the stairs imagining all manner of horrors.

The cold wet day had long since closed in and yet it was not teatime and to her despair she had been thinking longingly of the dull late afternoons that she had spent at Mr Hedley's tall narrow house, trying to think of conversation, anything to say to his sister or his mother. She had even, God help her, thought how much less lonely she had been at the back of the shop.

As she hurtled down the stairs she called out hopefully, 'Aidan, is that you?' though to her knowledge she had never yet called him by his first name but the once she made a mistake, so why on earth she should do it now she didn't know. It must be nervousness because she didn't pretend the dim figure in her hall was Aidan but it was not a woman and her heart fluttered in sudden fear. She had never felt quite so alone.

She stopped before she reached the bottom. Two candles burned in the hall but for all the lack of light there was something about the tall figure that made the man look as though he had not come in through the open door but had stepped out from an invisible portrait and indeed from the very innards of the house itself. She felt for the first time there that she was a visitor.

'Forgive me,' he said, 'I did knock and the door was unlocked and then I shouted. You really must learn to lock your doors though to be honest I know of at least a dozen ways to get in despite having grown too large for the scullery window. I'm your cousin, Ralph. I don't doubt you've heard all about me.'

She was conscious of walking the rest of the way and that when she reached the bottom step she got her first proper look at him and was suddenly shy.

'Alas, yes,' he said, with a smile in his voice, 'it is indeed the dreaded cousin. Don't worry. I haven't deflowered a maiden in her own hallway all week.'

She couldn't help but laugh as he shook his head sadly and by the light of the lamp that she held she thought him so easy on the eye that she determined not to stare.

He was nothing like she had thought he would be from the scandalous stories she had heard, that he was profligate, negligent, careless and somehow basically northern because above all else somehow his voice was perfect, not a trace of accent, like the gentleman that people imagined from London, and his whole appearance was a kind of unstudied perfection, the hair neat and shiny black, her own eyes, a pale flawless skin and he was smiling and he wore what she knew were the most expensive clothes that she had ever seen. He offered her a bouquet of white flowers.

'I robbed somebody's glass house,' he said, and in the other hand, like a magician conjuring luxuries out of the darkness, he flourished a bottle of champagne.

'How very kind,' was all she could manage, accepting both and being afraid to drop them. 'The only place I have a fire is the kitchen.'

'My favourite room.'

'Is it?' she said, half believing him.

'Hell, no, I don't think I was ever in it,' but he followed her through and sat down and she managed to unearth moderately clean glasses from a cupboard. He took the bottle from her and with a twist of his hand he unpopped the cork.

'We should have been drinking tea at this hour,' she said.

He looked seriously at her.

'My dear girl, don't say such things, tea rots the guts, I never touch it.'

'But the weather is cold for champagne, surely.'

'Champagne is appropriate at all times,' he said and handed her a glass which he had half filled and then let the fizz die down and then filled almost to the top.

She didn't like to tell him that not only had she not tasted champagne before but she had never had anything stronger than coffee.

'It's very nice,' she said.

'Is it, indeed? I should bloody hope so,' Ralph said.

She was aghast and rather admiring of the way that he swore, like it was usual conversation, not something men didn't say in front of women.

'Is it so expensive?'

'A king's ransom,' he said.

He topped up her glass but said wisely, 'Drink it slowly or it'll go to your head. So, are you planning to sell the old place?'

'Why,' she said, emboldened by half a glass of champagne, 'are you planning to buy it?'

He looked taken aback and then laughed.

'Unfortunately not. I expected to have it, you know.'

'So Aidan said.'

'Do you know Mr Hedley that well?'

'Only as my solicitor.'

'Do you find him dull?'

'I find his family dull.'

'I often wish it was something that could be said of the Carlyles.'

'I don't think anybody would call you dull.'

'They call me a lot of other things. What about the business premises?'

'I'm not going to sell those either.'

'Really?' He looked interested, eyes narrowed on her face in concentration. 'What are you doing to do with them?'

'I don't know yet.'

'I wouldn't want to sell any of it either.' He sat back in his kitchen chair and she thought she had never seen a man look more out of place in a domestic situation and how did he make it so easy for her to say things she would not normally have uttered? He drank half of his champagne and then in a very proper manner got up and said, 'I ought to go before it gets dark. Will you come and eat with us on Saturday and stay the night? My brother's wife said so and the rest of the family would like to meet you.'

'Even though I've taken their inheritance?'

'You're a Carlyle,' he said and she thought that he almost meant it.

# Five

'Did you go and see Miss Carlyle?' Aidan enquired of his sister when Lorna had been gone from their house for three days.

'I haven't had time.'

'You will make sure she's all right and ask her to come to dinner on Saturday and to stay the night.'

He was therefore astonished when Bea reported that Lorna had said she was going to Black Well Tower that night.

'She's what?' He looked up from the papers on his desk.

'To meet her family,' Bea said sweetly.

Black Well Tower was the kind of house which Lorna would have wanted to live in if she had been married. It was old, fourteenth century, but square in a friendly way though it was a stone house built for defence and had a small tower and a courtyard. The west wing had been built originally as a dower house, the kind of place for women of the house who were widowed and could be left there to their own shut-off lives quite away from the rest of the house where the newly married people would take up residence.

Lorna's rooms lay here but it was no reflection on her she was assured, and it could be reached easily from the landing so she need not feel insecure, it was just thought that she might prefer her own set of rooms and she could hardly complain since it had its own living room which was half library and study and half sitting room. It got the sun all day and had double doors which led into its own little garden and in front of the windows was a pretty writing desk and the furniture was dainty so that if she wished to be alone she could be though Lorna couldn't imagine wanting to get away from her new family.

Above all the house was comfortable and the people in it were jolly. There were a lot of servants and in spite of the winter weather it was warm. Her hostess came to her the moment she entered the house and kissed her and said how pleased she was to see her.

Lorna had never had a family before and was pleased with

all of them, even though the uncles and the aunts were stout and
red-faced and the uncles drank too much. Every room had a fire
and the dinner put before her was lavish. She was only sorry that
she had no decent dress to wear and she told Ralph so though
she was aware that she should not have done so.

'You're still the prettiest woman in the room. Why should you
care?' he said.

If he had called her 'beautiful' it would have been suspect but
'prettiest' was nothing more than a compliment.

'I know it's silly,' she said, 'but I've never had nice clothes and
I long for them.'

'Camille is the one who knows about such things,' and he
waved at his sister-in-law and she came across and addressed the
problem and when he had gone away she said,

'There is a very good dress shop near Elvet Bridge. We'll put it
on Ralph's account. Stay with us for a few days. I have no female
company but the aunts and all they do is doze in their chairs half
the afternoon. We'll go into town and have a good time.'

Lorna would have protested if she had remembered how but
they drank champagne all evening and she was developing a taste
for it. From somewhere there were musicians as though it
happened every night. She could not imagine such a thing, as
though once again Ralph had conjured what she most wanted.

He asked her to dance with him and when she was obliged
to confess that she did not know how he said he would teach
her and she could not think of learning being as pleasurable as
this, with Ralph's hand so slight upon her waist and his reassuring arm delicate and to be so close, his body so near that she
began to wonder what his mouth tasted like and then was ashamed.

'Do stay with us,' he said, 'I could teach you to ride a horse
and what different kinds of champagne taste like and you could
have wonderful gowns and feel a fur coat against your skin and
the dew under your bare feet—'

She pushed back from his arms and looked at him.

'Ralph – if what you want is the property that I own then
please don't pretend.'

'Of course I want the property, I have no money and I thought
it was mine. I don't pretend to anyone. I tell you what. You're all
alone there so if you like I will give you a maid to look after

you and a man to protect you and you need never bother with
us again.'

Lorna turned over. For a moment or two she had no recollec-
tion of where she was and then remembered. She sat up. She was
in the pretty bedroom at Ralph's house and she had had what
seemed to her a lot of champagne to drink. Strange, she had
always thought people felt bad when they drank and were not
used to drinking but she felt fine.

She was indeed a true Carlyle, she thought sighing and not
altogether pleased. Sobriety, however, had reached her now and
she remembered that his sister-in-law wanted to take her shopping for new clothes and that she might stay here for as long as
she pleased and that Ralph had offered her help and protection
and she felt comfortable once again.

A maid had been sent to help her wash and dress. Lorna knew
nothing of such things, would have dismissed her had she known
how, but the girl was helpful and friendly and when Lorna's appearance was as neat as she could make it she went downstairs to the
morning room where Camille sat alone at the breakfast table.

She enquired for Ralph. Camille laughed.

'He never gets up before noon and this is Sunday.'

'Do you go to church?'

Camille laughed again.

'Only at Christmas, Easter, weddings and funerals.'

The breakfast, under silver dishes on a sideboard, was bacon,
eggs, black pudding, sausages but Lorna was not hungry. She had
tea and bread and one egg by which time other members of the
family had come down to breakfast and finally Ralph appeared.

He smiled at her and said good morning and sat down beside
her with a huge plateful of food which he demolished at speed
and then enquired whether she was interested in going down to
the stables as he thought he might teach her to ride a horse.

She could not remember how to say no, even though she had
never met a horse. When she said this he laughed and they walked
down to the stables together, Camille having found her some
riding clothes which fitted her perfectly. She looked in the mirror
and saw not herself but a Carlyle.

'These were Sylvia's, Ralph's wife. I hope you don't mind.

Ralph is hardly likely to notice and you're exactly the same size
as she was. You aren't superstitious about wearing a dead woman's
clothes? Only I'm shorter than you and we've nothing else which
would fit.'

'How awful for him to lose his wife that way.'

'Two years ago and they had a son. Ralph was devastated.'

It was one of those sparkling frosty days which December does so
well and in her borrowed clothes and with her cousin at her side
she felt the kind of happiness which she had not known before.

He introduced her to a pretty grey mare. She laughed at being
introduced to a horse but the mare was so obliging and had the
softest nose and the best manners, he assured her, of any horse
in the stables and when he had mounted his own horse they left
the stable yard and began to walk slowly away from the house.
It was bliss. She felt that she had come home.

The little mare did exactly as Lorna bid her and so it was easy
to learn to trot and then to feel the loping strides of the horse
as she picked up speed and broke into a canter. The glistening
grass flew past under the horse's hooves and the trees beside the
river were white with frost. A yellow winter sun made the day
perfect and she was only sorry when he said they should go back
and told her that she would be sore and stiff the following day
if they should linger any longer.

By mid-afternoon when the sun set the Carlyles sat down to
eat a Sunday meal. There was red wine, though Lorna didn't
touch any of it, and Camille had found her a dress which though
pretty enough she assured her had not been one of Sylvia's.

'It's not very fashionable,' she said but Lorna was happy to
wear anything except her old clothes and the men of the family
told her how very good she looked when she came downstairs.
Later Ralph came to her at the fire and said, 'Are you going
home or will you stay with us for a few days at least? My offer
stands, I can send people to go with you.'

She felt so ungrateful and she heard the uncles laughing as
they played cards at the table and she looked at the thick velvet
curtains which shut out the night.

'It's snowing!' Camille declared, drawing back a curtain and
Lorna shivered at the thought of the enormous house.

'I think I would like to stay if you don't mind.'

'Not at all,' he said, 'now if you come over here I'll teach you to play poker. Camille is an expert but we will beat her,' and she got up and went with him.

# Six

Aidan had a good idea of what Ned Fleming wanted that Monday morning as Mr Gray showed him into the office. Ned, Aidan thought, always looked as though he had no money, his clothes were so shabby. Though Ned's father was one of the biggest pit owners in the area, Ned ran the local newspapers and lived with his wife and small child in a tiny terraced house in the town.

They had gone to the same school and always been friends though since Ned had married and Aidan had been left to run the solicitor's himself they had seen little of one another so he was rather pleased that Ned had come in though Ned would not do so without a good reason. He was no time-waster.

'What's happening with the premises next door to mine? I thought you'd have done something about it by now.'

'Miss Carlyle doesn't want to sell. I think she has plans for them.'

'Really?' Ned looked surprised. He hesitated and then he said, 'I hate to be intrusive, my son, but rumour has it that she's penniless.'

'Naturally I can't tell you anything about it.'

Ned sat back in his chair.

'I hear she stayed with you. Poor girl, a seamstress from a pit village with a thick accent and no airs. I'm sure your mother and Bea loved it.'

'She was a milliner.'

'Is she pretty?'

'Ned—'

'I hear she's as plain as she can be, little and skinny, and is galli-vanting around the countryside with Ralph.'

It wasn't a question though Ned looked quizzically at him.

'Doesn't it bother you?' he said finally when Aidan had said nothing for a long time but all Aidan said was,

'It's not my business.'

'Isn't it? It reminds me rather of that bloke who was thrown into the lion's den.'

'She wouldn't stay any longer.' Aidan hoped he didn't sound impatient and defensive.

'I wouldn't stay long in your house either and neither would you if you could think of some place better to go.'

'She insisted on going to her own house and then—'

'And then Ralph arrived on a flaming white steed and took her off to Black Well. Some people think it's a paradise on earth.'

'Oh, shut up.'

'You do feel bad about it, then?'

'Of course I feel bad about it. What was I supposed to do? She wanted to go and live in her inheritance. I can't just barge in.'

'An innocent girl from the fell tops?'

'I know!' Aidan glanced at the door, he had spoken so loudly. 'I advised her to sell both places to begin with or at least to let them. She would have had the money then, enough to set her up for life. She could have bought a neat house in town, had sufficient money to set up a small shop if that was what she wanted and have as little as possible to do with her family and especially him.'

'There is another solution, of course.'

Aidan frowned across the desk at him. 'And that is?'

'You could marry her yourself.'

Aidan looked patiently at him. 'And why would I want to do that?'

'I don't know, except that you seem concerned. How could you leave the kind of situation you have, where Bea frets herself into flinders, your mother terrifies the servants and holds everybody to emotional ransom?'

When the silence had grown sufficiently to fill the room Ned said, 'It doesn't have to be like your parents' marriage was. Annabel and I are happy. I think you really like this girl.'

'I don't know what brought you to that conclusion. You've never met her and you've never seen me with her.'

'You're just different somehow, that's all. So you're going to put up with your situation like it is for good?'

'What's wrong with it?'

Ned gazed at him as though he was stupid. Aidan tried not to notice.

'There are cemeteries more lively than your house. You don't live there, you live at the office. You know what'll happen. You'll get tired of being alone and then because your mother insists you'll marry suitably just so that you can shut the old buzzard up—'

'Leave it,' Aidan said.

Ned did. And when it was so quiet that Aidan could hear Mrs Manners talking to Mr Gray in the outer office he relented slightly.

'Have you not considered that I have five women in my household already?' he said.

Ned got up to leave.

'Yes, but unless I mistake your tendencies you aren't actually sleeping with any of them,' he said.

Lorna didn't go back to her own house, she stayed at Black Well. The allure of warmth and good food and the magic of Ralph's company was too much for her to resist. She tried to talk herself out of it several times but there had been too many days at the back of the shop.

Camille took her to Imelda Watson's and bought her a riding habit and a ridiculous hat with a feather which was as good as anything she could have made herself, everyday dresses in prettier colours than she had seen women wear before now, bright green and blue, underclothing that looked like froth and best of all evening wear, including a ball gown in black taffeta which rustled when she moved.

Lorna looked at herself in the shop mirror and surveyed her bare shoulders, white skin and dark hair and knew that she had never looked better. She had put on weight since she had stayed with her family and her hair was glossy and she had been to Camille's hairdresser so that it was fashionable and thick and her skin glowed and her eyes were the colour of sherry. She had lost the gauntness, the unhappiness. She even thought she might look reasonably pretty but when she saw the woman in the ball gown she was carried away at the idea that she was almost beautiful and she was so surprised that she stared into her own eyes, she could not believe it.

Every morning she and Ralph rode out into the Durham countryside and the fields were white with frost. One morning it snowed and she thought she would remember it as the happiest day of her life, galloping across the changing land, tasting snowflakes on her tongue and the sting of the falling flakes on her cold face and the contrast of the big square fast-melting snow as it clung to her black velvet riding habit.

When the horses were out of breath they stopped. Ralph helped her down and she looked back at the city from the hill where they were and she could see the grey rooftops, the cathedral and the castle and the thought of going back to warm fires and good food and the promise of Christmas to come, parties and dancing and music and the pleasure of her family made her feel as though she would burst for joy.

When she got back there was a letter from Aidan Hedley, asking if she would call on the Friday morning. Ralph offered to go with her but she went alone, making sure that she wore one of her new outfits and the hat she liked best. Her heart pounded. She couldn't understand why she was so nervous, she hadn't seen him in weeks. She thought about his sister and his mother and their narrow brown house with its thin terraced garden. The trees beyond the windows would be bare and black and spindly with nothing to obstruct the view across to Wharton Park at the very top of the city and down the winding of North Road into the town.

She had forgotten how orderly Aidan's premises were, quiet and shadowed, with Mr Gray and Mrs Manners in the outer office. A huge fire burned in the grate but was somehow not sufficient to ward off the coolness of the room. Luckily it didn't matter. Ralph had bought her a fur coat, no point in keeping it for Christmas, he'd said, you need it now. It was sable, a wonderful blue grey, and she wore blue and grey with it, right down to her gloves and boots and the tiny blue grey feather which ornamented her hat. She enjoyed buying hats much more than making them.

She was shown up to his office and all was neat, the brass door-knobs shone, her footsteps echoed on the white stairs and then Mr Gray opened the door and Aidan got up from beyond the desk.

She had forgotten how free and easy her cousins were by comparison to everyone else. Aidan's office was almost like a church, it was so hushed. He was wearing a dark suit and a white shirt, he was impeccably dressed, the fire burned in its brightly polished black surround. She gave him good morning and then wandered across to the window, noting before she did so that he could not hide the astonishment on his face at how she looked.

'I didn't notice your view before. It's really very pretty,' she said.

The snow was lasting and decorated the riverbanks like big white paint blobs which had been artfully placed here and there to best effect and the river ran slowly as it negotiated its way, meandering into an almost full circle around the city.

'Do sit down,' he said.

She sat and then she was pleased because he was not merry-eyed like Ralph or as amiable in any way though he did have disconcertingly searching eyes which she felt saw everything and made her feel uncomfortable. Perhaps it was his profession, she thought, which made him like that or his ghastly home life which she and Camille had laughed over many times as they sat by the drawing-room fire. It made her want to shudder when she thought about it.

His eyes were almost navy and very cool on her now and she began to wish that it was the day they had first met when she had been so impressed with him. He was so formal, she longed to throw his papers out of the window. He gazed down at them as though trying to make sense of them, frowning just a little. He looked tired, she thought, and the way that his eyes were so dark made his face very pale and he had a rather beautiful face which was shadowed in that room as he was sitting in front of the window and made the cheekbones look prominent. On a bad day, she thought, Aidan looked like some kind of superior orphan, as though nobody but his tailor cared for him. The thought made her want to smile and then he dispelled her good humour just by looking at her. Why did he look as though he knew more than you did? It was so annoying.

'I've had an offer for the premises,' he said.

'I'm not interested in selling the premises,' she said.

'Are you certain?'

'Quite sure.' She was already beginning to feel like the meek little milliner she had been. In spite of her rich clothes, her make-up and her carefully dressed hair this man could reduce her to nothing in seconds because he knew everything about her, he had seen her when she was poor and desperate.

She didn't think he was aware of this, so it was all in her head.

He was dull, she thought. He told her the details. She barely listened. She thought of going back to Black Well and sitting over tea with Camille, while the uncles snored, the aunts drank sherry and Henry ate buns until he was shiny-cheeked. They were making plans for Christmas, it would be more fun than anything ever before in her life.

'You still intend doing something with the premises, then?' That 'still' was slightly stressed.

She was annoyed with herself that she couldn't tell him what she intended to do because she didn't know and she thought back to how excited she had been when he had first shown her around.

'You make it sound like it's been years.'

'It isn't that,' he said, 'it's just that Ned Fleming needs more room and I think if he can't buy premises nearby then he might move from the city altogether and we would be losing both newspapers. Also,' he said and then stopped and he looked her straight in the eyes and said, 'you owe money to the bank. How are you proposing to pay it back?'

'It's only a small amount.'

'A good deal larger than it was.'

This was true. She had discovered expenses which she did not want her cousin to have to pay and had borrowed more. She wasn't sure whether Aidan knew or was just guessing.

'Ralph says everybody owes the bank. It doesn't matter, they don't expect to be paid.'

'The amount soon creeps up, especially with interest over time. You have no capital.'

'I have—' What was the word, Ralph had told her? 'I have assets.'

'They are of very little help since you aren't using them to make money or selling them and if Ned Fleming moves there will be two sets of empty premises right next door to one another so this is your best chance of a good sale.'

She thought of the business premises and how excited she had been about her plans. Now they seemed to count for nothing. She was ashamed and he had made her feel like that. He had no right to and then she looked down at her hands and knew that Aidan was correct in all he said.

'Will you think, over Christmas, about what you want to do

and if you are planning to make a long stay at Black Well then the house should at least be boarded up and made weather-tight. If you let me know I can attend to it.'

She couldn't bear any more, he was spoiling her day with his incisive remarks. She was now thoroughly uncomfortable and eager to get out. As she got up he said, 'Lorna—' and then he stopped and she looked at him because she had never heard her name on his lips before and she could hear it repeating sweetly in her mind. 'You will be careful, won't you?'

She felt herself tremble and realized it was with anger.

'I don't know what you mean.'

'I know that Ralph has been very kind to you but he has everything to gain and you are—' He stopped again as though he was aware every second that he should not say such things to her.

'I am what?' she said.

'You told me you wanted to go and live in your own house.'

'I cannot afford to make the place habitable.'

'Don't you understand that people are talking about you and that you have a reputation to lose? That you are becoming the name on everybody's lips? Ralph Carlyle is a byword for profligacy and debauchery and you have the bad luck to be his cousin.

'You need to leave his house and live somewhere respectable. If you don't want to stay at Snow Hall then let it or sell it. There's nothing to stop you except sentiment. You had no childhood there, you could have a future in some other house, you could have money to bring about the business you said you cared for. Ralph will do anything to gain that house and the money to keep it going. He has wanted nothing more all his life.'

The silence after this was complete. Aidan was very pale. Lorna went on listening to the silence until she could hear voices faintly in the front office and then she smiled slightly and left.

When she got home she flounced in, ignored everybody and went straight up to her bedroom and then she saw herself in the full-length mirror and went on looking and she thought she had turned into a spoiled young woman, somebody whose every whim had to be satisfied, and she hated Aidan for making her feel like that.

She recovered her temper in the early evening and dressed and went down for dinner. Ralph had been out all day but he was back now and asked her quietly before the meal how she had got on and she told him.

'He wants me to sell the premises.'

'It sounds like a good offer to me. They wouldn't be worth nearly as much to anyone else as they are to Fleming and you have no use for them.'

'I might have.'

'Really?' Ralph looked interested.

'I might open a stationer's myself, have a bookshop and a lending library.'

He looked for a moment longer and then began to laugh.

'Whatever for?' he said.

'To make money, of course.'

'But you would have money if you sold Fleming the premises. I knew it was a mistake not to go with you. Just because you don't like Aidan Hedley you don't listen to him. He's not an idiot, you know.'

'I never said I didn't like him.'

'What did he do?'

She looked down, she suddenly couldn't meet Ralph's beautiful eyes.

'He found me.'

'I'm glad he found you and you should be too. You could be back in that ghastly little shop with no future beyond ruined eyes and empty nights. It's not a vision to be looked on lightly.'

He always made her laugh. They couldn't talk any more because the dinner was ready. To her surprise she was bored. It was always the same. Too much wine was drunk, the talk was nothing new unless she sat next to Ralph. Camille's conversation was all gossip and fashions and to her irritation she kept seeing Aidan in her mind's eye, how very strained he looked for somebody so young and how white-faced and angry with himself when he had said things he should not have said.

They played cards after dinner but she didn't even like that and after a while she wandered off into another room, a little sitting room which was used for nothing in particular. It had lots of books which were never taken from the shelves and comfortable chairs which the older members of the family slept in after lunch. She stood there by the fire.

Ralph came in.

'Why don't you let me go and see Hedley for you?'

'No,' she said and turned away.

'If you don't sell the premises to Ned Fleming he'll have to find some others.'

'Aidan says Ned will probably move his newspapers to a bigger town.'

'He'd be mad not to.'

Ralph had hold of her hand. He brought it to his lips and kissed it. He had not done such a thing before and she wasn't happy about it. She drew the hand away. He very carefully turned her and drew her towards him and then held her almost at arm's length and he said, 'This time next week we will be at a party and you will be wearing a gorgeous dress and dancing and there will be lots of people and music and you will have forgotten about it.'

'I ought to make a decision.'

'I doubt Fleming is going to do anything drastic before Christmas. You have plenty of time to change your mind if you wish.'

She liked being there in his arms, it was comforting and new. The only time they were close was when they danced and he had taught her and it had been quite impersonal but this was not and she was able to put her hands on the lapels of his jacket and smooth them and then smile up at him because he had finally said what she had been waiting all day to hear.

# Seven

One cold evening shortly before Christmas, Aidan left the study when it was late and he thought he had done sufficient work for the day and he went through into the sitting room where the fire still blazed comfortably and Bea let him sit down and then offered him brandy since their mother had gone to bed. He liked it, he liked the silence in the night.

'I saw Camille and Lorna Carlyle today at Imelda's. I must say Lorna is looking very fine these days. She seems to be living with them.'

'So I gather.'

Bea looked down into her brandy and then she said almost in apology, 'I couldn't make a friend of her.'

'I didn't ask you to.'

'Well, if it's of any comfort I regret it. I couldn't see past her dreadful accent and her lack of table manners, I didn't want to in fact.'

Aidan looked curiously at her. 'Why not?'

'Because you seemed to like her and she's a Carlyle.'

He stared, irritated. Why did everybody think this?

'I did?'

'Didn't you?'

When she looked back at him Aidan considered his own brandy.

'I had a definite desire to protect her, if that's what you mean. I knew what would happen if I couldn't.'

'You can't be responsible for every young woman you have to deal with.'

Aidan thought of the first time he had seen Lorna. He often thought of it, how she had stood in the doorway, blinking in the sudden light. He had wanted to rescue her. Now he felt guilty, that he had not done enough, that he had not done the right thing, that somewhere between then and now he could have achieved more. When she had so recently stood in his office dressed in all the finery which Ralph Carlyle had no doubt provided for her, including furs which must have cost a fortune, he had felt sick. The words Bea had said reverberated in his mind.

She said, 'I'm sorry, I was wrong and now it's too late for me to try and make a friend of her. When I saw her in Imelda's I hardly recognized her. She's quite beautiful.'

Yes, she was, he thought, standing by his window talking about the view as though she was nervous. Ralph Carlyle had brought out that beauty. Aidan didn't want to think about how he had done so.

Bea smiled and it was against herself, he thought as she said, 'She ignored me.'

'Perhaps she didn't see you.'

'It's not that big a place. Camille is better too. I used to think she was so common.'

'Perhaps Lorna has made her less so.'

'She had no woman friend of her own age and everybody snubbed her. Now they are a united front and Camille is lovely too. She was giggling and talking and . . . I felt left out.'

The ball was two days before Christmas. Lorna wore, from Imelda Watson's, the dress of black taffeta. She stood looking at herself in the mirror, saying to Camille who was standing behind her, 'Isn't it rather daring?'

'Of course. All the other unmarried women, poor souls, God help them, will be wearing white. I shall bear wearing white too of course but then I suit white, because unlike the other women wearing that colour I am married and therefore couldn't possibly look insipid. There is nothing worse for inexperience, shyness and giggling than white.'

Lorna looked at her reflection and knew she had never looked better. The dress accentuated her tiny waist and rustled when she moved. It was off the shoulder and her skin seemed to shimmer above it, glistening just as it had in the artificial light of Imelda Watson's sanctuary of female indulgence. Somehow the black was full of different colours and when she turned the folds of it were darker and the cream lamp caught blue and purple and grey somehow within the material. She had known then that she could not leave the shop without that dress.

'I have a feeling it's very expensive,' she had said.

'Would you want it if it wasn't? You must have it, if you never have another ball gown. This is your first and you must always remember your first ball. I want you to have the best time that you ever did.'

Lorna thought that wouldn't be difficult since she had never been to a dance before. She was very excited about the whole thing and couldn't wait. The evening of the dance when she was almost ready there was a knock on her bedroom door and when her maid, Marie, opened it, Ralph stood there. The maid left without being asked.

'May I come in? I want to speak to you privately and everybody else is already downstairs.'

'Yes, do,' she said, turning with a swish of skirts and Ralph stared before walking into the room. He said nothing and she was nervous and prompted him. 'Do you like it?'

'I never liked a dress more,' he said, slightly mocking.

'Just as well as you will be receiving the bill for it shortly.'

That made him laugh and then he came inside and shut the door and he had blue velvet jewel cases in his hands.

'I thought you might like to wear these,' he said, 'I didn't know what colour the dress was but it seems to me that they will be perfect,' and he opened them on the little table nearest and showed her. They were sapphires set in white gold, long-drop earrings and a necklace. 'They're family things,' he said in a throwaway fashion.

'What if I should lose them or break them?'

'You won't.'

'Shouldn't Camille have them?'

'The last person to wear them was my wife. I hope you won't mind.'

'But Camille—'

'Camille is wearing diamonds,' he said. 'Wear them for me, just this once.'

Lorna was trembling so much that he had to fasten the necklace and thread the fastenings of the earrings through her ears. They couldn't come off, he told her, they fastened at the back, below her ears but hidden away in a neat clasp.

When she looked at her reflection in the mirror Lorna was astonished. Was this really the little milliner? Who had she become? And they went downstairs and she put on her sables and was helped into the carriage and went off to the ball, feeling like the world's most fortunate Cinderella.

The ball took place at the Royal County Hotel and during the early evening dozens of carriages stopped there and let down gentlemen in black and white evening dress and top hats and ladies wearing dresses in a myriad of colours. Lorna was very excited and from the moment she got down from the carriage was ready to dance, to laugh, to drink and to make the best of her first dance.

They were late of course and the music had already begun and when she stepped into the ballroom on Ralph's arm she was delighted to see couples waltzing about the floor. They joined them immediately. She looked about her a little and concluded that Ralph was the most handsome man in the room, taller than most and more expensive and elegantly dressed, and he danced brilliantly, so it was easy to dance with him.

He smiled at her and she looked into his eyes and thought that she could not be any happier. When the music stopped she caught sight of the Hedley family across the room, Mrs Hedley dressed in funereal black lightened with a diamond tiara, long white gloves and glittering with bracelets. Bea wore white which made her look pale and even older than she was with gold jewellery which looked all wrong.

To her own dismay Lorna found that she would have given a great deal for Aidan to come across to her with his mother and sister and chat and ask her to dance but he didn't. She was astonished to see how good he looked too, just as good as Ralph, and she didn't like that. Ralph was the sort of person who glittered at such an occasion but she liked the lack of ostentation in Aidan, she liked his quiet elegance, she hadn't realized.

She found that she was watching him dance, which he did effortlessly, and he danced with a different girl each time and they were always very young and smiling and looking up at him and making conversation because he was well off and important. He had a good name in the city and there was nothing better to have, she knew now.

And she thought it was because of the way she was dressed that Aidan did not come to her. Aidan was talking to several people in a circle and everybody was smiling. How she wished to know what they were speaking of.

She was glad when it was time for more champagne and she ignored Aidan Hedley and found a good many things to be glad of and by the time she had had three glasses of champagne she no longer cared and could not imagine what she had been thinking of.

Camille's plain white gown made the pair of them look as though they had turned society upside down on purpose and she was so slender against Henry's oversized figure though he was resplendent in evening dress which fitted him well.

Ralph and Henry and the uncles were by mid-evening apt to gather with other gentlemen in circles and talk and Lorna discovered that nobody asked her to dance. Plenty of other young women were dancing. Nobody asked Camille either but Camille seemed used to that and not to care and Lorna found herself alone again outside which was not how she had envisaged her first ball.

As she stood there she heard a noise behind her and when she turned a tall elegant young woman very plainly dressed and all the better for that was smiling at her. She wore black too but she had a wedding ring on her finger and when she spoke it was with a very well-bred southern accent. She was lovely, Lorna thought, and carried herself so well and had manners that everyone might have admired.

'I do hope you don't mind, only I was curious to meet you. I'm Annabel Fleming. My husband, Ned, runs the newspapers in the town.'

'Oh yes of course,' Lorna said. 'You have the building next to mine and he wishes to buy it, at least he did.'

'I think he still does but there seems to be little hope of it.'

'Mr Hedley says that your husband will move his business to a bigger town.'

'It's news to me,' Annabel said, 'and if he does go he will be going alone. I have no intention of leaving Durham.'

Behind her somebody said, 'There you are,' and the young man who came forward, smiling, was tall and dark and with a friendly open face and he said, 'How do you do, I'm Ned Fleming and you, I know, are Lorna Carlyle. My wife deserted me.'

'You were talking,' his wife accused him, 'the one thing men should not do at a dance.'

'My apologies. Would you care to dance, Miss Carlyle?'

'Goodness me,' his wife said, 'do take him up on it, he may never ask again, though you will be glad of that, he is an appalling dancer.'

Lorna found that she was very grateful and also that when they waltzed people watched.

'Are you sure you wish to be seen with me?' she said.

'Oh, absolutely,' he said with a grin. 'The question should be the other way about, I'm poor, married to an outsider and produce newspapers for the working classes.'

Aidan was not enjoying himself. He had known he would not. He was tired, he thought longingly of the fire in his bedroom and a book and a glass of whisky and somehow the sight of Lorna Carlyle, in her black shimmering gown and her beautiful flushed face, made him feel worse. He could see how shocked people were and although he thought them narrow-minded he knew that she could not afford to be thought racy or fast and he could see by the pursed mouths of various middle-aged people that it was exactly what they were thinking.

Ralph saw him and came across, smiling, and Aidan could not help saying, though he knew it was unwise, 'Could you not have looked after her better than this?'

'My dear boy, what do you mean?'

Aidan tried to look beyond Ralph's amused expression.

'Oh, don't be an ass,' he said.

The smile disappeared and Ralph watched Lorna dancing with Ned Fleming and then he said, 'Isn't she beautiful?'

'You're causing people to talk.'

'It's what I do. My scandalous life keeps people amused, rather like Ned's newspapers. He's brave, isn't he? Nobody else asked my darling girl to dance but of course rather like the Carlyle family he has very little to lose. It would have been nice if he could have afforded a decent dress for his wife. Not that she needs it, of course. Mrs Fleming is like a peach, ripe and sweet.'

Ralph excused himself and sauntered away. Ned and Annabel were standing talking to Lorna Carlyle and Ned spied Aidan and came across.

'Aren't you going to dance with Miss Carlyle? She needs you

to, you're so damned respectable,' so Aidan felt that he had no choice and went over to the two women. Annabel greeted him with a kiss and went off to dance with her husband. Aidan told Lorna how lovely she looked.

'Don't be nice to me, please. You don't think anything of the sort. I saw you before, frowning at me.'

'That wasn't at you, that was at everybody in general.'

'Don't tell me,' she said, 'you'd rather be in the office.'

'Not quite.'

'At home then, with your slippers and a book.'

'Close. Will you dance with me?'

'Certainly not. Every matron in the room is watching you, your reputation would never stand it.'

And that was when Ralph arrived.

'Excuse me,' he said and then he led his cousin away and within moments he was waltzing her elegantly about the floor.

Aidan went to Bea because she was standing alone.

'Where is Mother?'

'Getting ready to go home as soon as you've had enough. I'm bored. Nobody's danced with me except two friends of Father's and one of them put his hands on my bottom.'

Aidan bit his lip so he wouldn't laugh out loud because it really wasn't very funny even when his sister intended it to be.

Aidan could see Lorna dancing with Ralph and he was holding her close and talking softly to her and she was looking up into his face and it was so trusting like she had been with Aidan when they first met.

'Let's go now,' Aidan said.


Ralph and Lorna were alone in the carriage on the way home and it was beginning to snow. She was snuggled into her furs and he put his arms around her and she thanked him.

'What for?'

'It's Christmas and I'm happy. I've never had a real Christmas before.'

'What did you used to do?' Ralph asked her.

'Nothing, really. We had no friends. My aunt used to shut the shop and we would go for a walk in the afternoon and sit over the fire in the evening.' She thought back to Felicity and was slightly guilty that she was having such a good time not knowing whether the woman who had looked after her for so many years was all alone. 'I would like to see her again.'

'She could come and stay.'

Lorna was so pleased at his generosity that she reached up and kissed him and after a brief hesitation he slid his arms around her, drew her closer and kissed her properly for the first time and it was just as wonderful as she had dreamed her first kiss would be. When he let her go she hid her face against his shoulder so that he held her tightly all the way home to Black Well.

Everyone had gone to bed but the fire was still lit in the hall and there were lamps burning and the dogs looked up sleepily from the fire. She got down and petted them and they went back to sleep. Ralph picked up the lamp and gave her a candle and they went upstairs. As they reached the top landing Ralph gazed down the corridor which led to Lorna's rooms and said, 'There's no light under your door. Didn't Marie stay up for you?'

'Of course not. I'm not a great lady to do such things to people.'

'How are you going to get out of that dress?'

'I looked after myself for years before I came here.'

'And wore ball gowns?'

'I shall manage.'

He went in with her and Marie had obviously not been long gone, the fire was blazing up behind a guard. He put down the lamp he was carrying and lit hers and then he turned to her and she looked at him and then she was in his arms and he was kissing her. It had not been what she intended. She had not thought before she set out that evening that she would end up close to her cousin in her bedroom like this.

She had felt quite different. She didn't want him to know how disappointed she had been, she had wanted to have friends there and although Annabel and Ned Fleming had been kind she did not think she would see them again and she remembered how Aidan had looked at her as though he had expected better of her.

This was the only place that she could be, it was part of who she was, and Ralph had made it possible. She tried not to think about the part that Aidan had played in her coming here. It was Ralph who had looked after her, brought her to this house and bought her beautiful things. He was her only real ally. The Carlyles were her people now. She liked the way that he was kissing her, drawing her closer to him. The house was in complete silence. In sudden panic as she felt the need for his mouth she pushed him steadily from her and he let her go.

Lorna tried to organize her breathing into something regular. He stood quite still and then moved as though he was going to leave and she lifted one hand and then he got hold of her again.

It was as though the disappointment had to be made up, as though she could not bear the evening to get away from her without it being a success, without her being able to look back on it with joy and somehow this was the only way left. It felt like when she had decided not to go back to the shop, when she had taken the train to Durham. There were certain things which decided your fate and this was one of them.

She would never be accepted anywhere but here, and she had not known how badly she wanted to be. She wanted people to hail her with a smile in the street and they did not, she wanted to join ordinary young women and have them be her friends and every time she thought of Aidan's house she remembered that she had not fitted in, that they thought she was beneath them, she imagined them laughing at her thick accent and how Bea had smiled behind her napkin the first time they had sat down to dinner and Lorna had not known which cutlery to use.

They had despised her from the beginning and Aidan – Aidan Hedley had let her down, had left her to the humiliation of his family's snobbish ways. Nobody would ever be able to do that again because she would never put herself into the position where people like that could despise her. She would be beyond it, she would not care for anything beyond the boundaries of her own family and her own places and it would be enough.

# Eight

She had not intended to let things go this far. Where she had intended them to go she did not remember. All she remembered was that she had thought she could stop Ralph at any moment and she was sure that she could have, he was not pushy or frightening or did anything which made her wish herself elsewhere. The problem had been that she could not stop herself.

Now for the first time she was aware that it was not that people did not miss what they had never had but having never had anyone to herself like this she didn't think she would ever stop wanting him. There had to be a balance in life and her balance of having people care and having someone as exquisite as Ralph close like this she had been unable to stop herself. Never had she felt as much a Carlyle as when she had Ralph in her bed. It was not only men that had appetites, she was part ashamed and part deliriously pleasured whereas he was perfectly casual and even went back to his own bed in case Marie should discover him there and be scandalized.

She had not expected that either. She had, because she had seen it so often in him, expected excess, even lewdness of a kind because she had seen him drink too much and play cards all night and sleep all day. Everything Ralph did he did to breaking point but this was different. She was the one who slept almost until midday, Ralph had got up early and gone out with his favourite horse. He came back for lunch and merely nodded at her across the table so that she kicked him until he grinned and then she was almost happy.

After lunch she dragged him into the tiny sewing room at the back of the house and demanded, 'Where did you go?'

'I had to see a man about a horse.'

'Fool.'

'No, I did.'

'And this afternoon?'

And that was when he went back to the door and turned the

key in the lock. Not that she imagined anybody would come in, the fire burned there every day and she was the only person who ever sat in it, when she wanted peace and was reading. It was the best place for lovers to undress one another and take slow and pleasurable satisfaction though at one point he put his hand over her mouth because she cried out so much and then began to giggle.

It was left to him to say, 'Do you love me?'

'I have loved you since the moment you walked into Snow Hall, nobody was ever as kind to me as you. You are all those things that women want in men.'

'Ah,' was all he said.

She watched him for a few seconds, the firelight played upon his face. The baskets of logs were almost empty now and someone would eventually remember that the fire was down or would turn the doorknob and discover it locked probably for the first time ever. Lorna did not imagine that lovers had often taken one another on the rug here or perhaps they had in former times done just the same and she liked the idea.

They were obliged to put on their clothes and then go upstairs to bathe and change for dinner but it was very difficult not being able to touch him and after dinner, which she did not eat, she pleaded a headache and went to bed and dismissed Marie and waited. And waited. Nothing happened. The evening crawled past She did not dare to leave her room, but half-past two she ventured downstairs and it was ablaze with light and the men were sitting in the smoking room playing cards.

It was just past four when Ralph finally came upstairs and into her room.

'I'm sorry,' was all he managed.

'You are drunk.'

He sat on the bed and then lay back and closed his eyes.

'I couldn't do anything about it. I've never refused to play cards before, I can hardly do it now.'

'Surely your inventive mind could have thought of something.'

'I couldn't. I lost too.'

'How much?'

'Lots,' Ralph said and he turned on his side and went to sleep.

She couldn't rouse him but some time before dawn he realized where he was and stumbled off to his room.

Now she was included in all his doings. He took her with him when he went into town and she would go off to Imelda's with Camille and he would go to a pub with some of his cronies and he slept in her bed every night and every night she fell more and more deeply in love with him.

She occasionally thought back to her bed above the shop, listening to Felicity's breathing and smelling her foul breath, and she would cuddle in against Ralph's silken back and breathe in the scent of him and kiss him and often he would turn over and respond. He told her he had loved no one before like this, she assured him she never could grow tired of him and his lovemaking was exquisite. He knew how to give pleasure, she had not imagined such a thing, she felt drunk on it, she needed no wine but they drank freely in the evenings, had champagne in bed, they had long since given up worrying about what Marie thought or anybody else for that matter and it was generally acknowledged in the household that they were sleeping in the same bed.

She wrote to her aunt, asking her if she would like to come and stay, she so dearly wanted to make up with Felicity, she could never be comfortable at the way that things had been left. There was no reply. She wrote again but the same thing happened and after the third effort it seemed like such a waste of time, that Felicity would never forgive her and that there was no point in maintaining contact with a woman who so obviously wanted nothing more to do with her.

One day in February when she was in town without Camille who had stopped at home by the fire with a heavy cold she met Annabel Fleming and was delighted when Annabel took her to the Silver Street cafe and ordered coffee and cake. Annabel chatted about her little boy and her husband and Lorna was so flattered to be in her company that she let down her guard and said, 'Has Ned bought new premises?'

'No, but he is actually looking at some. You still don't want to sell?'

'Not until I decide what to do next,' and Annabel asked what she thought she might do with the premises and seemed animated with the idea of a stationer's, a bookshop and even a library for popular fiction and they discussed it for so long that they had to have lunch and Lorna thought she had never liked anybody better than this woman and then felt guilty remembering Camille blowing her nose and not talking because of her sore throat.

Ned Fleming was looking at bigger premises further up Saddler Street so Annabel said she was not to worry because they were definitely not moving away from the city and if Lorna was to open the shop they would be in touch often because most days Annabel still spent part of her time at the newspaper.

She wrote columns now and was thinking of starting a magazine. Her mother loved to look after Thomas so she had free mornings or afternoons and they talked about the magazine, what kind of stories they would want in it and Lorna became so excited that she did not want to go home.

Annabel took her back to the newspaper office and Ned did not seem to resent the fact that she would not sell and he listened to her ideas. He said that he knew of people who could supply pens and pencils and that the journals and writing pads could be given special covers with her shop name on. He also knew of people who made office furniture though he had seen the lovely mahogany counters in the shop and said that was one thing she wouldn't need.

He showed her around the newspaper office. Lorna had never been into such a place and liked the back rooms best where the big rolls of paper lived and she could smell the ink and the machinery was all there to produce the newsprint and Ned told her that he could place advertisements on the front page when she opened her shop and Annabel said she would write an article about women starting up their own businesses and that it would be good publicity.

When she finally got home she had to be quick to change for dinner and Ralph said, as they sat down, 'Wherever have you been? I was worried about you.'

'I've been having lunch with Annabel Fleming. She says that Ned is finding new premises further up the street and I told her of my ideas for the premises and she was so supportive. I'm definitely going to open it as a stationer's.'

Ralph frowned at the food on his plate which he should not have done since it was duck that he had shot and was always wonderful.

'You don't think it's a good idea?'

'I'm just surprised. I don't think you've thought it through. Where is the money coming from to equip it? Before you sell things you have to have the money to buy them.'

'I thought I would borrow it.'

Ralph helped himself to vegetables.

'From?'

'From you.'

He looked at her.

'Me?' He laughed in genuine amusement and held her gaze with merry eyes. 'What makes you think I have money?'

'Well, you – you buy things. You bought me sables and diamond earrings.'

'I didn't pay for them,' he said as though she had uttered swear words.

'Then I shall go to the bank.'

'You already owe them money and you can't pay that back. They're not going to lend you any more.'

'I thought that was what banks were for?'

'Not in my experience but by all means go to the bank and ask them.'

'I will,' she said and began to eat.

When they went to bed she had gone up ahead of Ralph and since there had been a lively card game going on when she left the dining room she was quite surprised to find that he followed her into her bedroom, knocking softly before he came in.

'I thought you'd be busy losing money again,' she said. 'Didn't you tell me you always have to be there?'

'I don't always have to be there and besides, I think I've upset you. I would help financially if I could but you see I can't. I didn't mean to be dismissive either, I'm sure it's a splendid idea.'

Her mind filled with relief and she went across to him and put her arms around him and kissed him. 'I knew you'd want me to do whatever I wanted to do.'

'Of course I do but—' He stopped.

'What?'

'I thought we would get married. I know that's a terrible way to propose and I haven't considered such a thing since my wife died but I think we get on very well and will do well together and I'm just jealous that you are planning things without me. I shall never stop you from doing what you wish. I love you very much and I want you by my side. Do you think you might be able to bring yourself to think of me as a husband?'

She wanted to say yes, she wanted to say that it was too sudden, that she had not expected it, that she must think but she couldn't say anything somehow just the bald, 'Marriage?'

He looked amazed. 'Well, yes. Why not? I know that people do these things the other way round but we are already in the same bed. Surely it follows that we are married?'

'I've never thought about marriage.'

'Haven't you? I thought it was the only thing that women did think about besides clothes and dancing and such.'

'It never entered my mind.'

'So you weren't expecting me to ask? You don't want to marry me?' The expression in his eyes was cooling fast, she couldn't make out whether it was disappointment or annoyance or perhaps a mixture of both.

'I'm quite happy to go on as we are for now.'

'Well, in that case I might go back downstairs and play cards.'

He made for the door and all she said was, 'Ralph—' but he was gone and the door had shut with an irritated click.

The next morning she went into town and there to the bank where she enquired for the manager and the man looked her up and down and told her that the manager was busy all day and she must come back. She told him it was important and identified herself to him and he asked her to sit down and then she waited for almost an hour.

During that hour she remembered her first experience of bank managers and how kind he had been and how he had put her at ease and given her tea and biscuits. Here at the end of the hour she was ushered into a small room.

She explained to the man behind the desk what she wanted and when she had he coughed and then he said, 'I understand that you have two properties but if I am correct you intend selling neither of these, is that right?'

'One is my home and the other I intend to set up business in.'

'It is most unusual, Miss Carlyle, for ladies to come here unaccompanied and it is difficult to be blunt in these circumstances but the fact is that the bank cannot lend you money because you have no capital.'

'If I had capital I wouldn't need to borrow.'

He smiled politely. 'But the bank is not in the habit of making loans to single ladies to start businesses. It's too big a risk, you see. What if the businesses were to fail?'

'But mine won't.'

'I'm sorry, but your assurance is not enough.'

'I thought that when people owned property the bank would be willing to lend.'

'I understand that the house you own is in very bad repair and therefore not saleable and that you would need the other premises to start your business. I'm afraid it just isn't possible for us to help you. You could try another bank, of course.'

Lorna managed to thank him politely and then he coughed again and said that she must pay back what she owed, the interest was mounting, and then she left. Back at home she had no appetite for dinner and afterwards Ralph followed her into the little sewing room and asked what was wrong and she explained.

'Perhaps if you came with me—'

'To a bank? If they knew you were my cousin you'd fare even worse,' he said. 'I don't understand, I thought you were happy here with us. With me.'

'I am.'

He kissed her and she let him.

'I do love you very much and being here with you but I'm not Camille, I would like to have something else just for me. Is that so awful?'

There was a definite frostiness about his manner towards her after this and she didn't like it. She thought that perhaps she was jeopardizing any future they might have together and for what?

# Nine

The weather after Christmas was much the same as it always was at that time of year, dark streets and freezing alleyways and fires which people jostled to be near and the river running slow and cold over icy grey stone. Aidan was interrupted in his office by Mr Gray, knocking perfunctorily and then looking around the door and saying, 'Mr Fleming, sir.'

To anybody else Mr Gray would have said his employer was busy but knowing how friendly the two men were and also talking Aidan over with Mrs Manners they had come to the conclusion that Mr Hedley worked far too hard for a man of his young age and never had any enjoyment.

Aidan had no idea that Ned came under the category of enjoyment as far as his staff were concerned but Mr Gray let the shabby-coated newspaper man into Aidan's office with a nod of his head and Ned sat down and then because he couldn't see Aidan moved a whole pile of papers off the desk.

'A drink?' Ned suggested.

'In the afternoon?'

'It's past six o'clock.'

'Is it? Good Lord, everybody should have gone home by now,' and he went through to tell his loyal staff to leave because they wouldn't until he did though they were meant to finish at half-past five and when he told them that he was going out with Mr Fleming he did not mistake the look of satisfaction on their faces.

Sometimes Ned and Aidan went to the County to drink but they would see people they knew so Ned walked past it and into the Three Tuns across the street so Aidan followed him and found a comfortable corner and Ned went to the bar for beer. Aidan liked whisky but he couldn't be seen drinking anything but beer when he was outside of his home and his office, it wasn't considered polite for men of his age to drink spirits and foretold a drunken future to the townspeople, so he accepted the beer gratefully.

'What's happening? You were going to look at premises further up the street.'

'I did.' Ned paused. 'I don't think I'm going to need to. I think the premises next door will soon be mine.'

Aidan frowned. 'What makes you think that?'

'Rumour has it that the young lady in question will be married to Ralph within weeks. She's sleeping with him.'

Aidan had never known Ned to be misinformed and he reminded himself of this now because all his senses screamed at him that this was not so.

'She wouldn't do such a thing,' he said, remembering the girl he had met and then he thought of how confident she had been before Christmas when she came to his office, dressed in furs and expensive clothes and how she had changed in the past weeks, how she had been almost like someone different that morning. 'No,' he said, 'no, she – she wouldn't. She couldn't. Besides, if Ralph wants to marry her—' Aidan's lips had gone quite stiff and were not obeying him.

Ned drank a quarter of his pint in one go and then put down the glass and there was silence between them while Aidan tried to accustom himself to the unwelcome news.

'Maybe it was the only way he could land her,' Ned suggested, 'he plays a good game, you've got to admit.'

'She can't marry him.'

'No, she can wait until she's expecting. The gossips will love that.'

Aidan stared at his friend as Ned got up. 'Where are you going?'

'I'm going to the bar to get you some brandy.'

Aidan tried to protest but couldn't manage beyond, 'I don't need it.'

'You've gone so white we don't need a lamp for the corner,' Ned said crisply.

'Ned—' Aidan protested but his friend had already set off across the room towards the bar so he sat there and tried not to imagine Ralph Carlyle making love to Lorna. He blamed himself, over and over even before Ned got back. Ned put the brandy in front of him.

'Nobody saw me,' he said in answer to the way Aidan glanced around.

'I don't know what makes you think—' Aidan said from between his teeth but got no further.

'Oh, come on, you look as though you want to break his neck. She was never your social equal, she was well below you and now – go on, tell me you don't care.'

'Of course I care,' Aidan spoke too loudly and tried to modulate his voice but it was early and not that many people were in the bar and besides, it was a big room. 'She wouldn't listen.'

'When do women ever listen to men?'

'She cannot marry that bastard, she really cannot.'

'I only wish I could be there when you tell her that.'

'Doesn't she see that he only wants the house—'

'And to sell the premises to me. You see, I knew good would come out of this.'

Aidan regarded his brandy as the besieged party regards rescuers and without even sniffing it he drank the whole thing down.

'That was expensive,' Ned objected, watching him.

'Let's go somewhere we can drink brandy in peace. I'm buying,' Aidan said, getting up.

Lorna could not have told anybody what drove her back to Snow Hall that day. She was being frustrated in her aim to open the shop, she could not think what to do next, the winter had seemed to go on for so long now and she was tired of the cold, the damp, the dark days.

She could have ridden but she chose to walk. It wasn't far, the morning was bright and for once was dry so she put on a sensible coat, hat, gloves and scarf and stout boots and walked and she did not regret it.

She regretted, when she got there, that she had left it for so long, she felt guilty though without money she was not sure what she could do and she knew that it was unlikely a shop of the kind she wanted to open would provide funds to maintain such a property.

She knew that she should sell before Ned Fleming went elsewhere, perhaps even now he had signed a contract for a building which would render hers unsaleable. She knew that Ralph would not be pleased when that happened and she thought over everything that Aidan and Ralph had told her and she began to think that they were right even though her instincts said otherwise. How could she start her shop on nothing?

She approached the house from the front and everything was even more neglected than the last time she had seen it and it was so long that she felt worse than guilty and her mood went down and down as she reached it. She unlocked the door and heard the silence throughout the house and was inclined to sit down and cry and told herself how stupid and pointless that was so she didn't. She wandered about, going from cold room to cold room, wondering whether she had been wrong not to sell this place.

She could have bought a really small house in the town and had enough money to set up her business but somehow she could not and she knew that it was nothing sensible, it was nothing to do with reason or business, it was to do with never having had any home except upstairs from the milliner's shop and never feeling right there.

This place was her family home and she could not sell it or let anyone else live in it. She went back downstairs and lit the kitchen fire and when it began to warm up it was soon a good blaze and cheered her. The room was too big ever to warm up completely and she went through into the little blue room which she thought might have been a study and was her favourite room in the house, she liked the little Dutch tiles of windmills and clogs.

It was much smaller than the kitchen and square with only one window which unlike the windows at the front of the building did not reach up from floor to ceiling so the draughts were much less in there.

A fire would soon make the room warm and she comforted herself because she was not short of fuel. The outside buildings down the back yard were filled with a mountain of coal and tons of very dry wood which had been there for so long that it was light and caught a flame easily and burned well. It would do the house good to have some fires lit if only for a little while.

She thought she would even clean the room and make it habitable. Why not? So she went back out to find dusters and a mop and when she came back a big piece of plaster had broken and fallen off the wall. She went over and swept up the small pieces, managing to lift many of the bigger pieces off the floor without breaking them. As she did so she looked up at the piece of plaster next to it on the wall which she was pleased was still holding on to whatever had been holding it beneath and she thought there was something sticking out from the wall, a kind of small squat package.

She put down the pan and brush and went to it and it was a long thin brown envelope, the end stuck down. She put her finger in under it and it tore. Inside was a big wodge of what looked like paper, all the same size, all together with a neat piece of paper across the middle. She pulled it from the envelope and then stared. It was money, a good deal of cash.

She sat down there on the floor and counted it. There was five hundred pounds. Lorna couldn't believe it. She sat for several minutes. It was like a godsend, it was perhaps an omen, it was exactly what she needed. She wondered whether someone had broken in and left it there for safekeeping but that seemed silly because nobody had broken in, the money had been there beneath the plaster for some time and she had found it at exactly the moment that she needed to. Now she believed in herself, this was a sign that she should open the shop, she had never been more sure of anything in her life.

The last thing Aidan expected the day after he and Ned had gone out and got drunk was a visit from Lorna Carlyle. He never got drunk, well, hardly ever, and had had gone to a great deal of trouble not to let his two outer-office people know that he had the worst hangover of his life and had no idea that when he closed his door they looked across their desks at one another. Mr Gray shook his head and Mrs Manners raised her eyes to the ceiling and then both had a quiet smile that their employer seemed human after all.

Miss Carlyle had not made an appointment but he had few appointments that day, something he was very glad of, he had been hoping to cut through some of the paperwork which threatened to slide from his desk it had grown so heavy but that day he was only pretending to work and all he hoped for was that nobody would interrupt and he could sit there in his little fortress by the fire and Mrs Manners would bring in lots of coffee. She had already done so twice and with it large biscuits to help soak up the state of his head and stomach and then Mr Gray knocked, put his head around the door apologetically and said, 'Miss Carlyle is in the outer office. She said she didn't need to see you, she just needs the keys of the business premises, but I thought it best—' He stopped delicately here.

'Show her in, please.'

She looked different, he thought savagely, now that she wasn't a virgin any more and he wanted to go across and shake her and ask her what the hell she had been thinking of except that the look on her face did not coincide with what he was thinking. She was tentative, softly spoken and met his eyes happily.

'I didn't mean to disturb you. All I want is the set of keys for my business premises.'

He didn't know quite what to think. He wanted to ask all manner of questions but couldn't and got to his feet because he had forgotten the courtesy when she came into the room. The room was not quite steady and he felt a wave of nausea and then he controlled it. He found that he wanted to talk, to say just anything in order to hold her there, and yet he was so angry at what she had done that he wished her gone.

'They're in the safe in here,' he said hurriedly.

This was a fabrication, he knew exactly where they were and she had been right, he did not need to be disturbed. They were in the cupboard in the outer office and were clearly marked.

When she didn't move he waited for her to sit down so she did and then he asked her whether she would like some coffee since Mrs Manners, knowing that her employer needed vast quantities, was making more and the smell of it was wafting through the office and when Lorna Carlyle dumbly shook her head he went to the door anyhow and shouted through to Mrs Manners in a way which made that lady lift her head in surprise. He never did such things except when a close friend was there and he could be informal but it was not an ordinary day in the office and she comforted herself with the thought that things would be better tomorrow.

The coffee, freshly made, was brought through and Mrs Manners, God love her, he thought, brought in biscuits which were shaped like stars, covered in chocolate and impossible to resist so while he got down and made a great show of unlocking the safe and going through it he noted that Lorna drank the coffee as though she needed it and ate a biscuit and when he got up in supposed regret that he could not find the keys he poured her out another cupful and then he apologized for his disorganization and went through into the outer office where he knew he could have put his hands on those keys in the pitch-black darkness.

He came back slowly, not sure whether to just give them to her or enquire as to her purpose. If he spoke he risked rejection but if he didn't his curiosity would not be satisfied and he was not at all happy not knowing what was going on.

He sat down as though the visit was not ended though by rights he knew it should be. He placed the envelope with the keys in it on the desk and assured her that he had another set, should she need them.

'Are you thinking over Ned Fleming's offer?' he said.

'I want to go and see the place,' she said.

'I could come with you.'

She looked surprised and he tried to think of any good reason why she would want him there and he also tried to look as though he had nothing else to do which anybody could see was not the case.

'I'm sure I can manage,' she said.

'Yes, of course.' It was as though they were dancing and he had trodden all over her toes and he tried to think how he hated the idea that she had given herself to Ralph, so why did he want to keep her there?

And then to his surprise Mr Gray gave his usual soft knock and put his head round the door as he would never have done when Aidan had someone in with him and he said, 'There is the meeting with Mr Kemp, sir.'

Aidan was astonished. He had not realized that Mr Gray had the kind of intuition which most men only dreamed of. Lorna got up.

'I mustn't waste your time,' she said.

'I'm meeting Mr Kemp a little later in that part of town so I can keep you company and open the doors for you.'

She could not, he thought, refuse without being rude so she let him accompany her out of the office. Mr Gray put a brief-case into his hands as he left. The meeting with Mr Kemp was indeed true but was not for some time.

They walked in silence across Elvet Bridge and Aidan made a

great show of looking at the river on both sides though there was nothing of interest to see. They walked up the steps which led into Saddler Street and next to the busy newspaper offices sat her premises, empty, cold and dark as he had predicted.

He opened the door and the sounds echoed. She went in without a word, making her way slowly around the rooms as though she had not seen them before, as though she had forgotten, and from time to time she would stare from the grimy windows as if she could see a great deal further than across the street.

He wished that he had known what she was thinking, and then she turned, faced him and said, 'You don't need to wait, I shall manage, I just want to be here.'

'I thought I might be able to help,' he said and he hadn't known that he was going to say it and he hadn't wanted to and he wished himself long gone, he wished that he had never left the office, he wished that Ned had not told him that she was sleeping with Ralph, he was beginning to wish that he had never seen her and it was like his feet were glued there to the floor because he knew that she didn't want him, that she wanted to look round by herself and yet he stayed there, like a tailor's dummy in a window. She didn't encourage him, she just stood there, waiting for him to leave but he didn't.

'I told you, didn't I, when I first came here that I wanted to have a stationer's and – and do other things perhaps and Mr and Mrs Fleming offered to help and – I do think I might be able to achieve something here.'

'Why don't you ask Ned Fleming whether he would like to rent part of it from you? You have three storeys here and a cellar and all you really need for a shop, unless you're planning to live here which considering you already have one house and are living at Black Well anyway isn't likely, is some storage space and enough room so that people feel comfortable making their way through the shop.'

She stood for a moment and then turned to him.

'Do you think he would be interested?'

'We could go and ask him.'

He could see the excitement in her eyes and was pleased that he had had the idea though whether it was any good he was not sure but he prayed that it would be.

They called in next door. Annabel was in the front office and she called Ned through as soon as they came in and all Aidan said was that he wanted them to go into the other premises and take a look and when they got there he showed Ned over the building and when all four of them were together again Ned Fleming turned to Lorna and said, 'I think this might work. And you could do much more here too if you chose.'

'Like what?'

'Like publishing. I have machinery and compositors, I know a book-binder. There are other things you could think of which are less ambitious like greetings cards, business cards, I could make and you could sell and you and Annabel together could design greeting cards if you wanted to. Also I know a joiner who could put up extra shelves for you and do other things, depending on what you decide you want, and if I could have all that space at the back of the premises we could knock through.' He glanced at Aidan. 'Though that takes us into legal territory and you might not want that. I'm sure there's a way round it.'

'I'm thinking of starting a women's magazine,' Annabel said. 'We could do it together. I write a women's column and various articles for the newspaper but we could do much more if we tried.'

Lorna was so excited about her new friends' latest ideas that she thought she would burst.

'You could sell newspapers and periodicals to suit all kinds of people,' Ned said.

Eventually Aidan had to go off for his appointment and when he came back they were drinking tea in Ned's office at the newspaper and eating pieces of shortbread and then they discussed how much would be a fair price for Ned to pay in rent and whether it was sensible to knock a hole in the building and how it might cause complications later and Aidan said he would draw up something which might suit both parties.

They were in such accord by the end of the afternoon that if it had not been that Annabel's mother had had the little boy all afternoon they might have stayed where they were but she invited Aidan and Lorna to their house and Lorna was very keen to stay longer and Aidan said he should get back to the office but he didn't go.

The Fleming house was a shock to Lorna, being used by now to the size and scope of Black Well Tower. It was in a street just below the hospital halfway up North Road which led out of town towards Newcastle and on to Scotland. Small dirty children played around the doors. When they went in Annabel put the little boy on the floor to crawl about and Lorna decided that she liked the tiny house, it had good furniture, bright walls and as many books as its bookcases could support.

Annabel reheated a stew which was already made on the stove and then they sat around the dining-room table, Ned with his son on his knee. They had a kind of sticky pudding with custard to follow and then went into the sitting room and drank coffee.

'Is there any more coffee?' Ned asked.

'You must be awash by now,' she said. She looked at Lorna. 'They went out and got very drunk last night. My husband came home at three and had to sleep on the sofa.'

Lorna stared at Aidan. 'You got drunk?' she said.

'Ah,' Ned said, 'no longer the whited sepulchre.'

'Oh, shut up,' Aidan said and that was when Lorna laughed.

'How did you get home?'

'I don't remember,' he said.

Lorna couldn't help but laugh again at the idea and the comical look on his face.

Ned and Annabel took their son to bed.

Aidan took the opportunity to ask, 'Does Ralph know you're planning to start a shop?'

'I don't think he was very happy about it.'

'Well, he wouldn't be, would he? He needs you to sell the premises, he needs the money badly.'

There was silence and in it Aidan could hear the soft tones of his friends talking to their child upstairs and he felt very left out. How wonderful it must be, he thought, to have nobody to come back to but your wife and child, how private, how easy.

'Are you going to marry Ralph?' he said.

'You think he's going to make it impossible for me to refuse?' she said, not looking at him.

'Hasn't he already?'

He thought the colour came into her cheeks but perhaps it was just the fire and then she said, 'I think I ought to go home.'

'I'll take you.'

Ned and Annabel came softly downstairs at that point and Lorna thanked them and Aidan insisted that she could not go home by herself in the darkness. Nobody spoke on the way and she hurried, she wanted to get away from him, he knew and he cursed himself for saying all the wrong things to her and even worse, he had been incredibly rude.

He hadn't meant to say any of it, he kept thinking back over what he had said and couldn't believe that he, who was normally so adept at these matters, after years of dealing with the law and people, could have been so incredibly clumsy and offensive but he didn't know the words to take it back. You could never unsay things, however much you wished.

# Ten

Ralph was waiting for Lorna when she and Aidan stepped into the hall. The lamps were burning, the dogs got up making a fearful row with their barking and Ralph appeared from the shadows, looking narrowly at Aidan as Lorna took off her coat.

'Hedley,' he said. 'I was getting worried as to my cousin's whereabouts.'

Lorna said hastily, 'I had supper with the Flemings and – and with Mr Hedley.'

'How are Ned and his wife? Do come in,' Ralph said. 'Maybe I could give you a drink.'

'That would be nice,' Aidan said and suddenly Lorna thought it would be anything but nice and she had a real desire to get rid of Aidan. They went into the little sitting room and she warmed her hands by the fire and Aidan and Ralph followed her inside and Ralph poured whisky from a decanter which was always put on to the sideboard in the early evening.

'So, what prompted this supper with the Flemings?' he said, handing Aidan a heavy squat glass of golden liquid.

'He's renting part of the premises from me,' Lorna put in before Aidan could speak. Somehow she didn't want him involved, she wanted Ralph's mood to fall on her and not their blameless visitor and then she remembered that it had been Aidan's idea in the first place and she wished that he had not thought of it, that she had not accepted it and that she had come home and forgotten all about her plans.

Ralph said nothing more and Lorna wished that she did not feel quite so nervous around him.

'I didn't know things had got so far.'

'I shall have enough money to take care of things and enable me to open the shop. Mr Hedley is going to draw up the papers so it will all be legally right.'

'How kind you are, Aidan.'

'It's not kindness, it's just business,' Aidan said in icy tones and

Lorna panicked, looking from one to the other. She had never thought of Aidan Hedley as being difficult but he was being now, looking straight into Ralph's face in a way that made her think somebody was going to hit somebody in a minute. What had happened to her cool-thinking lawyer? She wished he would finish his drink and leave. And then she remembered what he had said about herself and Ralph, how he had implied that he knew they were lovers, and her heart thumped in her chest.

She loved Ralph, she did not have to explain herself to anyone and especially not to this man who was making her angry now and she knew why. It was because he was partially right in his thoughts and words and she didn't want him to be right. She wanted him to think well of her because she respected him but she didn't like him any more.

She didn't want to care what he thought or what he said. He had no right to sit in judgement on her or on Ralph and especially not on their behaviour. Of course Ralph did not want her to start the shop, it would ruin all his plans and it would mean that she was not the obedient woman which she was certain the Carlyle men expected and she would not be at his beck and call and he resented that and more somehow. She could not work out exactly what the more was but she knew that the situation here was very dangerous.

She turned to Aidan and looked beseechingly at him and after a moment or two he swallowed the rest of his whisky and said he really had to go and she saw him into the hall, shutting the door of the room behind her. She hastened him along the hall and opened the front door and thanked him very politely for seeing her home and then she said, 'Goodnight,' so that he had no choice but to let her see him outside and close the door quite firmly after him.

She went back into the little sitting room where Ralph was standing by the fire with his drink untouched in his hand and he said instantly, 'How could you make such a decision as to rent the premises to Fleming and allow Hedley to draw up papers and not consult me?'

'You didn't seem to want to be involved.'

'I don't see the sense to it.'

'We've been through this and really you have no rights here.'

'No legal right certainly but morally I have every right. Those premises belonged to my grandfather—'

'And mine and he left them to me.'

'I thought you wanted to help the family. I don't think you understand. I am going bankrupt. I have nothing more to offer. I have huge debts, I owe money everywhere and if I can't find some from somewhere I shall lose this house. We shall have nowhere to live and since you have denied us, your family, access to the house where we have lived for the last several hundred years what on earth do you think we will do then? And you can think of nothing more than selling journals and pens to the ladies of the town. Are you completely out of your mind?

'You are a Carlyle but you are going to let us go under because you will not acknowledge that what you regard as your sole inheritance belongs to all of us, can't you see it? You have no right to it other than the rights the rest of us have. You would see your family put out rather than sell these premises when there is a perfectly good buyer and the money would get us out of the mess we are in.

'The business premises are worth a great deal of money and it would save us but you don't want to do that, you think that by renting out a little you can manage your shop and that is all that matters. You think you can set up in business and make money selling pencils to scholars. Lorna, you cannot do this to us, in all conscience, you cannot. You have to sell the premises to Fleming. It will save us. We can move back to the house and get rid of this place which costs me a fortune to run and everything would be right. Without it we will lose everything. Now do you understand?'

'You won't,' she said, losing her temper in turn, 'you'll squander the money and there is not enough money to put right the house so that we could live comfortably there. It's falling to pieces, you must know that. Nobody works here, that's what I see. All Henry does is sleep, all Camille does is shop and all you do is—' She stopped there because she saw the change in his face.

'Do tell me what it is that I do.'

And then she was afraid of him, of his intense gaze, for the first time and didn't answer.

'I have kept my family together despite my father dying and my grandfather deciding that a slip of a girl was more deserving of my inheritance than I was. I have to keep everybody and take responsibility for everything.'

'But you don't,' she said.

'Neither do you. You have the ability to save your family and you will not do it. How selfish.'

'How dare you call me selfish?' Lorna had not known she was capable of such anger, she could hardly see for it and she was shouting. 'All you wanted from me was the house and the business premises so that you could do what you wanted with them.'

'I would do anything to save my family.'

'Then why didn't you?'

'What was I supposed to do?'

'Whatever it was you didn't do it,' Lorna said. 'Blaming other people for your shortcomings is no good.'

Nobody said anything for a few moments during which Ralph gazed into the fire. Then after a long time he said, 'So you won't sell the premises. What are you planning to do with the house?'

'Nothing yet.'

'I think we should move into it.'

'You can't unless I say so.'

'Is that right?' he said. 'What makes you think you can stop me from doing anything that I wish to do?'

'Your regard for me, perhaps?'

'My regard for you prompted me to ask you honestly to marry me but you won't. You don't want a husband, you just want a lackey.'

'That isn't true.'

'I thought you cared for me.'

'I care very much for you.'

'So much so that you prevent us from living in the house that our family has owned for hundreds of years. What kind of love is that, Lorna? You see us unable to pay the most basic of our bills and yet you do nothing. I don't think you love me at all, I don't think you love any of us,' and he slammed out of the room.

Lorna didn't sleep and in the morning when she and Ralph were alone in the breakfast room together she ventured to ask him what he was going to do that day and he said blithely that he was going to visit friends in Gateshead.

'Shall I come with you?'

'No.'

'Ralph—'

'Wives visit family friends. Whores don't,' he said and he got up and walked out of the room.

That day Lorna went for a long walk and ended up at her house and she knew that if she was not careful the whole family would live there and eventually she ended up in town. It was Sunday so the town was quiet, only the bells rang out from the cathedral for evensong, and she found her unwilling footsteps in the direction of North Road and Aidan's house. She didn't want to go there, she had no intention of ringing the bell and then the door opened and Heather smiled in recognition and said, 'Hello, Miss Carlyle, do come in.'

'Is Mr Hedley at home?'

'He's the only one at home, Mrs Hedley and Miss Hedley have gone to some special service at the church. Go right in.'

She did. The fire burned up brightly in the sitting room and for once she wished that Heather had been more formal and announced that she was there because Aidan was asleep in an armchair and his face was softer and younger and then he sensed that she was there and opened his eyes. As he focused she said, 'Yes, it's me. I'm sorry to bother you but I have a problem and I don't know what to do and I could have gone to the Flemings but I didn't like to disturb them on a Sunday and I'm completely at a loss—'

He got up, rather quickly for somebody who had been asleep just moments ago. He told her to sit down, he offered her tea.

'No, I don't want Heather back in here, if you don't mind.'

He reassured her and when she had sat down he took his seat again.

'Has something awful happened?'

'No, at least – no. I know that you don't approve of me, I know—'

'Just tell me.'

'I said nothing did. Ralph is very upset about the business premises. He wanted me to sell them, he thought like you did—'

'No, he didn't. I wanted you to sell them because it was a

sound business proposition and it was a good offer, Ralph wanted
you to sell them because he wanted the money.'

'We had an argument, he was very angry and he thinks that
I should let my family go and live at Snow Hall and there is part
of me that sees the reasoning and—' She stopped there. Aidan
was shaking his head.

'If you let them have Snow Hall it will not be yours and I
don't think you will like living there with them for any real
length of time.'

She ignored that and she said what she had not even thought
up to now.

'I don't think Ralph loves me. I did think he did for a while,
he was so very affectionate and funny and entertaining and – all
the things I thought I wanted in a man and he was patient – but
he wants the house, he really does.'

Aidan got up and wandered about the room for a moment or
two, stopping in front of the fire and then at the window and
there was very little to see since it was raining and all that time
Lorna was aware of the grandfather clock ticking heavily in the
corner and that very soon his mother and sister would come
home and she would not want to be there any longer. And then
just when she had almost completely lost patience he said, 'There
is an alternative.'

'What is it?'

'You could sell Snow Hall.'

She gazed at him.

'But – nobody knows I want to.'

'Do you want to?'

'I cannot afford to keep it.'

There were tears, she didn't know where they had come from
but they had to be dashed away before they reached halfway
down her cheeks. 'Now you're going to tell me that it could take
months to sell and that in that time Ralph will have worn me
down with his good and bad humours and I will have given in
and there will be nothing that can be bettered and I will somehow
lose everything because the money from the shop will be eaten
up by Ralph and the house and everybody's needs and—'

He didn't say anything for several moments and then he said
slowly, 'There is a way round that.'

'What is it?'

'You could sell it to me.'

She stared at him because she could not have imagined that he would think of such a thing.

'Why on earth would you buy Snow Hall?'

'Because I need a bigger house,' he said simply. He named a figure, more generous than she thought it was worth but she was not going to argue on that score.

She sat for a few moments, ever more aware of the afternoon closing in and that at any moment his mother and sister would come through the door and she would not be able to speak to him any more.

'Why don't we go out?' he said and they moved into the hall and she was grateful that all he did was collect his coat and then they left and walked quickly enough down the hill towards the town so that even if his mother had come back she would not see them.

They went to his office because of the rain or just because there was nowhere else to go. She had never been there before when it was empty and the fires were out. He got down and put a match to the fire in his office and then they sat one on either side of it in his uncomfortable straight-backed chairs and watched it burn up.

'How long would it take to draw up the papers?'

'I could do it this evening if you will wait.'

'Then do it.'

'Are you quite sure?'

'It's the right thing to do,' she said. 'I want you to keep the money for me. I have a feeling that Ralph will somehow get his hands on it. There must be a legal way round it so that whatever the circumstances it will be mine.'

'If you will trust me I can pay you a penny for Snow Hall and I will invest some of the money in both our names and I will keep the rest for when you need it.'

'To me only?'

'Certainly,' Aidan said.

She insisted on going back.

'I won't tell him yet what I've done.'

'I think you should stay here.'

'I don't want to stay in your house, you know what Bea and your mother think of me, and in a day or two I'll be able to move in above the shop when I work out what is needed. I want to go back tonight. Ralph was so angry this morning and he won't be by now.'

Nothing he said could persuade her not to go back to Black Well Tower. He saw her most of the way and then she stopped before they reached the last turn of the corner at the driveway and she said, 'I want to go by myself. He doesn't like you, it would only make things worse.'

'Be careful, then.'

# Eleven

She watched him watching her as she turned the corner and she had vague regrets about him and she had other regrets about selling him the house. It was such a betrayal of Ralph but her instincts were not wrong, she could no longer trust Ralph with the house or the business premises, she could no longer wait, the money had become important to him, so important that she thought he was concerned for nothing else.

She didn't know what had happened, she only knew she had had to do something about it but she wanted to see him again because she felt now as though the relationship was over, much as she loved him, and she would like another day or two just to complete things somehow.

After that she would be able to leave Ralph, she knew that she would but she thought Aidan was right, she must tell him nothing until after she had gone. She thought of the premises and the rooms above it with a small wave of excitement. She would be able to go forward, she would be able to leave Ralph. She had to.

She waved and then she started up the drive and it was a moonlit night so it was not until she got most of the way up the drive that she realized the house was in complete darkness. That was unusual, it was not late and none of the family ever went to bed at this hour, but not a single light burned in the windows and there was no noise. She thought it was especially strange that she could hear her footsteps as she approached the building. There being no light she went up to the front door which was never locked until the last of them went to bed but it was now.

The place had a strange feeling about it and she didn't like to have to go round to the side door. That too was always open but now it was locked and then the back door and that too was locked. She walked down the stable yard and the stables were empty and the carriage houses were too.

She knew what had happened but she did not think Ralph could have done such a thing, not in a few hours, it was impossible. She gazed through the windows and there was furniture in the rooms, not all of it perhaps but she could see now what he had done and she walked in the moonlight to where the drive to Snow Hall began and she had been right, light blazed from the house for the first time in fifteen years and as she drew nearer she could hear the sound of music, voices and laughter.

The front door was closed but not locked and she went inside and light fell across the hall from the drawing room and it was just as though they were at Black Well, the fire was lit in the hall, the dogs were sleeping, there was even a rug down for their comfort. She followed the light and the music and a table had been set up in the dining room there and the table was filled with half-eaten plates of food. Somebody had spilled red wine over the white cloth. Henry and Camille were dancing and the head stable boy played the fiddle. The uncles and aunts were snoring in their chairs and Ralph saw her immediately and came towards her and ushered her out into the hall.

There he picked her up and carried her upstairs while she protested and tried to free herself and soon they were in one of the bedrooms and the fire there had not yet taken the chill of so many winters from the room but there was a bed made up, nothing much else, a chest or two which must have contained clothes or his belongings. He let her down on to the bed and he said, 'I thought you'd gone for good and I was so disappointed when I had such a surprise for you. I saved you some champagne.' He indicated the bottle and glasses on one of the chests.

She twisted away from him.

'What on earth made you do this?' she said.

He got up and went over and opened the champagne.

'I don't want any.'

'You love champagne.'

He brought it over. He took the glass and slowly poured it over the front of her coat and dress. She said nothing.

'Did you honestly think you were going to get the better of me?' he said.

'I wasn't trying to get the better of you. I was trying to do the right thing.'

'That's very funny. I haven't heard of a Carlyle who was

trying to do the right thing before. You should learn not to take on people you can't better.'

'Is that what you do?'

'Oh, it's what I always do. What is the point in fighting the fights you cannot win? Do have some champagne.'

She moved away and he got hold of her.

'No, don't,' she said but he didn't let her go and he drew her off the bed and over to the bottle where it stood and then he poured the whole thing all over her, while she said, 'No, Ralph, don't,' and started fighting to get away. 'No, stop it.' When he let her go she went over to the door and tried to get out but it was locked. She hadn't seen him do this, why hadn't she seen him? 'Can you let me out, please?'

Ralph had conjured another bottle of champagne from somewhere and was opening it.

'Did you know this was the biggest room in the house? My grandfather and grandmother slept here. This is my bed, though, I had it brought over specially for tonight.'

'Do I not have a bedroom?'

'Right here.'

'I'm not staying here with you.'

'Oh, I think you'll find that you are. You have nowhere else to go and nobody else to go to and tomorrow we're going to be married in the chapel here. I procured a special licence to make sure that everything was as it should be.'

'I will never marry you.'

He smiled.

'I do like the way you say these things. Come over here. Come on. I'm too tired to fetch you, I've had a long day arranging things. The old place has improved already. You must have thought so when you saw the lights.'

She didn't move.

'I imagined you would have been pregnant by now,' Ralph said. 'That would have been so much easier.'

'I would still not have married you.'

'You know, that did occur to me. You are not the usual kind of woman who can be browbeaten by society's stupider ideas. It was one of the first things I liked about you. You wanted to have fun, black dresses and pink champagne, and to ride across the fields until you were breathless. Come on, don't let's quarrel about it any more and take those clothes off, they must be sticking to you.'

She didn't answer. She didn't move. Ralph drank the champagne. He got up and stood by the fire for a while with a glass in his hand and kept replenishing it.

'You can't keep me here indefinitely.'

'I don't have to, we'll be married tomorrow and then you will sell the premises to Fleming and everything will be fine.'

Nobody spoke after that. Ralph fell asleep on the bed but when she moved from the door, thinking she might look for the key, he woke up straight away. He hadn't had that much to drink, she thought. She was close enough for him to grab hold of her though he didn't do anything, he just held her, and even worse she was so cold by then and so uncomfortable and the bed was soft and he wasn't doing anything objectionable.

His arm around her relaxed but if she moved he woke up so she lay still and wondered what on earth she was going to do to get out of here. She wished now that she had not let Aidan go before they reached the house because he would have seen the darkness and he would have at least insisted on coming here with her and that would have been a bigger mistake because he might have got hurt or he might have prevented her somehow, though she didn't see how, from coming here at all.

As soon as it was light she would find a way out, she would escape. In the daylight everything would be different.

She didn't sleep, she kept thinking about Aidan's house and his mother and sister and how they disliked her and how she wished she had agreed to go to them, how much easier it would have been than this. She dozed off from time to time but every time she tried to move even just a little Ralph drew her close, she was convinced he could do this even in his sleep. She called herself all kinds of names before morning but none of it made any difference.

It was a bright morning, the sun came up and lit the windows and Ralph stirred and then went back to sleep and after a very long time there was a knocking on the door and he got up and went to open it and he brought a tray into the room. There was tea and bread and butter, eggs and bacon. She felt sick.

He came to her and he had poured tea and cut bread and butter. She went to the door and tried it and then hammered on it and then she shouted and shouted. Ralph didn't take any notice, he just continued eating, yawning from time to time and then staring out of the window as the sun warmed the countryside.

'I always loved this view,' he said, 'when I was a small child I used to come in here in the early mornings and Grandmother would get up and put an arm around me at the window. Nothing's stirring, not even a rabbit.'

'You can't keep me here,' she said, a little desperately.

'Oh dear,' Ralph said, 'and I had convinced myself that this would work. Now there are plenty of ways of making sure you do but you will not make a scene at the altar. How we arrive at that is up to you.'

She left the door and went to him and tried to find the person she had loved.

'Don't you care for me?'

He looked quizzically at her.

'You didn't really think so?' It was almost a plea. When she didn't answer he said, 'I did suspect you were that naive because of where you had come from and the life before you came here but no Carlyle has ever been that stupid and I reasoned differently. You did think so? I'm sorry, I thought we were like-minded, you certainly are difficult for a female, I haven't had much experience of diffi-cult women, usually they succumb so easily. You have surprised me often, which is why it took me so long to get to here. I felt so certain you would give in, give up or fall in love with me.'

'I did.'

'People who fall in love do not think as clearly as you or make the kind of decisions which you did.'

'Then what was it?'

'I fear it was what men usually feel, it was lust. Easily confused, don't you think?'

'I never felt anything for anyone before.'

'A disadvantage. You will know next time. Do have some tea before it grows cold.'

'If I promise to sell the business premises will you let me go?'

'Nothing will make me let you go before we are married. I did try very hard so that it wouldn't get to this but you were too clever for me, you knew that I was indolent and self-centred and you decided to get out and I don't blame you, I see why. I almost left it too late. I thought you wouldn't come back, I thought you had gone to Aidan and he would never have let you come back the way that things were. He's quite clever really, though something of a cold fish. I was sure you were in love with him but he's not your type, he could never make you want him.'

'How can you make somebody say yes at a wedding ceremony when they don't choose to?'

'Did you think this was a matter of choice? It never was. Not for either of us. If I thought even for a second that you would refuse I would knock you across the room. You aren't very big and the damage could be permanent. Is that what you want? I would so hate to risk breaking your neck, it would complicate things unduly.'

She couldn't think of anything more to say and the time passed and he poured more tea for himself, since she hadn't drunk hers, and he ate what was left of the breakfast, having, she assumed, waited a decent time before he did so just in case she should want something to eat – manners were Ralph's forte, after all. There was another slight knock on the door and when he opened it something white was handed to him and he closed the door again and then turned almost apologetically and he said, 'This was my mother's wedding dress but I shall quite understand if you don't want to wear it though it is more suitable than your present clothing.'

'What did your wife wear?'

'I was drunk throughout so I don't remember. I married her because she had money.'

She took the pretty satin garment from his hands and took off her clothes. He didn't even watch, he wasn't like that. The smell of old champagne was strange and sickly, it was like peeling off skin, it had stuck so thoroughly. She even poured water from the jug into a basin and washed her body completely and he didn't react at all, he just gazed out of the window, brow creased slightly as though he was thinking about something else entirely.

When she was dressed and had brushed her hair and made herself as presentable as she could she gazed at herself in the mirror. It fitted as well as though some clever seamstress had spent days sweating in the cold gloom of a back shop. The idea of a back shop made her think almost affectionately of Felicity and then almost to blame her for what had happened, which was ridiculous, she knew.

She had never imagined that someone could make her so afraid without actually doing anything that she would agree to do what he wanted but it was so now. She did not doubt him and could not bear the idea of being hurt physically. It was not cowardice, it was simply common sense. Aidan had been right about Ralph all along. She found comfort, for a few minutes, in the idea that Aidan would find out what had happened and then she thought, even if he did, it would be too late. Ralph was not to be put off.

It was a cold wet morning, the grass was soaking and the bottom of his mother's wedding dress was inches deep in rain and mud by the time they had walked the short distance to the chapel. All the Carlyle family were there. Neither Camille nor Henry looked at her and everybody else stood silent. She made her vows so softly that she did not think anyone would be able to hear her faltering voice and her hand shook when she had to sign the register.

Back at the house the rest of the furniture arrived and there were lots of boxes which the servants were unpacking.

'By tomorrow,' Ralph said, pouring champagne for her which she did not accept and which he put down on the little table beside her, 'everything will be here, the transformation will be complete, the Carlyles will be back where they should be.'

They were in the little room where she had found the money, the room she decided she had liked best with its small square Dutch tiles of windmills and clogs and tulips, so charming. The rest of the plaster had not fallen off the wall yet and the fire burned up and soon heated the room.

'Now may I go?'

'On your wedding day?'

She didn't say anything and Ralph looked at her for a long time and then he said,

'There are several ways to do this. I do like you but I had more important things to consider than you. We're married now and since I'm thirty I don't think I'm going to be going anywhere for a very long time. You like living with us or you did until you found stupid notions of shopkeeping. I blame Fleming for that. So, will you drink champagne and let it go?'

'I will drink to Snow Hall and its future.'

'I'm happy to do that.'

So they drank the champagne and after that Ralph led her upstairs. It was the first time in her life she had wished she had a weapon about her. She could see why people carried guns and if she had had one she would have shot him the moment after they entered the bedroom. And that would have been a waste because she would most surely have hanged for it.

Ralph maintained pleasantries throughout. She did admire it in him. He didn't do any insisting though she thought that if she had struggled even for a second he would have done but she had seen him in every mood now and there was a part of her which would not play the victim here.

He had her and that was all it was. He didn't hurt her, he didn't pin her down or hit her or make crude remarks or laugh and she was sure it was nothing more than many a woman endured on a Saturday night in dozens of pit villages and worse their husbands were drunk and dirty and clumsy, their breath was not sweet for champagne nor their bodies young and smooth. He even gathered her into his arms afterwards and told her to go to sleep as they had often done and she did, she was exhausted by then. She had not cried that day, she began to think she could not do it and that even her tear ducts had frozen on her.

# Twelve

When Aidan had arrived back after seeing Lorna to Black Well, Bea came into the hall.

'Heather said that Lorna Carlyle had been here.'

He went into the study and she followed him. He didn't say anything, he didn't know whether to take Bea into his confidence or not but he didn't want his mother to hear anything they might say.

'Is something going on?'

He hesitated.

'I feel so guilty about it all,' Bea said. 'Perhaps she should come back here and stay?'

'I've bought Snow Hall.' He hadn't intending saying this, somehow it said itself. Immediately afterwards he regretted the fact that he could obviously not control his mouth. Bea stared at him and nobody spoke for such a long time.

'Is that what the visit was all about?' Bea stood for several seconds and then she said, 'She's afraid of him, isn't she? My God, Aidan, you shouldn't have let her go back there.'

'She insisted. What could I do?'

'She has no real choice after living like that with him,' Bea said wearily. 'Either she has to stay with him or leave the area altogether.'

'She wants to open a shop on the business premises and to have Ned rent a part of it.'

Bea shook her head. 'Ned and Annabel Fleming are not typical of people in this city. Other respectable people wouldn't go. You didn't let her think such a thing, surely.'

'I would have supported her.'

Bea was silent again and then she looked at him in a way that he thought she had not before and she said, 'You couldn't marry her.'

He was astonished at this and turned the sentence over and over in his mind and he knew that this had been what he had thought all along, that there was no way in which he could marry this woman and there were so many good reasons, a dozen of them at least, and he had explained it all away, used logic and made excuses and yet always he saw her as she had been for the first time, poorly dressed and standing in the doorway, like an animal emerging from a hole in the ground. He pushed away everything that he felt and said, a little hoarsely, 'Who said anything about marriage?' and he went to the fire so that Bea would not see his face.

'Are you very much in love?'

'Not at all, how ridiculous,' he said and then realized that he was almost shouting and he turned away from her and said into the fire, 'Oh, Jesus Christ,' in a way which would have made his mother pass out if she'd been within hearing.

Instead of reproving him or leaving the silence of disapproval or making a dreadful joke Bea only said in a soft voice, 'I'm so sorry, Aidan.'

'I think I loved her from the beginning but the last thing I ever wanted to do was marry after what we put up with. Years and years of shouting and screaming and days and days of silence and that horrible feeling that they hated one another so badly that it was crawling up the walls. I can't stand the way Mother wears black as though she cared for him and she pretends, she has made up a life that never existed, a time in which we were happy.'

'She has to do that.'

'Sometimes I just wish that she would die,' he said and then was horrified not just at what he had said but at his shaking voice.

For the first time in many years Bea went to Aidan and he put his arms around her.

Aidan knew that he shouldn't go to Black Well, he would think of several reasons not to, he had appointments the following morning and so many urgent things to attend to that he made himself go to the office and begin to work as though he had nothing on his mind other than that.

He made himself stay though his concentration was low and after lunch he couldn't help himself any longer, even though the rain was coming down hard. He astonished the staff by saying that he had an urgent appointment as they knew very well he hadn't and went off to Black Well. When he got to the point where he had left Lorna the night before he paused for some reason and then went on around the corner and there he stopped.

His instincts had not betrayed him, something was wrong, and as he drew nearer he realized that the house and its surroundings were empty. The curtains were gone from the windows, the rooms were bare.

He didn't hesitate, he hurried across to Snow Hall. Everything was quiet there but it was inhabited. Servants were still carrying boxes and items of furniture through the hall into the rooms as he came in through the open front door.

He had amused himself the previous evening after Lorna had gone by imagining what Ralph would look like, what Ralph would say when he was told that the hall was now Aidan's property. He had not thought that he would walk in like this to find that Ralph had taken possession. It meant that Lorna had, for some reason, told Ralph that she had sold the place and he had moved in and made sure that all his household moved with him.

Ralph had either heard him or been told he was there because he came into the hall, saying carelessly, 'Why, Aidan, what are you doing here?' He smiled broadly and Aidan knew it was not the expression of a man who was aware that the house he had wanted so badly belonged to another man and that man was standing in front of him. Neither was it the expression of a man who had moved here out of desperation. Aidan could not work out what Ralph's expression showed.

'I came to see Miss Carlyle.'

'Ah, alas, we have no one of that name.'

Aidan didn't understand. Was Lorna not here with her family? Had she and Ralph quarrelled badly? Had she left? Was she back at the other house? He cursed himself for not lingering there, for not going inside somehow and finding her. Was she hurt, was she alone? He did the only thing he could think of. He said, 'Is Lorna not here, then?' and he felt as though he stumbled over each word.

Ralph went back out into the hall and said something Aidan didn't catch to one of the servants. Eventually he came back in and after a few moments Lorna came in too.

Aidan was so relieved to see her that he didn't know what to say and since Ralph didn't leave he couldn't say any of the things he wanted to and turned each would be comment over in his mind and as he did so he looked at her and he saw, with dismay, that she was quite different from the worried girl he had left the evening before and he was angry with himself for having left her.

She looked steadily at him. She was pale and had dark smudges under her eyes as though she hadn't slept but she was calm.

'Aidan,' she said, 'how good of you to come.' It was the first time she had called him by his name since the once she had done so by mistake, shortly after they first met, and he did not pretend to himself that he was pleased about it or that she did it out of friendship. Her voice was cool as ice.

'I just wanted to see how you did.'

'I'm quite well.'

'I didn't know that you were moving.' He included both of them in this remark.

'I was going to come and see you today,' Ralph offered. 'You can tell Fleming that he may have the business premises. We no longer have need of them. If he agrees then you can draw up the papers for signing. I take it he still wants the place?'

Aidan was so taken aback that he didn't answer immediately and then all he could say was, 'So far as I know.'

'Good,' Ralph said.

'I thought you were going to rent part of the premises and start a shop?' He directed this at Lorna.

'There will be plenty to do here. With the money we plan to do this place up. God knows it needs it,' Ralph said.

And then Aidan realized. He couldn't think what had taken him so long.

'You're married,' he said.

'This morning,' Ralph said with a beaming smile. 'I got a special licence. In the chapel here. Very fitting, don't you think?'

Aidan couldn't remember the last time he had done something without thinking about it and he prided himself that he never lost his temper so he had no concept of who the man was that hit Ralph Carlyle.

One moment he was himself and the next he was possessed by the kind of loss of temper which he thought with slight regret he must have inherited from his mother because his father had never lost his temper through all the years of his mother shouting and screaming and throwing various objects in his direction.

It all came back, her working herself up into a frenzy, calling his father names in front of other people, the way she had somehow forced him to move out of the bedroom, the days of Bea and himself moving so quietly, afraid that at any moment the storm would break once again.

It had broken here because he knocked Ralph right across the room, he saw with satisfaction how Ralph, taken by surprise, went back, staggering and then losing his balance and falling and he could hear, for days afterwards the cry that Lorna uttered, 'Aidan, no!' As though he had killed Ralph instead of just inflicting a little damage and losing his own dignity in the process.

Ralph must have shouted, though in his fury Aidan didn't hear him because two big men appeared in the doorway and they got hold of him and even then Aidan couldn't contain his anger.

'You bastard. You miserable snivelling—' The rest of the words were not said because he ran out of breath and when he remembered who he was and where he was he was standing over Ralph though held back and there was blood on the turkey rug which Ralph had wiped from his face and then touched the rug as he got up slowly and carefully and Ralph's henchmen had come in and they got hold of Aidan to stop him while Ralph smiled. It was the worst smile that Aidan had ever seen, Ralph wiping more blood away from his face and grinning.

'Throw him out!'

They did. Aidan found himself sprawling at the front door of the house he owned, knowing that he could do very little about any of this.

The bar of the County Hotel was always a busy place. Mid-afternoon in other parts of the hotel ladies drank tea and ate fancy pink-and-white cakes. The older ones talked about their grand-children and the younger ones about their children. It was quiet in the corner of the bar, though. The lunchtime drinkers had gone and it was too early for those people coming in after work.

People drifted in and out, even the barman, polishing glasses and chatting. Aidan liked the chat, he liked the seat there in the shadows which the bar cast somehow because it was after all a discreet place. He had no doubt that lovers met there and could not be seen and various noises floated through, scraps of conversation and the chink of glasses.

In the early evening it became busier but nobody bothered him until he gradually became aware of a tall figure moving towards him and it emerged into Ned Fleming.

'Aidan?'

Aidan scrutinized him.

'I was going to come and see you.'

Ned sat down on the tall stool next to his.

'Would you like a drink?' Aidan offered.

'Aren't you ready to go home?'

Aidan considered his glass on the bar. It still held some brandy.

'Not quite yet,' he said.

'Isn't Bea expecting you back for dinner?'

'I never get there. My father never did either, you know. He would stay at the office sometimes until we'd gone to bed. So much to do.'

'I could come with you.'

'I wouldn't recommend it,' Aidan said. 'The food is awful.'

Ned caught the barman's attention.

'Jack, can we have some coffee?'

'Wouldn't you rather have a drink?' Aidan said.

Ned pushed the brandy glass away from him.

'Jack, put another double in there,' Aidan said.

Ned shook his head. Aidan didn't argue. He got very carefully off his stool when Ned got up and they moved not very far but around the corner where there were comfortable leather chairs and once Aidan had sat down he didn't understand why he hadn't moved there sooner.

The coffee arrived and Ned poured it out and gave him the cup and saucer.

'There's no milk,' Aidan objected.

'It tastes better like that.'

It didn't, it was hot and bitter and somehow fought with the brandy as it went down. Ned poured some more and he insisted it was drunk. Aidan didn't want to argue with anybody else for a long time so he drank it and then looked about. There was nobody in that part of the room and for a while nobody spoke and it was like velvet, that silence, he was so glad of it, it was the reason he had gone there in the first place, space and silence and the slow pull of the river somehow was right and soothing.

'You feeling any better?' Ned enquired after a small eternity had passed.

Aidan looked across at Ned, who had drunk only half of his coffee. 'How did you know I was here?'

'I went to half a dozen pubs and then it occurred to me that you would hardly be thinking of subtlety. Mr Gray was worried about you.' Ned glanced at him. Aidan pretended not to notice. 'What happened?'

'Well – Ralph Carlyle has decided to sell you the premises next door. There, I knew you'd be pleased.'

The silence after that took in at least another eternity. Just when Aidan was beginning to think he might politely ask for another drink Ned said, 'You hit him?'

'How did you know that?'

Ned reached over and touched his hand and to Aidan's aston-ishment the knuckles on his right hand were slightly bloody. It was nothing to be concerned about, he thought, regarding them with interest.

'He didn't hit you.'

'He didn't need to hit me. He won.'

'And her?'

'He didn't hit her either, at least not that I could tell.' The need for brandy was going off now. 'Somehow he induced her to marry him.'

Ned was silent for a few moments and then sighed softly, as though he had known something of the kind had occurred.

'She didn't have so many choices, you know, Aidan.'

'That's more or less what Bea said. I thought the idea of the shop was something real, something that could be achieved in spite of everything that happened. The trouble is that we've put women into small boxes and told them what their choices are, no wonder everything is such a mess. I don't understand why I couldn't get this right.'

'Do you want some more coffee?'

Aidan shook his head. Ned got up.

'Come on, then, we can go back to my house and have something to eat.'

The air outside was surprisingly cold somehow as he met it. Aidan was glad of that.

# Thirteen

Lorna had not known that she could be so unhappy at the place she had loved so much. She was glad of the warmer weather as the weeks went by into spring and then became summer because Snow Hall was not sufficiently weather-tight to shelter people well. The summer showed neglect too, the grass long in the fields, the broken fences, the shabby outbuildings and in all the rooms the plaster was cracked and the wallpaper mouldy or peeling.

She had hoped that Ralph would use the money from the sale of the premises to begin to repair what he could afford but nothing happened until one day when a new carriage appeared and two showy black horses. She found Ralph down there at the carriage house admiring his latest purchase.

'And this is what you spent my money on?' she said, angry but not very surprised.

'Isn't it beautiful?'

'We already have two carriages. What did we need with a third?'

'I couldn't resist it. And don't you think these two horses are beauties?'

'They won't keep out the wind and the rain next winter.'

'Oh, don't be boring,' Ralph said, smiling amiably at her. 'We can deal with those things when they happen.'

'You forced me to marry you and took my money for this?'

'There's plenty left and besides, the tradesmen don't expect to be paid straight away—'

'The butcher came to the house the other day, Camille said, and will give us no more meat because we owe him so much and he isn't the only one.'

'We'll find somebody else to deal with. There are plenty of butchers about. And besides it will be autumn soon. There'll be plenty of game and geese and ducks coming into the big ponds past the house. There are fish in the stream here, rabbits and pigeons aplenty in the woods. Details, my darling, just details,' and he patted the two horses and rubbed their velvet noses.

She thought that Ralph, having attained his goal, would no longer sleep with her but he came to her bed every night and it occurred to her that he was determined to have a child, to make an heir for Snow Hall. In the circumstances it could have been laughable but it was not. She hated his very touch and would turn her face away when he tried to kiss her lips. He seemed not to notice or to care.

Nobody made her stay at the house now that they were moved in and she was married and eventually when she had enough courage she went into town and made an appointment to see Aidan and the afternoon when she turned up at his office she remembered the last time they had met and how he had hit Ralph and she could not look Aidan in the face.

He said stiffly, 'Mrs Carlyle, do sit down.'

'Oh, don't,' was all she said. Aidan closed the door.

'What is it?' he said and he got down beside her chair so that she felt better and worse all at the same time.

She didn't want him that close or that compassionate, it made her think of the look on his face when he had understood that they were married and how he had lost his temper and hit Ralph.

'I just wanted to get out. I wanted to see you, that's all, and I walked up and down for an hour before the appointment and—'

'Let's go for a walk,' he suggested.

They left the office by the back way and went along the towpath. It was a pretty day to go out of town, the leaves were just beginning to turn. She could not think what had happened to the summer. She told him what Ralph had done with the money so far.

'I didn't understand how he felt about the house—' she said and Aidan said impatiently,

'He doesn't care about the house. Has he done a single thing to improve it since you got there?'

She too became angry, she could not understand why, Aidan had always done everything he could to help, this was not his fault. She only wished she had listened to him. She wished they could go back to the beginning and she would sell everything and have a little house in town and run a shop and she thought, yes, I really am Felicity's niece, I still see myself behind the counter. I have come no further.

'How could you understand? You live in that – appalling little house with your – your dreadful family.' Lorna thought back to Bea's room at the house which was so over-furnished that there was hardly room to move. If ever a woman should have a house of her own it was Bea.

And that was when he said what she felt he had been waiting all afternoon to ask.

'What did he do to make you marry him?'

'Nothing.'

She didn't like the way that he was looking at her. They had stopped. There was nobody about.

'Did he force you?'

'No.'

'He must have done.'

'He made me believe that he would. He's the only person I could have married, that's the truth of it. We all know it and what a fool I made of myself. How I ended up caring for things that didn't matter like fine clothes and dancing and—' She stopped there, unable to go on any further because she couldn't trust her voice not to break.

'In fact the worst you can accuse yourself of is that after almost twenty years of unremitting drudgery, boredom and poverty you wanted to waltz in a beautiful dress.'

She shook her head. They didn't talk any more, he put her hand through his arm.

When they came back into town Aidan took her to Saddler Street and left Ned to show her the premises and she could not help regretting what could not be. The sign outside now read 'Durham Guardian and Chronicle' right across the front of the two build-ings in big letters and it looked as though it had always been like that, to her slight regret. It took in the rooms which she had been going to use for her shop but when they went inside it was almost as she had imagined.

The smell of paper and ink held the air and there were shelves of books for people to buy and others for them to borrow. Expensive pens sat in leather and satin cases and hard-backed journals bound in blue, red, black or brown leather stood on the shelves. The counters were polished, the floor tiles had been washed and buffed. There were newspapers and periodicals for sale, coloured pencils and chalks with small blackboards for the children and even puzzles and games for them to buy, cheaply priced, she noticed, so that even the poorest might find a small treat.

Ned came through and showed them where he had broken through and extended the back rooms now full of machinery and there were new offices. Annabel also came in when she heard their voices and managed to hug Lorna without commenting on her marriage and then took her to the Silver Street cafe where they had tea and scones and she said, 'I was wanting to get in touch. I'm starting up my women's magazine. I'm going to call it *Ladies' Forum* and I would like you to write some articles for me.'

Lorna was astonished but she could not help feeling a small lift of excitement such as she had not experienced since the giving up of all her hopes of independence and work she might love.

'What could I possibly write about?'

'Hats. What is fashionable, what is unfashionable, what women ought to look for in a hat, whether they should be worn on every occasion. What is suitable, where and how different hats are made, the materials used, the ideas behind them, wedding hats, everyday hats—' Here Annabel ran out of breath and ideas but Lorna was very taken with the notion.

'We could call it Fashion Chat and incorporate all kinds of clothing,' Annabel said. 'It would mean that women of every back-ground would have something to read and also we could tie it in with advertising. I would go to the various shops who sell women's wear. I could talk to them about what is likely to be all the mode at various seasons and we could put the article in the middle and the advertisements around the outside or some-thing like that. I would have to ask Bert what would be best. We could give you a by-line.'

When she explained that this meant it would read 'Fashion Chat by Lorna Carlyle' Lorna thought not.

'I can't possibly let Ralph find out what I'm doing,' she said and that was when Annabel looked frankly at her and said,

'I'm so very sorry about your marriage. I had to stop Ned, he was so incensed for you that he would have come to the house.'

'I wish you had been able to stop Aidan too. It didn't help.'

Annabel thought for something positive to say, Lorna could see, and she came up with, 'You would be paid properly for your work,' and Lorna thought she couldn't have said anything which would have suited better though it took time to sink in. Lorna could not believe that she could make money in such a way but when they had finished their tea and scones Annabel took her back to the newspaper premises and they talked to Bert about how the layout would look for the proposed articles.

Lorna liked the tall thickset man who looked after the sub-editing and the printing. He was enthusiastic, his passion for work showed in his eyes, and Annabel introduced her to all the other men who worked there and they were all the same, she felt better than she had felt in a long time, it was like a homecoming, here in the bowels of the newspaper business.

Then they went into the front and Annabel introduced her to Eliza Grahame who did the typing for the offices and explained what she wanted but also said to Lorna that there was a great deal of work and if she could learn to type herself it would be a great help. Lorna thought there could be no more interesting place on earth than Annabel's office which was very large and had three desks in it.

'I'm going to run the magazine from here. If you like you could have your own desk.'

Lorna was entranced.

The rest of the afternoon was caught up in thinking of new ideas for the magazine and included articles on general fashion, also, keeping in mind those who had no ready money, how to make clothes you already had look more pleasing, crafts such as embroidery, knitting and sewing, reviews of popular books, articles about child welfare and upbringing and those of politics and general matters which were of especial concern to women.

The day was far advanced when Annabel had to go home and see to her little boy. Ned volunteered to take Lorna home and said as they walked briskly down the street, 'I'm very sorry for your situation. I had no idea things were that bad.'

'Don't worry about me, I shall manage.'

'I suspect you have always done so.' She kissed his cheek when they reached Snow Hall and waved him away and then she went inside and up to her room to change for dinner, hugging to her every word that Annabel had said about the magazine.

She was quite distracted when they sat down at the table but nobody noticed and her mind was free to range over the first of her articles for the magazine and she was so excited that after dinner, while Ralph and the others played cards, she took the journal which Annabel had given her and a pen and wrote by the fire.

'What are you doing?' Camille asked, coming over to her.

'I'm writing a journal, just the day's doings and so on. I can stop if you want to talk,' she said and she put down her pen apparently willingly and kept the smile on her face but behind it the voice in her head played on and later when she and Camille went to bed and left the men playing cards, she took the journal and her pen upstairs and began again and it held her attention until Ralph came to bed. He was drunk and only just managed to undress before he fell into bed, snoring.

Lorna wished she could have had a typewriter but she didn't want to arouse any suspicion in her husband so she confined herself to writing by hand, and going into town on the pretext of shopping, she would call in at the office and Miss Grahame would show her the basics of typewriting, starting with the middle letters and memorizing them on the left and the right and Lorna's enthusiasm carried her ahead so far that within days she was producing fairly good copy.

She liked being there with Miss Grahame and Annabel and all the men so much that it was only with reluctance that she went home but sometimes she had to go shopping with Camille or stay at home so that Ralph was left in ignorance but Camille hated reading which was Lorna's excuse for being alone and would leave the room in search of other amusement so Lorna was left for hours to do her writing.

As for the money she was paid, she was obliged to keep it in a small locked box which Ned provided her with and he kept it hidden away on the premises. She did not see that she would ever be able to spend it but it was nice just to think that she was able to earn from something she enjoyed doing so much. It was not work to her, it was freedom.

The magazine went ahead and she became Yvette, Fashion Editor. She and Annabel also wrote articles on how to make Christmas gifts for your family, Easy Ways to make a Christmas wreath for your door and Paper Chains, What's New. For those lucky enough to be attending dinner parties and balls there were fashion tips and what was the latest style in accessories, for the less lucky who were at home there were articles on how to keep your children happy with homemade toys, what your Christmas dinner might consist of and Mrs Hatty's Best Ever Christmas pudding.

Annabel took Lorna to meet Mrs Hatty, who ran the Garden House Hotel, and they ended up in a back bedroom at Mrs Hatty's, under cover of buying early Christmas presents in the town for their loved ones, sitting by a fire with a couple of typewriters on a rickety table and two of Mrs Hatty's less good dining chairs, drinking lots of tea and thinking up new ideas in front of what Mrs Hatty called 'a roaring fire'.

Mrs Hatty would interrupt frequently, so interested was she, bringing more tea and building up the fire and asking from time to time whether they had considered articles on special sage stuffing for the chicken, dried fruit stuffing for the goose and special leftovers for Boxing Day.

Camille came into the front hall one particular day shortly after this and said, 'Are you going into town? May I come?' She said it quickly as though it was all one sentence so that Lorna could hardly refuse. She couldn't think of an excuse though she was annoyed but Camille's face lit up at the idea of shopping and so in the end, despite having promised Annabel they would go to the Silver Street cafe and discuss the magazine, she ended up taking Camille. They were early for the meeting and she was just working out what she would say to Annabel, it didn't have to be much, Annabel was very quick, when Camille said to her,

'I'm sorry about what happened. I feel so guilty and so awful for you and I know you don't feel as if we can be friends any more.'

Lorna was surprised and then looked into Camille's glittering eyes and Camille looked down and didn't cry but when she would have spoken Camille said, 'I married Henry to leave a – a very bad situation. I didn't think I was getting myself into another and I wanted to help you but I didn't dare.'

'Is it so hard?'

Camille didn't answer and then Annabel turned up so Camille was obliged to hide her tears but when Annabel sat down, Lorna having said they had come into town to shop, Camille looked up and said,

'I know you had planned this meeting. I won't keep you,' and she got up to go but Annabel put a hand on her arm and said,

'No, don't go, I think you might be able to help,' and while Lorna sat she told Camille about the magazine and their ideas and a kind of light dawned in Camille's face which Lorna had never seen before.

'Oh, how wonderful,' she said.

Annabel agreed with this and after drinking their tea they went on to Imelda Watson's and had coffee with her and talked about the new fashions, what they thought might be popular with the women of Durham next season. Camille turned out to have a fair eye for colour and design and made a number of very good suggestions, including that she could write a column about seasonal events, the idea being that it would let people know what was happening before it happened and then there would be some gossip about it afterwards which she could also report, if she was fairly discreet about it.

'One of us would have to be seen everywhere,' Annabel said.

'It shouldn't be difficult, between us we cover the hunt balls, the dinner dances, the church and chapel services, the various parties—'

'And Ned could cover the things women don't get invited to.'

That week they were including Mrs Hatty's special stews and warming soups, and a knitting pattern which Annabel hated because these were so awful to proof-read but they would prove very popular they all agreed, and were including patterns for babies' and small children's hats, scarves and mitts in the Christmas issue.

When Lorna and Camille reached home just before dinner Ralph eyed them suspiciously and said they seemed to be doing a great deal of shopping and Camille lifted her chin in a way that Lorna hadn't seen her do before and said that they had to be discerning in such matters or did Ralph want the women of the family to wear ghastly clothes and he retreated and said nothing of the kind, he wanted them to be elegant of course, like a man who wishes he hadn't said anything.

On the days when Lorna and Camille did not go to town sometimes now Annabel came to the house and occasionally she would bring Thomas, her little boy, with her and Lorna would watch him and wished that she could have been pregnant. She didn't see why she wasn't and she imagined what it might be like to hold a child of your own close. Perhaps you needed to feel affection and passion for such things to happen and then she thought of the pit wives with their huge broods and pale, weary faces and thought that it was not so. There was certainly no lack of closeness to Ralph, he had nothing to complain about there.

One day after Annabel had gone Camille watched her down the path with the little boy and Lorna could see longing in her face.

'Isn't he gorgeous?' Camille said.

'He's wonderful.'

'I wish I could have a child.'

'You've been married a long time.'

Camille shook her head. 'Such things between Henry and me stopped – or never really started.'

Lorna gazed at her and Camille faltered and then she said, 'He only likes to look at me, you see.'

'Look at you?'

'Why yes. Very often he doesn't want me at all and,' Camille shuddered, 'I can't say that I want him.' Camille turned to her impulsively and she said, 'Be careful, won't you?'

'What do you mean?'

'I mean that Ralph got tired of his first wife. I don't want to alarm you but—'

Lorna stared. There were footsteps in the hall, one of the servants, so they were silent after that but when it was late, when the men were drunk and playing cards, Camille and Lorna went off into the little sitting room and sat over the fire and Lorna, who could contain herself no longer, said, 'Did he go to other women?'

'He treated her badly. She thought he cared about her and she argued with him.'

Lorna shivered.

'I would never argue with Ralph any more, he gets that look in his eyes, like nothing would stop him. Did he really not care when she died?'

'He cared very much about the loss of the child, he wanted a son, as I suppose they all do.' Camille stopped there but it was not the kind of thing which meant she had said what she wanted to say but just a pause and after Lorna had waited while she thought Camille debated whether to say any more she went on.

'She didn't die when the child was born but she was very weak and she slipped and fell over the balcony in front of their bedroom at Black Well and hit her head on the ground below and died.'

Lorna felt sick. 'Was it really an accident?'

'It was taken as such. Some people thought she was so miserable after losing the child and that he treated her so badly that she did it on purpose.'

'Oh God. He told me he only married her for her money. He married me for that too and if I can't bear a child—' She couldn't stand the thought and put her hands over her face.

Camille said nothing and then another thought occurred to Lorna and she looked at Camille and she said, 'What if he did it?'

Instead of smiling at the idea and shaking her head Camille said, white-faced, 'She was told there would be no more children, she had had childbed fever and was so ill and he cares very much for this place and the family name and he was the one that found her but of course it was all smoothed over.'

The idea of Ralph as the kind of man who would do anything for an heir made Lorna want to faint for possibly the first time in her life. She thought back to her wedding day and how she had married him before he even put a hand on her in anger.

# Fourteen

The magazine flourished and Lorna and Camille spent most of their days in Annabel's office. It was even better than Lorna had imagined it because the front office dealt with the buying of stationery, the back of it was the setting up of the printing but they were involved in everything, including the cover which changed with every fortnightly issue and was a subject of great discussion.

Then one cold winter day Bea Hedley came into the office, rather crimson-faced. She looked dismayed when she saw that alongside the editor there was Miss Grahame, Camille and Lorna and tried to retreat but Annabel was not the kind of person who would see anyone backing out of her office and she took Bea's arm as the blushing woman tried to get away and brought her inside.

'Is it something from the church?' she asked helpfully.

'It's a short story. I know you don't publish such things but I—'

She went no further but Annabel said that she fully intended publishing the kind of short stories which women might enjoy because she thought there was a definite place for fiction in the magazine. Bea again would have left but Annabel sat her down and gave her coffee, while to Bea's huge embarrassment she read the story through and when she looked up she said, 'I think it's excellent. Women want to read about women, their problems and their affections, and this is a wonderful love story. How much do you want for it?' and Bea's face crimsoned even more with pleasure. 'It will have appeal to everyone who reads it,' Annabel said. 'Have you any more?'

'You would like to see another?'

'I would very much like to. We could do with such fiction in every issue of the magazine.'

'I couldn't use my name.'

'You can be anyone you choose,' Annabel said largely.

Lorna saw the reserve drop from Bea like never before.

Annabel gave her coffee and then Lorna asked about the story and Bea said, her gaze dropping, 'It's about a girl who has an inheritance and how it changes her life.'

Lorna, recovering quickly, said, 'Oh well, nothing that any of us knows about,' and the tension went from the room.

'Perhaps, later, you could write a serial,' Annabel said, 'if you could make it so that it stops at a very exciting place each time it would mean more magazines sold as people wanted to know what happened.'

'That would be wonderful, though I must keep it secret from my mother. She would be scandalized.'

Annabel looked about her as Lorna had known she would and said, 'I think there's room for another desk in here.'

When Bea had finally composed herself and left Ned came in and Annabel told him about the idea of a serial and he said that if it was really good he might think of publishing it as a full book afterwards so that it might reach a wider audience.

Camille became Yvette, Fashion Editor and Lorna moved on to writing other kinds of articles. She did a series of articles on Women at Work, interviewed those who made quilts and some who were good at lace-making and shopkeepers of all kinds and women who helped their men folk like the farmers' wives who made butter and cheese and the butchers' wives who made black puddings and sausages and brawn and tongue and boiled hams and pease pudding.

There were painters and poets – Annabel, not averse to gathering any kind of copy which she thought would do, discovered two very good poets who had not been published before and Ned talked to them about publishing slim volumes of their work and after that Lorna suggested to Bea that she might start a writing group at the offices in the afternoons.

Bea was very excited about this and so the first Wednesday in February a dozen women gathered in a semicircle around a big fire in the biggest of the back rooms and Lorna thought that eventually they would be able to have poetry and short-story and serial readings in the front of the shop where the journals and pens were sold.

Annabel asked Bea to write some children's stories and on

Saturday afternoons they gathered the children and their mothers and sometimes even their fathers, having put a notice in the newspapers and in the front windows to let people know and Ned had leaflets posted and that late winter people would listen to the readings and keep out of the cold and go home happier when the afternoons gave way to dark nights.

One such early evening Lorna saw Aidan standing outside, waiting for his sister. She had not seen him in so long that she found herself going outside into the cold. She went towards him, smiling, and found that he smiled in return and she was glad of it.

She greeted him and then tried to decide whether to ask him a question which had been on her mind for some time and then she thought she did not know when she would have another opportunity so she blurted it out because she was afraid that she would lose her nerve and not say it.

'Do you know anything about Ralph's first wife?'

Aidan frowned at the suddenness of her question and looked surprised.

'Like what?'

'Like how she died?' There was silence. 'Was it anything to do with Ralph?'

'There was no evidence that Ralph had done anything or been anywhere near at the time.'

Bea came out at that moment, her step was light and her smile wide. She tucked her hand through Aidan's arm and wished Lorna goodnight so happily that it made Lorna smile again before she went back inside.

Aidan had a visitor shortly after this, a doctor from Castle Bank Colliery, a man with whom he had had various dealings over the years because the firm had always been his solicitor but his news was not about him, it was about Felicity Robson.

'I understand that you dealt with the inheritance of her so-called niece so I thought I should come to you. Miss Robson is dead and someone will have to pay for and arrange the funeral. I thought you would know how best to get in touch with the niece since you have been acting for her.'

★　★　★

Ralph, seeing Lorna come home late one afternoon with Camille, came into the hall, a sure sign that he had been waiting for her.

'You got a letter from Hedley this morning. Your aunt died.'

She wanted to ask him fiercely why he should open her letter but she knew that there was no point.

'There must be something in it for you. He suggests an appointment.'

She said nothing. She took the letter and read it. She did not know what she felt but she could not help the tears coming into her eyes. She wished things had been better between herself and Felicity. Felicity was the only person who had cared sufficiently to give her a home and though it had not been much of a home it was still a lot better than some people had.

'Did she own the property where the shop was?'

'I don't know.'

'Well, we can certainly use the money,' Ralph said.

So far Ralph had done nothing to Snow Hall. She had no idea how much of her money he had left but as far as she could judge it had gone on things they could have well done without. The house was cold and draughty, the roof leaked and Ralph was always swearing and complaining about it. The whole place was damp and the windows were rotten and rattled at night. He had spent money on the stables. Camille was fond of saying that they would be more comfortable sleeping with the horses though she only said such things when they were alone.

He drew her into the study and she let Camille go on upstairs without her to change for dinner. There was no fire in that room, nobody ever went in there. It was dark and gloomy and only a single lamp was lit against the night.

'If there is any money I want it, do you understand?'

He smelled of whisky. He was drinking more now, she thought, though she was not there during the day to know quite what he did.

'Of course,' she said.

'What were you doing in town?'

'Oh, the usual. We go and visit, we shop, we have coffee.'

'Every day?'

'Well, yes. Surely you don't mind?'

'I suppose not.'

He kissed her. She would have turned away but he caught her by the hair. He didn't hurt her but if she had moved it would have hurt. She knew that he was becoming more and more frustrated because there was no child and every opportunity now that he was given he wanted to have her so that she did not get a chance to change for dinner and since the dining room was always freezing now she was glad at least that she didn't have to wear an evening dress, it was so little protection against the cold.

The following morning she went into town to see Aidan and to hear him say how sorry he was that her aunt had died.

'I still think of her that way. Do you know what she died of?'

'Apparently it was her heart.'

It most likely broke or wore away from lack of use, Lorna could not help thinking savagely.

'Did you contact her after you left?' Aidan said.

'Several times but she didn't reply and I hadn't the courage to go back. I didn't want to hear her say any more of the awful things she said to me when I walked out.'

'You don't regret it?'

She shook her head.

'Are things getting worse?'

Now she regretted having questioned him the other night. She cursed herself silently for somehow giving this away and Aidan for his perception.

'No.'

He didn't believe her, she could tell by his expression.

'You could leave him.'

'Where would I go? I have a life now with Annabel and the others at the office and—'

Aidan said nothing to that.

'What Ralph really wants to know is whether my aunt has left me anything.'

Aidan hesitated.

'I'm not sure that there is a will, I have to go there and look for it and you are not related as far as I'm aware. In the meanwhile there is the funeral to be paid for.'

'Naturally I'll pay for that but it will have to be a secret. Ralph thinks I have no money of my own so I'm afraid you'll have to pay for it for the time being. I don't want her in a pauper's grave or for the parish to have to pay. She looked after me all those years and then I walked out and left her.'

'Lorna—'

'Oh, don't.' She got up. 'Don't tell me it was the right thing to do, I don't think that I can stand it. I've made such a mess of things, I can hardly bear myself any more.'

'You could at least stop lying to me,' he said.

She stared at him. Aidan looked straight back at her. She sighed and shook her head.

'You were born for this job.'

'What an appalling thought,' he said with a vestige of a smile.

'Oh, you were. Sometimes I think you see straight through everybody. He isn't treating me any worse than I suspect most husbands treat their wives. He's beginning to drink very heavily, he hardly goes out, the house is falling apart—'

'There's no evidence that he mistreated his first wife.'

'How do you know?'

'Because he wasn't there.'

'You don't have to be there, though, do you? You just have to make someone hate themselves and it seems to me that women are good at these things.'

'Are you telling me you think she might have killed herself?'

'Isn't it possible?'

'I suppose so. It was a frosty night, it was assumed that she slipped.'

'If it was that cold what on earth was she doing out there?' Lorna argued, sitting down again in her eagerness to shift the focus of the conversation from her own relationship with Ralph. 'Unless she had lost her mind because the child had died.' She stopped this line of thought abruptly, knowing that it would not help. 'I have to go, I'm meeting Annabel and Bea at eleven.'

'Shall I organize the funeral?'

'I'll do it.'

'Then I'll come with you,' he said and she nodded in agreement and left.

# Fifteen

Castle Bank Colliery in the dead of winter with slushy streets and dark days was the least good time to go back, she thought. Ralph did not offer to go with her. When she told him what Aidan had said about the lack of will and lack of family between the two women he swore and then lost interest.

Sitting in the local funeral director's office she was only glad that Aidan had gone with her because deciding on the coffin, the burial, the flowers, was almost impossible somehow. She did not want to make any decisions and all she remembered afterwards was that she kept on saying yes to Aidan's polite suggestions. They trudged down Church Lane to see the vicar where a biting wind cut across their faces from the fell beyond the village because there was nothing to stop it and then they were sitting being asked what kind of hymns they wanted and she couldn't think of a single one.

'Your aunt did not attend church often so I have no idea what she would want,' the vicar said. 'Of course she was not from here. I believe her family had something to do with the iron and steel works at Consett.'

'There was so much to do,' she said.

'Some women have four or five children, get them ready, are here and still make a Sunday dinner when they get home,' the vicar said as though there was something virtuous in overwork.

'And come and clean the church, no doubt, mid-week,' she could not prevent herself from saying.

He agreed. Irony, she had discovered, was not the vicar's forte.

They did not have to pass the shop to go home, the road led from Church Lane up to the station, but she knew that being Aidan, he would have arranged everything.

'I'd like to go to the shop with you.'

'I would like an opportunity to search for the will but you don't have to come with me.'

She assured him that she wanted to go. She did not understand why, the whole place seemed like something she had never
been to before, she recognized no one but then they had had no
friends and people had only come to the shop when they must.
She didn't even want to wait outside while Aidan fitted the keys
to the door and she did not look around her and once inside
she shivered and it was not just because of the cold air, it was
the smell of damp, the air of poverty and failure, and she thought
of Felicity being there alone night after night, knowing perhaps
that she would not escape as Lorna had done. Did you ever
really escape? she wondered. The place seemed to echo with their
footsteps.

The hats for sale in the window had been there for years and
were dusty and limp-looking and even old-fashioned. She knew
about such things now, she knew what richer people wore and
what they ate and drank and how they lived and she knew that
they were no happier for it.

Nothing had changed at all, had Felicity not sold a single thing
after she left? It did not look like it. At the men's side everything
had gone but they found it when they went into the back room
where she had worked all those years, caps and hats for the men
who never came there, some of them had been expensively made
but the shine and sheen had gone and they were, like Felicity,
neglected and unused and unwanted. It was as though Felicity
had given up or perhaps lost Mr Humble. Had he died? He
certainly could not afford not to work, she remembered how
tired he would become, standing all the time, and his threadbare
clothes. What could have encouraged men to come into the shop
when they had such a scarecrow to receive them?

In the back there was some evidence that Felicity had carried
on with repairs. Some of them were still there, half done as though
she had grown tired or so ill that she could not go on and for
a few moments Lorna's fingers itched to mend them because
they were either clumsily finished or needed a younger hand and
sharper eyes and the more she thought of Felicity struggling the
worse she felt and knew that she should have been there or that
she could have or should have done more.

She went on up the stairs and was aghast at the furniture, so
very shabby and so little of it, and in the bedroom the wardrobe

door hung open as though broken and Felicity's meagre store of clothes was still there. Lorna remembered her in each dress, faded fabrics which other women had owned first and she could still smell Felicity on them and it was the smells of childhood, of biscuits baked and stories read and walks taken in magic places, it was not the grown-up version of herself that she saw, the disillusionment, the longing to be away, the desperation of youth when held by middle age and her resentment, how cruel it seemed now.

The bed had been left, presumably after Felicity's last night here. The sheets were grey with age and numerous washing and the bedcovers were frayed. So were the curtains and the carpet there in the middle of the floor.

The old desk where Felicity had done the accounts had piles of papers. Above it was a shelf which held the few books she had owned.

'What will happen to all these things?' she asked, turning to Aidan.

'It depends on the will. There isn't one at the bank or at any local solicitors but some people make a will and just leave it and I'm going to take a look through the desk,' he said.

Lorna watched him open the middle drawer and then she too set to work, she suddenly wanted Felicity to have made a will, wanted her to have left at least something to her, wanted her to have cared and yet part of her hoped she hadn't because then she would feel the more guilty that Felicity had cared so much and she had left. All the lonely and poor days and nights when she was dancing and drinking champagne in the days when she was happy with Ralph and still in love with him. Reason told her that it had not been much time but she thought that perhaps it had been more than Felicity had ever known.

There were three drawers at each side and Felicity had not been a particularly tidy person when it came to papers but she searched through the top two drawers at one side and Aidan, having found nothing, began on the other and in the bottom of the last drawer on her side she found something heavy, a box which she dragged from within and deposited on top of the desk at the same time as Aidan brought forth a document and said, 'Ah, this is something like it,' and he perused it and she waited and then grew impatient,

'Is it the will?'

'Yes.'

'Let me see.'

He ignored her for a few moments and then said, 'She owned the building and everything in it and it's all left to you so she had enough money to buy the place.'

Involuntarily Lorna said, 'Oh no,' and he said with a quick look of surprise,

'Who else should she leave it to? You worked for this.'

'That isn't the point.'

He handed the document over.

She read it, wanted to cry. Felicity had even mentioned each tiny piece of jewellery, none of it worth anything much, a string of beads in blue that she had bought at a little jeweller's in Bishop Auckland main street because they had been having a rare day out and she had seen it and liked it so much, Lorna could see now the look of longing on her face and remembered once again the party she had gone to when Ralph had insisted she should wear the Carlyle sapphires, and the contrast.

Felicity had never worn them, she had been asked nowhere, perhaps in those days she had thought she might, had thought she would, had hoped even that she might meet someone she could marry. Lorna even thought they were still most likely in the box they had been bought in. There was also a thin silver bangle, Lorna did not know where that had come from.

She handed back the document to Aidan. She felt sick and then she remembered the box on top of the desk and to distract herself more than anything else she opened it. It was full of letters tied up with ribbon, two bundles of them.

'What are those?'

'I've never seen them before.'

'We should go.'

He turned and Lorna, not sure whether she was meant to take anything from the premises until the law had sorted out every-thing, stuffed a bundle into each pocket and then she realized he had turned away so that she could take what she chose in private and she slipped her hand through his arm to thank him.

They left the shop, she didn't want to leave, she half thought that Felicity was standing there behind the glass or perhaps beating

upon it willing her, urging her, not to go because of the loneliness and yet, like the good parent she had hoped she was,
standing back and letting go. Lorna wanted to run back and open
the shop and have it be the childhood that she had wanted, the
one she and a million other children all over the world had never
had, comfort, opportunity, security, the idea of a future with a
loving family.

As they walked a bitter wind cut through the street and by
the time they reached the railway station it had begun to snow.
She was glad to board the train, she wanted to go back to anything
that was familiar, even Ralph and the house he would not keep
right. It seemed that some people never reached a goal as far as
love went. Perhaps the love which Felicity had had for her was
the best that she could expect.

Stupidly, she and Aidan had an argument. He wanted to see
her home, she wouldn't let him. They hadn't had an argument
in a long time that she could think of and she would never argue
with Ralph so in a way this was a luxury.

'Ralph hates you.'

'I won't come right to the house but you can't go. It's late, it's
dark and I'm not letting you go alone.'

'If he sees you he will be very angry.'

'He won't see me. Tell him I'm Ned, he won't know any different.'

On the way back she came to a decision and not long before
she reached the house she said, 'I don't want Felicity buried there.'

Aidan thought for a few moments and while he hesitated she
said quickly, 'I want to take her home.'

'We don't know where her home is.'

'Then we'll find it. Couldn't you make some enquiries?'

'Lorna, she lived there for twenty years.'

'I don't care. People there didn't want her, didn't make friends
with her — or she didn't with them. She must have come from
somewhere and I want her taken back there.'

She let him take her home and watch her towards the door
but he stood in the shadows and he was right, Ralph assumed
Ned had brought her back because he quite often did and Ralph
liked the idea of Ned being around because Ned was the man
who bought property. He had seen her though and as soon as
she got inside he asked her about the will and he was pleased

when she told him that she had been left everything and she let him assume that Ned wanted the premises there though why on earth he should she could not imagine.

When she went to bed she put a shawl around her shoulders and brought the lamp as close as she could and kept an ear open for Ralph's heavy feet on the stairs but he would be slow and deliberate because he was always drunk now so she would hear him in plenty of time.

She put one bundle of letters straight into the drawer of her bedside table and undid the first bundle and put all but the top one into the drawer too and she thought that if he should take her by surprise she could slip the letter under her pillows.

To her joy it was expensive cream paper and the ink though somewhat faded was legible and it was a man's hand, she thought, the ink was thick and black, or had been, and it was someone confident and educated. She glanced at the signature at the end and it was a letter from her father.

It was dated, October, 1888, Craster, Northumberland.

> My dear girl,
>
> Whatever am I to do? I cannot come back now, my father has chased me from my home and from you. I know you think little of me, I know you consider me cowardly. I will not ask you to forgive me, since I am not there I can comfort myself in the darkness here that you have already done so and until I hear from you I will hold on to that thought because if you do write to me you will take away that relief, the only warmth I have in the world.
>
> I have an upstairs room here which looks over the tiny harbour. The October tides are full and sweep across the harbour walls which come almost all the way round from both sides like encircling arms, stopping short only to allow in the fishing boats which keep the village alive. Cold foamy water coats the top of the walls and rushes down the other side shortly before the next wave arises to follow it.
>
> I think about her night and day and my beloved child –

Here, Lorna stopped. She had never on paper or anyplace else, she realized now, been referred to as a beloved child. She said it over and over to herself, and it was warm like a hot brick and comforting like a hug and now that it had been said, been written, it could not be unwritten and was therefore hers like a dear possession.

> I would give anything to come back. The minutes are hours and the hours days and the days are so endless, I am only glad when darkness comes and then I drink myself to sleep and I am so grateful for it like nothing else. Sleep takes me, gives me some place to go, and even then I see Cate in my dreams and always she is just out of sight and her shadow lingers. I long to touch her to feel her close, to think that she is real even though she is gone and to be with her once again. Oh, Cate, Cate, it will never happen, I know it.

Cate was such a pretty name, she felt. It laid itself upon the tongue like sweet jam at breakfast. It was somehow the prettiest name of all. It wound itself into one's heart. For the first time then she dared to think of her mother and she remembered being very young and Felicity's hand so warm, her fingers so slender, her voice lifted in song and in laughter. Where had it gone?

She heard the sound of Ralph's heavy footsteps and he hesitated as he reached the door of their bedroom as though lions were waiting for him. Was that how she made him feel? Was that why he drank? He opened the door with difficulty. He did not fall into the room, he did not even sway. He was smiling when he reached the bed, even managed to undress at least part way and then he very elegantly slid on to the side where he was meant to fall and by the time his head was upon the pillows he was asleep.

It was not the sleep of innocence, it was not the sleep of happiness, it was the drunken outgoing of an unhappy man. She listened to the breathing of brandy or whisky and she knew that he had calculated how much it would take until he needed no more. Was it like that with her father, with Shaun? It was a good name, such a pretty name, and yet she would not have used it. He would have been 'Father' to her. Why had he left? Why had he gone alone? Why did he write? And why did nobody answer him, go to him?

Cate and Shaun. It sounded so right, it sounded as though it would last forever.

She did not even try to rest. She sneaked away into the cold of the downstairs. Everybody had gone to bed, all she took with her was a small lamp. She huddled in the warmest room – the smoking room since that was where the men played cards after dinner. She sat there on the rug by the almost dead fire and read all the letters.

Felicity had obviously written back to him because the next letter was full of relief. He wrote still 'to my dear girl'; so that was no help. There were no new experiences to record and it gradually came to her that he was ill, that he could not go outside, that he could not leave the one small room above the harbour because he explained in great detail the comings and goings of the fishing boats, how the fishermen would sell the catch when people came to buy and how much of it went off presumably to Alnwick to be sold there in the shops and on the market.

He told her of the wading birds, the seagulls crying above the house where he lay, the comings and goings of the landlady and the landlord, who brought his meals to him, saw to his fire, changed his bed, washed his clothes, brought in books and news-papers. He knew that he would not see her again, that he would not see his beloved child. The letters had gone on for nine weeks. Gradually his handwriting became less and less legible as the illness grew worse. There was no final letter, no goodbye.

Lorna sat in the almost darkness and wished she could have known him no matter what faults he had. He had wanted to be with her so much and she had never known him.

She sat there as the dawn came late and it was only when one of the servants, Tessa, came in to light the fire and started that she got up, bundled the letters out of sight and went back to bed.

Ralph never got up for breakfast now. She left him slum-bering and went into town to see Aidan. It was lunchtime by then. He greeted her amiably and suggested they went out to eat and he took her to the Silver Street cafe and there at a little table in the gloom at the back she told him about her father and she gave him the letters to read.

'I want to go to Craster and see his grave. Let's go very soon, before the funeral is organized. Would that be any good?'

'Of course.'

The train which went from Durham was one of the prettiest routes in the world, she felt sure. Up through Newcastle's elegant station and then along the coast with the little farms and neat stone villages where the tide washed the yellow sand and there was a slight wind behind it so that the waves splashed the beach and bounced over the rocks.

They hired a horse and trap. Craster was tiny as her father had said in the letters, full of little terraced houses which looked out toward the sea and the smell of kippers which were smoked there. It was exactly as she had read about it, she even knew the building which had housed her father so long ago, a small hotel. They went inside, ostensibly to have something to eat but she tasted nothing, her mind was back there more than twenty years and her parent was dying in the room above and he had not family or friends to be with him.

They discovered that the parish church was at Embleton just a little way along the coast. The village had a fine ruined castle but all she was interested in was finding her father's grave. They spent about half an hour searching and she was the one who found it. She shouted and Aidan came over and they stood there. All it said was Shaun Carlyle and his dates.

She did not know what she had expected. Something more? Or that a miracle should occur and there would be no grave and she would find that he was still living there or that people had heard of him but he had moved on and lived, was prosperous and happy. She stood in silence for a long time. Aidan didn't move. He wasn't the kind of person who would urge people away when they needed time, she thought.

Eventually she began to walk very slowly away from the church-yard and it took a supreme effort as though she was walking much too fast up a very steep hill and was obliged to stop and catch her breath after a minute or two. The tears unbidden began to stream from her eyes but when Aidan took a step towards her she held up both palms against him. She was shocked at her instinctive reaction. She did not want to be touched, she did not want anybody near her. Ralph had ruined for her the sweet expectation of a man's touch.

The journey home was taken in complete silence. When they got back to his office she said, 'I need some money.'

'How much?'

'Quite a lot, I think. I want to make repairs to the house.

I can't go on with the place like this and Ralph is so drunk so often I doubt he would object any more.'

He said nothing though he looked as though he would have liked to and then he did. He said, 'It's my house, I'll pay for it.'

He saw her most of the way home and would have left her without a word but that she turned and thanked him. He shook his head and she smiled at him and said, 'I know. You're just doing your job,' and he nodded and smiled and went home.

Ralph was already drunk when she got home and she and Camille put him to bed but she did a great deal of thinking that night and the next morning when Ralph finally came downstairs she sat down with him at the table.

'Aren't you going to have anything to eat?'

He looked straight at her. He was pale and his eyes were dull.

'Since when have you been concerned?'

'What is the matter with you? You got everything you wanted. Why are you doing this?'

'Doing what?'

'You weren't like this when we first met, you didn't drink yourself into stupidity. You rode your horse and saw your friends and—'

'Because, as you say, I got what I wanted,' he said.

'And are content to let it drop to pieces around you?'

Ralph regarded the table as though there was interesting food on it instead of empty plates. The servants had grown lax, she thought, but then she didn't think they were ever properly paid.

'What do you do?'

He was still sharp, she thought, even hungover. She pretended to misunderstand. Ralph waved an arm.

'You tell me lies and think I'm so befuddled that I don't notice. You have been indulging my forbearance.' He smiled at the utterance and looked quizzically at her.

'Perhaps.'

'Perhaps nothing. You and Camille are like conspirators. That's what women do, they work against us in pairs.'

'I'm not working against you, Ralph.'

'Right from the very beginning,' he said. 'When I first saw you I thought I could do anything I wanted and it would be easy. Look at you now. The real Carlyle in the family,' and he got up and left the room almost steadily.

Lorna went off to the kitchen where the cook and the maid who should have cleared the table were sitting over the fire. She could have rung but she walked in and saw them and she went over and she said, 'You will be paid what you are owed this very day. Please, Tessa, go and sort the dining room out,' and she turned to the cook and asked what they were having to eat that day and the woman shrugged and said there was little left.

Lorna went into town and to Aidan's office where he gave her the cash she had estimated she would need and then she spent the rest of the morning going around the various tradesmen, into their back rooms where they did their accounts and kept their business papers, and she paid the butcher and the general grocer and farrier. She ordered what the cook had said she would need for the next few days and she even went to Imelda's dress shop and although Imelda was polite she said she wanted to see her in private and when they were alone she said, 'I've come to pay what we owe you.'

Imelda went white. They knew one another very well by then but nobody had ever mentioned money and Lorna had shrugged it off in her mind, thinking it was Ralph's problem and nothing to do with her and that Imelda had too much delicacy to refer to it when Annabel and Lorna had done everything they could to advertise her business for nothing by writing articles about what Imelda thought fashionwise and about the clothes she sold.

Even she was shocked by the amount because Ralph had paid nothing for years but she paid it anyway and she was glad that when she had glanced at the amount of money in Aidan's office and disclaimed all he had said grimly was, 'You'll need that and more,' and he was right.

By the end of the afternoon she had been to see a local builder and he had promised that he would come early the next day and they would discuss what needed to be done to the house. Aidan had insisted on paying for this but she would have cash so that nobody would be aware of what was going on.

She went back and stealthily, in the kitchen, she gathered the servants together and paid them not just what was owed but extra. She told them it was for putting up with the treatment they had had for so long, that she was glad they had stayed and that she hoped they would stay on now but that she would need them to put the house right. She told them about the builders and how the leaky attic rooms where they slept would be the first to be repaired and that there would be new bed linen and new beds and that when the weather was inclement every fire in the place was to be lit.

The coal merchant delivered huge quantities of coal the next day, she talked to the men who worked outside and gave directions about the gardens and the woods and she spent all that day with the builder, taking him from room to room, seeing what must be done as soon as possible and the weather was beginning to get better so that would help. The roof was the first thing but some of the rooms needed major replastering and they decided that each room would be done separately and carefully so that the household need not be particularly interrupted.

That night, with fires burning at either end of the dining room, the table and chairs smelling of polish and the food good and fresh, she had dinner served early so that Ralph did not have time to drink so very much before he ate. The result of that was that he fell asleep by the drawing-room fire and she had to awaken him to go to bed.

He was awake when she was the following morning and she persuaded him down to breakfast and then she said that she would like to go riding. It was a bright cold morning. Ralph didn't argue. They went out and rode all morning and when the horses were tired and they stopped under a tree on the far edge of the estate he got down and helped her down and when she gazed back towards the house he said, 'So, are you mistress of all you survey?'

She said, 'Ralph—' and he said wearily:

'Oh, don't. Every time you tell me a lie I know it, I can see by that expression on your face as though I was too young to bear the truth.'

She wanted to smile at that and gazed down at the reins in her gloved hand.

'This was what you intended all along,' he said.

'It's nothing of the kind.'

'No, I forgot. You wanted a shop. I fear that you are too common not to want to give up shopkeeping. It's a terrible fault in you and one I would have done anything to cure. Do you have any money?'

He had lured her so carefully that she was shocked by this.

'Not on me, no.'

'I need some.'

'For what?'

'For all kinds of things, of course.'

'Why don't you sell the carriage you bought and the horses that go with it? You never use them.'

'I did. What do you think we've been living on lately? We only have one carriage left. Of course we should have a motor next.'

'I want the roof repairing.'

'Lorna, I must have some money. I have gambling debts—'

'I'll get it,' she said.

She debated with herself, shocked almost, as to whether she ought to lie to Aidan about the money so she went to Ned and took the money he was keeping for her and gave it to Ralph. At the magazine she wrote articles on house repairs.

'Do women really want to know about such things?' Camille said, shocked, but Annabel said that as long as it involved furnishings and making things over as well as buying new she did not see why it should not be included.

The magazine was doing very well and Ned was about to bring out Bea's first book. It was a novel about two sisters whose parents die and leave them to fend for themselves, called *Kate and Amelia*.

# Sixteen

The book was being launched at the newspaper offices that week and Ned provided a lavish party. The big building was packed with people that night and lights blazed from every window. Even Ned's father, Tranter Fleming, who was a very important man in the area and owned pits, turned up and lots of others who read the newspapers and the newspaper employees and even people just happening to be around in the street.

All the doors were open, every room had food and drink and there was music, Ned had asked a local string quartet to play and since it was a fine night it turned into the biggest party that the city had seen in months, hundreds of people milling about in the area of Saddler Street and another band started up in the Market Place and people danced.

The novel sold out, Ned was obliged to reprint immediately, and Bea sat like the queen that her name implied and signed every copy. Lorna thought she had never seen her so happy. Lorna had persuaded Ralph to be there and Henry had come with Camille. Aidan even brought his mother. Mrs Hedley looked disapproving at the beginning but as the evening went on her expression changed when she saw how the book sold and how involved in all this Bea was but she said to Lorna when Lorna approached her merely from good manners, 'This was not what I wanted for my daughter.'

'Perhaps it was what she wanted.'

Mrs Hedley looked shocked.

'I always thought you would stir things in this city before you were finished, young woman, and I was right. You are what people of respectability used to call "immodest".'

Immodest. Lorna could not help laughing the moment she was alone only to find that Aidan loomed behind her.

'What's funny?' he said and when she told him he laughed too.

'Mr Gray said you came into the office today. We didn't have an appointment, I'm sorry I missed you.'

Lorna didn't like to tell him that she had waited until she thought he was out because the money from the newspaper earnings had not been enough and she knew Mr Gray was empowered to help her.

'If you keep paying Ralph's debts out of what you got from me for the house you'll have nothing left because it's bottomless.'

'What else can I do?' she said.

She didn't know where Ralph went or whether he played cards or other games, she only knew that he came very drunk and unhappy when that night was almost morning and climbed into bed with her and fell into the kind of sleep which is escape.

When he finally came downstairs it was almost lunchtime and she was about to go into Durham to the newspaper office. She paused in the hall. Nobody was about. She put on her gloves and then said carelessly, 'Did you lose all of it?'

'Every penny,' Ralph said and he went off into the dining room from where the smell of roast chicken wafted through the hall.

She did not tell Aidan that she intended looking for evidence of her mother's family, she didn't know why she wanted it but after finding her father's grave it somehow seemed important. She had gone to St Oswald's churchyard where other members of the Carlyle family were buried and was not very surprised when her mother's grave was not there.

She just wanted to see it as she had wanted to see her father's and if possible to discover if Felicity had had any real connection with either family. Nobody seemed to know what her mother's family were called, she asked Camille and Henry and the aunts and uncles who might have known but they did not talk to her, they had nothing to say about her mother or her mother's family, just that she had been a common girl from a pit village and nobody had thought anything of her.

After her enquiries, she could not think what else to do and Aidan came into the office when it was almost lunchtime and he said, 'Do you have a few minutes?' so that she was obliged to give him some time and he said, 'Shall we go to the cafe in Silver Street?'

She didn't want to go with him, she didn't even want to be seen with him. She didn't even know why, she didn't want him to know that Ralph had gambled away all that money in a single evening. She didn't want Aidan to think of her as stupid. She sat there in the cafe, gazing at other people as they ate and drank and talked. She might have known them, she didn't see properly, she wanted everything to be different, she wanted herself to be different, not to feel as though she was getting everything wrong no matter what she did or what she tried to do.

'I've been making some enquiries with regard to Miss Robson and your family because of the funeral and most especially your mother and father—'

He stopped there. She waited.

'And?'

Aidan hesitated.

'There is no record of your parents' marriage. I had a feeling there wasn't because I tried to find them when I was originally looking for you and I didn't unearth anything.'

She stared at him and all around them the hum of voices and the clatter of crockery and cutlery somehow ceased and a strange buzzing noise assailed her ears. She waited until it stopped and the cafe went back to normal and then she said, 'You must be mistaken.'

'I could be. I didn't want to upset you so I've been very thorough.'

'Why wouldn't they be married?'

'I don't know.'

'If they weren't married I would have no claim on the Carlyle inheritance, would I?'

'You were named specifically in the inheritance so yes, you would, and your father was Shaun Carlyle and most assuredly, from what you've told me, your mother was Cate.'

'They could have run away. They could gone to Scotland.'

'They could have.'

'But you don't think so.'

'Why would they do that unless they were very young and somebody was trying to stop them?'

'My grandfather?'

'Possibly.'

'So my mother's name could have been Robson and Felicity could have been her sister.'

'She could have been.'

'Why would she not tell me?'

'I don't know but I think since we are going to Consett to talk about the funeral we could look and see if your mother is buried there.'

Lorna had never been to Consett before. It was an iron-and-steel-making town a few miles north-west of Durham City and was truly industrial. The Consett Ironworks was huge and dominated the whole place and everybody who lived there worked either at the works itself or at industries connected to it or were shopkeepers to keep the whole thing moving. The town was covered in red dust from the works.

The parish church was the first place they went and Aidan had already made an appointment to see the vicar and he was most helpful, Lorna thought, since Felicity had not lived there in so long.

'Do you know anything about her?' Lorna could not help asking.

'About her family?'

'Yes, did she have a sister?'

'No, but I have looked into this since you asked me whether she could be buried here. Her father and mother and her brother are buried here and her sister-in-law.'

Lorna was disappointed and worse it made her feel depressed. The vicar pointed them in the direction of the area where the Robsons were buried after they had talked about the service which she wanted. Lorna tried to concentrate because it seemed fair to give Felicity what around there they called 'a good send-off' though she couldn't think who besides herself would come to any service. The vicar said there were no next generation and he said it with a shake of his head.

It was raining, fittingly somehow, as she and Aidan went into the churchyard and they had to look hard at first for the graves and then they found Felicity's parents' grave, John and Freda, and then her brother, James. He had not been dead long, Lorna thought, looking at his dates and then she came across another grave and she stared and Aidan who was standing beside her stood quite still. It read 'Catherine Robson' and the dates. That was all.

'Look, Aidan. That has to be her. She must have been Felicity's sister, that proves it.' She stared harder. 'Does this also prove that my parents weren't married?'

'It would be most unusual for her other name not to be on her grave. And if they had been married why is he buried in Craster and she here?' Aidan said.

'Perhaps they had quarrelled badly before she died,' Lorna said and then thought back to the letters. They had not quarrelled.

The vicar was making his way across to them, the rain had stopped.

'Do come back in and have some tea before you get your train.'

'I think this is my mother's grave,' Lorna said. 'Felicity Robson brought me up and claimed she was my aunt. I thought that it was wrong and that she had lied to me for a specific reason but it seems she was.'

The vicar stared at the grave.

'There was no sister. This woman was James Robson's wife. There were no children of the marriage, there would have been records.'

'She was his wife?'

'Yes.'

He went back inside and they had no option but to follow him. There was seed cake which his wife had made, but they drank their tea and left, hoping the vicar would not notice their inattention. It was not his concern and he had not the slightest curiosity about such matters. His wife, however, who was a local woman and had played little part in the conversation, saw them to the door.

'I knew the Robsons,' she said.

Lorna turned to her.

'Did you know Cate?'

The vicar's wife looked around her as though somebody might be listening.

'She ran off with another man. It was the talk of the place for years.'

'She ran off?' Lorna could hear how faint her own voice was.

'Yes. James was a hard-working man, a pitman from a respectable family, so it was all the worse when she ran away. She died and for some reason her family had her body brought back here.

I suppose they would do that but no one ever spoke of her again. She had disgraced her family. He never married after she died, I think he was so embittered, poor man. Everybody was so sorry for him and for his shame.

'Some people said that she wouldn't have run off without a good reason, how he must have treated her badly, knocked her around or kept her short of money, but he didn't. He was a good-living churchgoer, honest and kind, and as far as anybody could see there was no reason for her to leave that anybody could understand. She wasn't from here, of course.'

Lorna's head was spinning by now, she wanted something or somebody to lean against but all she could say was, 'Not from here?'

'No, not these parts.'

'Did you know her family?'

'No.' The vicar's wife's brow furrowed as she thought. 'I believe that they were Northumbrian. From the coast.'

And then Lorna's heart began to beat heavily. 'Were they from Craster?'

The vicar's wife looked as though a light had been turned on. 'Exactly,' she said, 'I had forgotten.'

'Do you know what their name was?'

'I don't think I do.'

They went back inside and explained to the vicar and he took them through into his study and Lorna was able to ask him who was vicar here when the couple were married and again, his wife remembered because she had been a member of the parish at the time and was able to tell them that the vicar was Mr Wynstanley who had retired now and lived in Blackhill, just nearby, and the vicar showed them that her mother's name had been Catherine Radcliffe.

They walked the short distance to Blackhill. There was no real break between Blackhill and Consett, just the big park which both claimed and a number of imposing houses. The retired vicar did not live in one of these but in a small house in a terrace which faced the road and ran at right angles to it. At the bottom of the hill was his, Number 3, Puddlers Row.

Aidan banged on the door and a small thin woman, wearing black, opened it. He greeted her politely and asked for Mr Wynstanley and was guided inside. Lorna followed. She didn't want to go first and hung back, it was so gloomy, she could see nothing and the hall was painted brown and the floor was brown linoleum with a strip of carpet in the middle.

The woman pushed open the first door on the left and ushered them into a small room which was crammed with furniture. It looked as though the vicar had taken all the furniture from the vicarage into his terraced house. She could hardly move. The vicar was a short fat man, who asked them to sit in uncomfortable armchairs and listened carefully and then thought and said, 'Yes, I remember the wedding, I have a very good memory for such things.'

'Do you remember it particularly for some reason?' Lorna asked.

'Oh yes, it was because there were just the two of them, I mean no member of either family came to the wedding and it surprised me because of course James had a family and they were good churchgoers and members of my flock but they had not mentioned it and even though the banns were read in church nobody said anything and I could not work it out. Whether Miss Radcliffe had any family of course I have no idea.'

'Did they as a married couple come to your church after that?' Aidan said and Mr Wynstanley looked down sadly and shook his head.

'Not for long. She ran off. There was a great deal of talk.'

'Could you tell us about it?' Lorna said.

He hesitated.

'Please. I am her daughter, you see, and I would like to know if I have any family and what happened.'

'Well, it doesn't become a minister of the Church to say such things but it's a long time ago and I held my tongue then. She met another man, I don't know where or how, but there was to be a child and it was said that the child was not James's.'

Lorna and Aidan walked back to the station in silence but when they got on the train and the carriage was empty but for them Lorna said, 'Why would my father go there when my mother was already dead? Perhaps he felt nearer to her like that?'

Aidan shook his head.

'Why not?'

'I don't know. It's just the kind of thing women think men do.'

'They aren't all made of stone like you,' she said.

'Perhaps her family still lives there.'

'Why wouldn't they come to her wedding?'

When they got back to the office Lorna looked at a map of Northumberland which Aidan had unearthed from a cupboard in his office. There was a tiny place called Radcliffe a few miles from the coast and, Aidan informed her, the Radcliffes who had lived at Dilston, not far from Hexham, were the Earls of Derwentwater.

'I believe it's a very common name though in that area,' he said.

'I'm going back there.'

He sighed.

'Something told me you would. Are you sure it's a good idea? Your parents are dead, it doesn't matter legally that they weren't married, you still got your inheritance. What do you hope to gain from it?'

'The knowledge that my mother was not the kind of woman who—' Lorna stopped. She could feel the burning in her cheeks and didn't look at him.

'Lorna—'

'Do you want to come with me?'

'If you insist on going.'

# Seventeen

It snowed the day of Felicity's funeral. It was the kind of day which Consett always had many of, the locals knew, there was a biting cold wind up on the tops and nothing to stop it sweeping across the little iron town other than the buildings which made it up, the works itself, huge and ugly, and the terraced houses where the workers lived and the big houses where the managers lived and the up and down of the hills where Consett flowed into Blackhill and the other villages which were almost part of it.

Lorna did not understand that day why she had insisted on having Felicity buried here, none of her family was alive to see, nobody turned up who might have remembered her. Lorna half hoped some forgotten school friend or family acquaintance would arrive to swell the numbers but in the end it was only the vicar, the men to carry the coffin, Aidan and herself. She had asked Ralph if he would go with her but all he said was, 'I never met her, why would I want to be there?'

Aidan made the arrangements, all she had to do was turn up at the railway station, sit beside him on the train, watch the fast-falling snow and remember what their life had been like when they had the shop.

She felt guilty now thinking of how she had left and what Felicity must have endured. She tried to defend herself, she had written to her over and over urging her to come and stay but she had known that Felicity would not spend time with the Carlyles, she knew more now than ever how she would feel. No doubt Felicity had wanted a good life for them and had managed as best she could and when it was a poor best and all her dreams had gone the child she had taken away had turned against her.

At least she had brought Felicity home, she felt better about that, she didn't want her stuck up in the wilderness of Castle Bank Colliery where she had made no friends.

At the end of the service she turned when the men came in

to carry the coffin the short distance to the grave and there was somebody standing at the back of the church. She couldn't make out much in the shadows, only that it was a man. He left and when she walked out behind the coffin with Aidan she could not see anybody. Nobody came to the graveside while the vicar said the last words over Felicity's body but Lorna could not help turning around once or twice in case anybody was near.

She thought she caught a glimpse of somebody beyond the bare black trees to the edge of the graveyard but she had not sufficient time to look and it seemed so disrespectful so she tried to concentrate, she tried to think of the good times she and Felicity had had together when she was a little girl.

As the gravediggers began to throw soil into the grave she and Aidan walked a little way off and she said to him, 'Did you see that man?'

'At the back of the church, yes.'

She might have known. Aidan never missed anything.

'Why do you think he didn't come forward?'

'Perhaps he was an old lover.'

'Don't joke.'

'I wasn't. He must have known her from way back if you didn't recognize him. He seemed about her age.'

Lorna looked hopefully at him.

'I didn't notice.'

The vicar came out and Lorna, on impulse, went to him and asked if he had seen the man.

'Oh yes.'

'Do you know him?'

'I can't say I do. I assumed he was an old friend. Many times people come almost to funerals.' The vicar looked quite apologetic. 'They do not announce themselves or claim anything, they hover at the back of the church in the shadows for all kinds of reasons, you see. It doesn't have to be relevant to this, he could just be remembering something from time past.'

It rained the second time they went to Craster and it was as unlike the pretty place which Shaun had described as it could have been and Lorna realized that she had seen it through her father's eyes and not how it really was now. The boats which came and went were to do with the whinstone and sandstone quarries which gouged the hillsides beyond the little town. That plus a fishing fleet made it a busy place, with comings and goings of people and boats and the distinct smell of fish and tiny particles of sand which covered the houses and was washed by rain so that the rivulets in the road were grey and ragged. The wet beach was littered with thick brown trails of seaweed and wind pushed the incoming tide hard against the shore.

The little pub was busy and when Aidan shoved his way inside through the mass of men she did not care to follow him and hovered just outside trying to keep out of the rain and wind. It seemed a long time before he came back and even then all he could tell her was that nobody had heard of her mother, she had not lived at the pub, so Lorna could not work out why Shaun had gone there after she had died. There were no Radcliffes in the churchyard.

It was late when they got back to the station and Lorna was tired and despondent but there was no train. They sat in the tiny waiting room by the fire until it was dark and still the rain came down. She fell asleep against Aidan's shoulder and started awake when somebody spoke.

'What is it?' she said.

'There's no train coming at all,' he explained. 'There's been an accident.'

They managed to get a lift back to the village although she protested.

'We can't stay here.'

'What else do you suggest we do?'

Lorna couldn't think. They went back to the pub which was the only place which had rooms and then they had just one free. She didn't like to say to Aidan that it wasn't his presence she objected to when they finally got up there, just that she was convinced this was the room her father had had all those years ago.

It looked out across the harbour, it was exactly the view he had described, and she could remember so many of his words, his loneliness and his despair, his failing health and his longing for Cate and for his child. She felt as though he had only just died and that some of him lingered there. She was afraid, she didn't know why, after all there was nothing to fear if her father's ghost, even if just a little of it, in some way haunted the place, she would have been glad of it, it was somehow her own self that she feared to meet, whatever of him there was in her.

'Are you uncomfortable about this, Lorna, because—'

She turned around.

'I hardly think you're going to ravish me.'

'Are you worried about Ralph?'

'He'll be drunk by now, he probably won't even notice I'm not there.'

'Then what is it?'

She sighed and went over to the fire where he was standing.

'I remember this room from the letters, my father spent weeks in it.'

'He died here?'

'Yes.'

'Possibly he didn't, it could have been another room or—'

'Aidan, I know he did.'

'All right, then.'

There was a knock at the door, Aidan had ordered supper and when it was all set on a little table with two chairs before the fire they sat down and had a glass of wine and something to eat though she couldn't manage more than a few mouthfuls. She could see the fire through her glass and there was something comforting about the whole situation that she couldn't deny.

The rain and wind were drumming against the window but thick curtains kept out the weather, the fire was big and bright and suddenly there wasn't a place in the world that she would rather be. She thought of the many meals taken in Ralph's presence and was happier now with the solicitor, who sat across the table, looking into the fire and no doubt trying to work out the problem which they had been set. He was holding his wine glass, he hadn't drunk much of it, no chance of him becoming unruly, he wasn't given to it except in male company and then he suddenly looked at her and said, 'What are you smiling at?'

'What have you thought of?'

He hid the smile.

'How do you know?'

'You have. Tell me.'

'I don't think Radcliffe was her name. There would have been some evidence, don't you think?'

'Then how will we ever find her?'

'You don't think that was perhaps the point?'

When she looked across at him he looked down as though the wine had some fascination for him and for the first time ever she found herself admiring his eyelashes which was stupid and – they really were very long and dark, what a dreadful waste on a man.

'What?'

'Well, I don't know, it just seems to me that this would have been much simpler if she—' He stopped.

'If she what?' Lorna prompted impatiently.

'If she didn't have something to hide.'

'Like what?'

'If I knew that we wouldn't be sitting here.'

'I'm glad we are sitting here,' Lorna said.

'Is that your second glassful?' he said. 'Maybe you've had enough.'

'Have you noticed how you're always telling me what to do?'

'If I am it never makes any difference.'

'It doesn't stop you, though, does it?'

'You pay me.'

'To tell me what to do? Are you charging me by the hour at the moment? It could be a very large bill,' she said.

He offered to sleep on the floor and then in a chair but the floor was bare and the chairs were no fit and besides, she told him, it was ridiculous. Nobody said anything for a long time when the room was in darkness. The rain was still hitting the window but the wind had ceased and she thought she could hear the sound of the waves against the harbour and she thought of her father lying here, alone and unhappy. She could hear Aidan breathing steadily and she turned over and moved nearer and put her face against his back and then he said clearly, 'Don't.'

'It's very dark.'

'It's called night-time.'

'I keep thinking about my father. I'm glad I'm not here alone. Do you think he died by himself?'

'No.'

'Who do you think she was?'

'I don't know but I don't think it's anything to worry about.'

She drew back a little and lay there for a while and then she turned over, away from him towards the window again. She shouldn't have but she felt comfortable there, like coming home should be but never had been. Was it because her father had been there for weeks or was it because Aidan was there and in the stupidest way she felt safe where he was? He didn't drink too much like Ralph, he didn't grab her or ask for anything or take advantage in any way, he didn't even touch her. She tried to think of any time that he had done and couldn't other than the odd chaste gesture.

It took her a long time to get to sleep and if he had moved at all, been restless or turned over and indicated in any way that he was still awake, she wouldn't have slept but since he didn't she gradually drifted off and when she awoke there was the warm intimate feeling of being very close against somebody and half conscious, she realized that she had turned over, was near to him, with an arm around him and he still hadn't moved. Then she said softly, 'Are you awake?'

'No.'

She went back to being close and fastened the arm around him again and she said, 'Thanks.'

The weather had moved on. It was a bright sunshiny day and when they had eaten breakfast she wanted to go for a walk so they went beyond the harbour and walked over towards the ruins of Dunstanburgh Castle, across the road which was well worn and lay above the beach and the rocks and the tide which was about halfway down. There was no reason to walk, nothing but the goal of the castle in sight.

Somebody ought to have made a decision but he didn't say anything and she didn't want to, she just wanted to walk towards the castle as though they had no reason for being here other than one another's company and when they reached the castle they walked around it for a while and then back towards the village. She stopped before they got there, she didn't want to go because there was the train to be thought of and Durham to go home to and this was almost like an unintended holiday.

'Must we go back?'

'I have an appointment at four o'clock.'

'You always say that, and half the time I'm convinced you don't.'

Going back was a horrible letdown, Aidan went back to his office with barely a word and she went back to Ralph. He had been so drunk that he hadn't noticed she wasn't there and she was relieved but Camille said in a whisper as she reached the hall, 'Wherever have you been? I was so worried about you and didn't dare to say anything.'

'I'm glad you didn't. I got stuck in Craster with Aidan Hedley.'

'I'm sure he behaved like a perfect gentleman.'

'Yes, he did,' and she thought about it and she thought that if he had even smiled at the wrong time she would have flounced away and because he hadn't she trusted him now as she had trusted no one before. She missed him, she wanted to go to him, to talk to him, to ask if he had any more ideas about her family.

'You like him,' Camille said.

'Do you think that's wrong?'

'Why shouldn't you? Tell me all about it.'

They sat down and she told Camille about her mother but not about the part where they had slept in the same bed. She kept the details such as they were to herself and went over them and that night while Ralph snored she remembered the warmth of Aidan's body and the sweetness of his temper. Having a secret between them made it better somehow and she knew that Aidan would never tell anyone and it was all the better for that. She wanted to see him again the next day.

When she got up however she was very sick and could only surmise that the supper she had eaten when she came home, little as it was, did not agree with her. All that day the nausea hung over her so that she had no inclination to do anything and Camille was unhappy and wanted to send for the doctor but Lorna assured her that she was already feeling better.

The following morning however she was ill again and Camille insisted on sending for Dr Menzies who was the family physician and he examined her carefully and then looked straight at her and said, 'I could be wrong, Mrs Carlyle, but I think you are expecting a child in about the early autumn.'

Lorna stared into the face of the little Scotsman.

'But I can't be,' she said.

'Ach, I hear this over and over again. Did you not notice any changes?'

'I didn't think about it.'

'So many women don't. They think it's one thing and then they think it's another when in fact it's the most simple thing of all and the most likely.' He smiled at her. 'Make sure you eat properly and get plenty of rest and if you can have a cup of tea and a biscuit before you get out of bed in the mornings it may ease the sickness. It will pass very soon and then you will feel energetic and well. You're a very healthy young woman, you need have no worries. No riding but walk if you can, get some fresh air, it helps,' and he smiled benevolently and went off back to the city.

Lorna didn't quite know why she wanted to cry, perhaps it was the change in things. Ralph came to her, his face brilliant with his smile.

'The doctor told me, how wonderful, Lorna. I will take good care of you, I swear it,' he said.

Ralph was so pleased, that Lorna didn't burst into tears until he had left the room and then she only had moments before Camille came in and she couldn't cry over her because Camille had no child and no expectation of one and no husband to speak of, just a large apparently jolly man who didn't really want her.

She couldn't say that her first reaction was that she didn't want the child, that she didn't want anything of Ralph's, that she was afraid, that she had never felt more a Carlyle nor wanted less to be one and the greatest stupidest thing of all was that she kept bringing to mind the walk to the castle with Aidan and it had been perfect and in the state she was she thought it was the only thing in her life which had been perfect.

She knew she was stupid to think that and it was only shock and she would get used to the idea of having a child but she thought that never again would she be that careless person who had walked across the field toward the castle with Aidan and she wanted that again, she wanted to relive that walk forever, other people hand in hand and children playing and dogs running about here and there and the castle with its strange tentacle-like reach for the sky and its somehow almost-permanence and she thought she had never loved a castle like she did this one.

She tried to remember what they had talked about but she was only conscious of Aidan in bed and his breathing and the sweet velvet of his back and how if she had but indicated he would have turned to her but he knew that she could not bear the dominance of a man's touch or will and that he had to give her time and space even in a bed and he had done that and she liked him for it, liked him more than anybody she could ever remember.

In spite of the way that he tried to tell her what to do he freed her and it was a rare thing in a man, he gave her room to be herself as no one ever had and then she thought that was not true, Annabel and Ned did the same and so did Camille and Bea too in a way, it was all part of the same thing but Aidan did it best. She wanted to run to him, she wanted not to be pregnant with Ralph's child and yet she felt guilty because she seemed to have given Ralph so little when he had demanded so much. She owed him this child, she owed the Carlyles this child.

She thought that the child was everything he had wanted, he wanted an heir for Snow Hall and for the Carlyles and why should he not?

He referred to the baby as 'he' right from the beginning so that she became anxious, wondering whatever would happen if the baby was a girl. She had intended telling no one but when she and Camille went into the magazine office Camille said, 'Lorna has some exciting news,' so this failed. She tried not to be cross, there was no reason why the baby should remain a secret and before long people would be able to see that she was pregnant but she didn't want Aidan to know, that was the truth of it.

Annabel hugged her and she told Ned when he came in and he hugged her and she was pleased at how glad they were but later, when she and Annabel were alone in the office, Annabel said, 'Don't you want this baby?'

What a dreadful thing to have to admit.

'I'm afraid it won't be a boy. I'm the only girl in generations of Carlyles and—'

'Look at what happened to you,' Annabel finished up. 'It proves that you and Ralph can have a child, surely that's the most important thing, and there's no reason why you couldn't go on and have other children and since there have always been boys there will surely be one.'

The future mapped out like that made Lorna feel better and worse. Annabel was right, she had time to produce an heir, the problem was there was nothing left for a child to be heir of and that nobody knew except herself and Aidan.

That afternoon Aidan came to the office and said to her that he had a story to talk to her about so they left the office and walked down to the river by way of the steps down by the side of Elvet Bridge, turned right there and began to walk along the towpath which took in the bend of the river and eventually came out at Framwellgate Bridge while the cathedral loomed huge above them. When they were alone and out of sight of other people she stopped and all she said was, 'Aidan—'

And he said, 'I've had an idea.'

# Eighteen

Ned had been in town at lunchtime and they had gone to the Dun Cow for a beer and Ned told him that she was expecting a child and it was like being socked in the stomach.

'So now Ralph will have everything,' Ned said. 'Pity it's all going down his throat.'

'Is he in a bad way?'

'In debt all over town.`

Just to get away from a subject he didn't want to discuss Aidan said, 'Have you ever heard of the Radcliffe family?'

'Well, yes, everybody knows the stories about the Earls of Derwentwater.'

'Lorna's mother was apparently called Radcliffe. They came from Craster, at least—'

'At least you and Lorna think so and went there?' Ned guessed. 'I wondered where you had gone. I came to the office. You didn't come back until the following day. If he finds out he'll kill you.'

Aidan became very interested in what was left of his beer.

'There are dozens of lovely girls in this town, why that one or is that the point?' Ned asked.

'I don't know what you mean.'

'Yes, you do,' Ned said, finishing his beer, 'you can't marry her so you relieve yourself of that burden, it's quite safe for you to love her because she belongs to somebody else—'

'Morally—'

'Oh, don't do morally,' Ned said impatiently and he went off to the bar for more beer.

Aidan didn't usually drink during the day but he couldn't stop himself from having another, the thought of Lorna getting bigger with Ralph's child was so depressing and he thought of himself and how hard he had tried to make her trust him. It seemed now that it was all for nothing and then Ned came back from the bar frowning in thought and as he put the beer down he said, 'Were there Radcliffes in Craster?'

Aidan was grateful for the change of subject, however relevant.

'There may be but we couldn't find a connection and Lorna's father went there after her mother died and he died there, his grave is there.'

'Why wouldn't he want to be buried with his wife?'

So Aidan told him about it until Ned's brow was furrowed.

'The other question is why on earth would her family want her back to bury her when she had behaved so badly?'

'Face?' Aidan said.

'Too late for that, leaving your husband and having a child with another man wasn't the thing to do and still isn't unless you're rich. And if they knew of the child's existence which they obviously did why did they let Felicity Robson run off with her?'

'They wouldn't want her. And the Carlyles didn't want her. They only wanted her when her grandfather left her so much. Presumably Miss Robson had nothing else.'

It was no surprise therefore that Lorna was desperate for the child to be a boy, Aidan knew.

'The obvious answer is that she didn't come from there and that he went there for another reason,' Ned said.

'Which would be?'

'Well, I don't know, do I?' Ned said and then grinned as Aidan said,

'I thought you knew everything.'

But the vicar's wife had said she came from Craster and then he thought, no, that wasn't true, Lorna had pounced and the vicar's wife, perhaps mistakenly, had agreed with her. Aidan could not think back to that bedroom without remembering Lorna there, so lovely and so afraid and so resenting Ralph and what he had done that she would not let anyone touch her. Aidan hadn't slept properly either then or since, he wanted her so badly.

She would never have forgiven him for a betrayal of that type, even the slightest touch, she had confidence in him, she trusted him, it made him groan just to think of it. Opportunities neglected seldom return, his mother would have said, but he knew that he had done the right thing, she looked at him now in a way in which she looked at no one else and he had kept that trust because it was not given lightly and even the smallest clumsiness on his part could take that look off her face forever.

He went back to the office, late and feeling guilty and worked doubly hard all that afternoon, not just because he had taken time off and gone to the pub but to try and rid his mind of Lorna in that room where she thought her father had died and listening to her sweet and even breathing through the night.

Now on the towpath he said, 'What if she came from a village just inland or nearby?'

'And had met my father in Craster? It's a bit far-fetched.'

'Have you thought of anything better?'

'If she lived somewhere around there she got to know her husband first—'

'Not necessarily.'

'But she must have done. Why would she not marry my father if she met him first?'

'If she was poor the Carlyles wouldn't want him to marry her.'

'So she went and married a pitman from Consett? I don't think so, Aidan.'

'How are you feeling?'

That silenced her for a few moments and then she said in a trembling voice, 'Like I'm having a baby. I'm so scared.'

It was the first time she had admitted this to herself, not that she was afraid to have a child, she wanted one, she was afraid that it would not do, that Ralph would not be satisfied. She turned away from Aidan so that she wouldn't cry or he wouldn't see her and that was when he turned her back to him very slowly and carefully and then he drew her towards him and held her there against his shoulder.

'I wish we were still at Craster,' she said when she could bear to move away.

'Why don't we choose a day and go up there and see what else there is to find?'

It cheered her so much that she managed a smile

A little further up the coast from Craster was Newton-by-the-Sea which was nothing much more than a square of houses at the bottom of the hill and detached houses set for their sea views further up the hill which led into Low Newton which was the first place you came to when you got off the train and there as they passed by Lorna saw a sign and it read 'John Radcliffe, Boat builder'.

They stopped and got down but the place was locked and it was shabby as though it had not been used in a long time. She went and knocked on the doors of nearby houses but either they didn't answer the door or they knew nothing. Aidan's suggestion that they should call in at the local pub was better.

'John gave over building boats some time back when his missus died,' said the man behind the bar. 'Lives down at Newton.'

So they went back to the little square at the bottom and next to the pub, when Aidan banged on the door, a man of about fifty filled the doorway. They told him who they were and that they were looking for the Radcliffe family and he invited them in. It was a neat little house, very clean and sparsely furnished though the furniture was good and it looked prosperous. Lorna explained that she was searching for members of her mother's family and he asked who her mother had been and when she said her name the bronzed outdoor look left the man's face and he said, 'She was called Cate?'

'Yes.'

'Nobody of that name in our family.'

'Are you sure?'

'Quite sure.'

They thanked him and walked out and once they were out of earshot Lorna, feeling despondent, said, 'I think you were right, she had things to hide. Now we may never find who she really was or where she came from or why my father came back to Craster.'

'It must have been that he had happy memories of her there,' Aidan said.

There was nothing to do but go home. She didn't want to leave Aidan, for the first time ever his house seemed more attractive than Snow Hall, but she could not linger. She was tired too, she had not imagined that being pregnant would make her feel tired, that plus the morning sickness, which had passed to some degree since Marie brought her tea and biscuits in bed, made her want to go and lie down as soon as she got in the door.

Unfortunately she could hear someone crying. She had good ears. It was not at the front of the building but there were open doors through the house and she made her way to the darkness at one side of the kitchen passage and there was a huddled form in the corner, weeping, quietly now, as though the storm was almost passed. It was Tessa, who was a housemaid. She didn't hear Lorna's soft approach so that when Lorna said her name the girl jumped and crouched further into the corner, wiping the tears away with the edge of her apron.

Lorna went nearer. Tessa drew further back. Lorna smiled at her, she thought that might reassure the girl, gave her a minute or two to stop crying and collect herself a little and then she said, 'I started life working in a back room at a horrible little shop in Castle Bank Colliery. I lived there with a woman I thought was my aunt. It was dismal. Where are you from?'

'Darlington.' Tessa sniffed. 'My dad works in the steel mills.'

'Are you homesick?'

'No, I like it here, I mean – I don't want to go back.'

'There's no reason you should, is there? You're very good at what you do but I could find you another position if you want to change? You might get lady's maid or—'

'It isn't that,' Tessa said and her voice quaked, 'I was happy with my position here since you – since you sorted things out.'

'What is it, then?'

'I think I'm expecting.'

'Oh,' Lorna said, and she thought she could tell that Tessa was a little nearer childbirth than she was.

'I can't go back there, my dad will kill me.'

'Is it somebody who can marry you?'

Tessa made the kind of noise which people make when they are ironically amused, the difference between a snort and a smile and then she sobbed and sniffed.

'No.'

'Can you tell me?'

'No.'

Lorna tried to think.

'There is a mother-and-baby place in Newcastle. You could go there until you have the baby and then – and then you could come back.'

'They would take it off me.'

'No, they wouldn't. You could bring the baby back here. Why not?'

Tessa burst into fresh sobs.

'You're too nice,' she said, 'I can't do that.'

'Why not?'

'Because it's his, it's Mr Ralph's,' Tessa said and she turned and ran, scuttled back down the passage and through the baize door and Lorna stood for a long time afterwards, thinking that if she had had any sense at all she would have realized from the beginning and yet how could she?

In the end she followed Tessa through the door and to the astonishment of the kitchen staff burst in on them as they were in the final preparations for dinner. There was the smell of roasting chicken. It made Lorna feel very sick. Tessa, suddenly very busy with the cutlery, looked up in horror.

'Come through, I want to see you,' Lorna said and she took the other door which led away from the kitchen and out into the main hall and then, with Tessa following, she opened the door into the little room she had always liked so much and made her own, with the little Dutch tiles. She concentrated on a windmill until Tessa came in.

'Close the door.'

Tessa did and when Lorna looked at her she could see how afraid the girl looked.

'Did he force you?'

Tessa's eyes widened.

'Did he?'

'He was – he was drunk.'

'Oh God.'

Tessa, slightly emboldened by the taking of the Lord's name in vain, said, 'It's not like he's old or nasty or – he knows how to make you want him. I did try to get away, I knew it wasn't right, but he pressed me and made me feel awful for resisting and then I was frightened. I'm nobody and nobody would believe me if he said I had just let him.' She stopped there.

Lorna knew exactly what she meant. Ralph could not help being charming even in the most awful circumstances. It was as if part of him stood back cynically surveying the fool that he was and it was so attractive, so devastating and so ultimately destructive.

Tessa, somehow made brave by the silence, stood up straight.

'I'm not a slut, you know,' she said. 'There was a lad last year and I wanted to marry him but he wouldn't because I wasn't good enough for his family and I lay with him, thinking that he would marry me and nothing happened and I was grateful but so ashamed because I thought we were going to be together. They were nobody special but he was above a house maid so his mother said, I wanted to marry him really bad but it never came to nothing but this – this was just ten minutes in the back hall. I'm sorry.'

'Would you want to go to the mother-and-baby home?'

The girl, made miserable by the suggestion, shook her head dumbly. Lorna took a deep breath, decision made.

'You shall stay here and have your baby here and be part of the household and if you are ill you are to come to me and when your time comes you shall have Dr Menzies. How do you feel?'

Tessa began to cry.

'Oh, Missus, I couldn't. You bein' so nice to me after what I've done.'

'Have you told the other staff about this?'

'Nobody, I didn't dare, but it's starting to show.'

'And Ralph?'

'Him least of all.'

'Right. If anyone says anything you are to say that I have said you shall stay here and I think no one will argue. If you have any problems you are to come to me.'

Tessa cried, hard and long. 'I feel like the worst girl in the world.'

'Women have been blaming themselves for things which were out of their control for generations. Let's stop doing it.'

Tessa looked confused but relieved and grateful. 'I should go, I should.'

'No, you won't. You belong here and I'll make sure you have lighter duties as you advance with your pregnancy. Don't go blaming yourself.'

Tessa left, happier than Lorna had seen her in weeks, and when she had gone Lorna sat down on the sofa and put her hands over her eyes and cried. There was nobody she could tell. Camille was too close, Annabel would tell Ned and Aidan – Aidan least of all, he was so set against Ralph already for what had been done.

# Nineteen

Even though Felicity had made a will it would take some time, Aidan said, for the legalities to be sorted out. Lorna made another visit to the shop that summer. She wanted to sort things out, to decide what should be thrown out, what could be given to other people to use and what she should keep. It was not going to be an easy thing to do but there was no point in putting it off. She was obliged to tell Aidan that she was going but she impressed upon him that she would rather go alone.

'I haven't been there by myself and I would like to.'

'Of course,' he said, handing her the keys and she left with barely a word. She had an awful feeling that he knew there was something wrong, that he could read it on her face and if he questioned her she would break down and tell him about Tessa being pregnant and so she got herself out of his office and on to the train in the shortest time possible. Luckily she had not told him she was going to ask for them and he had somebody waiting to see him.

She tried not to dwell on the bad memories and she waited for the train to take her home. Home. It was not home, it never had been, but it was difficult to divorce oneself from those feelings when she had lived there for the first twenty years of her life.

It was not as bad as she had thought it would be, but then things never were, she thought, if you faced them. When she got there she began cleaning, she swept and mopped the floors, she rid the place of dust, she cleaned the kitchen and then she began the process of sorting through Felicity's clothes and deciding that they were good enough, at least most of them, to be worn by other people so she folded them and fastened them into big piles and then she began on the furniture, thinking it could all be sold.

She went down the street to the shop where Mr Featherstone sold second-hand goods and she asked him if he could come and clear the house. He was enthusiastic and went back with her to look over the place. She had decided that the only thing she wanted to keep was the old desk and when he had gone back to get his cart to begin taking the furniture from the house she went through the desk with the idea of emptying it completely so that she could organize someone from Durham to come and collect it. There was nothing but receipts for the business, various letters, nothing of any interest, and she emptied all the drawers.

One of them came all the way out. She had tugged at it because it was stiff and then it shot out almost causing her to fall over and when she put it back there was something face down on the floor. She turned it over. It was a photograph of Felicity and a man. She wondered whether this was her brother but they looked nothing alike. Felicity was dark and this man was very fair. They were laughing.

There was something in the background, she couldn't quite make out what it was other than a building with some writing above it so she put the photograph into her pocket as she heard Mr Featherstone drawing up at the front door.

It gave her a certain satisfaction to watch him taking pots and pans, cutlery and crockery and various ornaments which he wrapped carefully in newspaper though she could have told him they were worth little. But someone might like them and they would bring a little money. He went off with one load and came back later for the kitchen table, the kitchen chairs, the bed, the bed linen, the armchairs.

Gradually the shop began to look quite empty and different, as though it was standing on the verge of being something new and it needed that, she thought, it had been shrouded in failure for too long. She only hoped somebody would come along and make it into the kind of place where people wanted to visit or something vital like a greengrocer's or a hardware store. She cleaned the windows and polished the counters and took down the worn and ragged curtains so that the light streamed into the building for the first time in years. The dusty old hats had gone.

She looked at the photograph again and wondered whether it was the same man who had stood at the back of the church during Felicity's funeral. If he had had nothing to hide he would have come to the front, she thought but she tried hard to remember any man in their lives except Mr Humble and couldn't. Would the photograph have come from a time before that? She looked at it again. Felicity did look very young and happy as Lorna did not remember her.

She put the photograph in her pocket and got the train back to Durham and she went to the newspaper offices. Annabel was alone there.

'What will you do with the shop?'

'Sell it, I suppose. I only wish I had somebody like Ned, waiting to buy it. I can't think.'

'It's not such a bad idea. We don't have a use for it now but I know he's intending to start other weekly newspapers in various towns and he'll need offices for advertising and for staff.'

'*Castle Bank Chronicle*,' Lorna said, laughing.

'I'm not joking. We'll ask him when he comes in.'

Lorna sat down at her desk and that was when she remembered the photograph in her pocket. There was a magnifying glass in the office. She took the photograph and looked at it in close up and showed Annabel and the building to the back with writing on it turned out to be a pub, The Red Robin was written large behind them.

'I've seen it, it's in Consett,' Lorna said.

She recognized the man, even though he was twenty years older. She walked into the bar of the pub with the usual smells of stale tobacco and smoky fire and the man behind the bar said, 'Would you not prefer the snug? That's where ladies usually sit.'

It was early, just before lunchtime, and there was nobody in yet, the stools drawn up neatly to the bar and the tables clean and the floor swept.

'I'm not a customer,' she said, 'and I hope you won't mind but you were the man who came to Felicity Robson's funeral, weren't you?'

He looked straight at her as he put down the glass he had been polishing. He hesitated for a few moments and said, 'You were the young lady there. I recognize you. How did you find me?'

She unearthed the photograph from her handbag, put it on top of the bar and he gazed at it for a long time and then he smiled a little and he picked it up.

'I heard she'd died and I wanted to be there, for no reason as it turns out. You are her daughter?'

'No, she never married. I am Lorna Carlyle. I wish you had come to the front and we could have spoken.'

'Nothing left to talk about. I lost track of her when she left here years ago. I wanted to marry her. You're a Carlyle?' He was looking at her very hard now. 'She wouldn't have me, she was convinced old man Carlyle was going to marry her.'

He pushed the photograph back at her and she returned it to her handbag.

'He was my grandfather, I never met him. Did he promise to marry her?'

'I don't know. I do know that he turned her head. I never saw her again after she took up with him. I laughed myself stupid when I heard he hadn't married her. What did she do with her life?'

'She opened a millinery shop in Castle Bank Colliery.'

She thought he was going to laugh again but he shook his head.

'Poor Felicity. Selling hats, eh? What's your connection with her?'

'She brought me up.'

He hesitated and then he said, 'I'd like to hear more about it. There's nobody in. Why don't you stay and have a drink? I'm James Radcliffe.'

Lorna stared at him.

'My mother was Cate Radcliffe. You wouldn't have known her, would you?'

'She was my cousin.'

Lorna wanted to kick herself. She had been looking for her family in the wrong place.

'I was told she came from Northumberland, from the coast.'

'Her mother came from there, her grandfather was a fisherman. Her mother never liked it here, she thought it was a comedown to live in a place like this. She said she never got used to the air and often she would take Cate to visit her family. I don't think there's any of them left now. Our fathers were brothers.'

He gave her sherry and came from behind the bar with a pint of beer and they sat down at one of the little tables which were set to the sides of the room.

'Now I see you better you look very like her.'

'Did you know her husband?'

John Radcliffe took a big sup of beer and only answered her when he had swallowed it.

'Aye. I never liked him.'

'I spoke to the vicar and they said he was a good man.'

'If going to church makes you a good man then he was. He was church daft, he was always there and he liked her staying at home and cooking and cleaning all the time. I don't think she got out from one week's end to the next.'

'But she met my father? At the coast?'

'Aye, I think somebody died and she went back there with her mother for the funeral. It was a huge disgrace when she ran away. I didn't blame her. It was no life with him for a lass like Cate. I heard she'd had a bairn to Shaun. The talk was terrible. She never dared show her face back here and then they both died. People say she got her just deserts but I thought it was hard.'

'Did they know about me?'

'I think everybody did but people pretended because the whole thing was seen as a shocking affair.'

'Don't you think my mother and father should have been buried together?'

'I expect nobody wanted it.'

'And his body was not brought back from Northumberland, it was as if his family didn't want him because of what he'd done and Felicity took me away after that because she was the only person who would. Didn't anybody care?'

'There was talk of an orphanage. In the end I think old man Carlyle paid her to take you away.'

'Then why did he leave me everything?'

'Did he? Well, Shaun was dead and Shaun had been his favourite son as I understood it. His father was heartbroken when he got tangled up with a married woman. He never forgave them for it. Stephen, his brother, was a wastrel, a drunk and a gambler, Shaun was better than that.'

'My husband Ralph is just the same as his father was,' Lorna said with a sigh. 'Did you marry?'

'No. I was so bitter after what Felicity did to me. I wish I had done but I couldn't think well of women after that. Now I have nobody, no children, no family to speak of.'

'Aren't any of my mother's family left?'

'I don't think there are but I can show you the house where she lived with her parents.'

How hurt they must have been, Lorna thought as John Radcliffe called in the barman from the back and asked him to mind things. It was called Berry Edge Farm. He told her it was the oldest house in the area. It stood alone away from the rest of the rows of houses and must have been there long before the steelworks. It was owned by other people now and a woman was hanging out washing in the garden.

'Shall I ask if you can have a look inside?' he offered. 'I know her.'

'It seems so rude,' Lorna said but he had already gone over to speak to her and she said cheerily enough that they would have to excuse any mess they saw but the house was neat and tidy and clean and as she passed through the garden Lorna could smell the washing as it dried.

You went in through the back and there was a long narrow kitchen which had a faint odour of sweet baking and then a step down into the dining room. The other room downstairs was the sitting room and both of the rooms had views way across the valley and they were big wide rooms such as large families of farmers would need. She could almost hear their voices as they sat around the table, having tea after a hard day's work, generations since.

John told her that her mother had been an only child. He remembered going there to play when he was small because he too was an only child. The rooms had lovely wooden ceilings, unpainted, but the wood was exquisite, and she wandered about upstairs for some time, trying to imagine this woman she had never met, wishing that she had any memories of her at all.

She didn't want to leave but this was somebody else's house so she could not linger for too long. In the end she tried to remember how it looked, committing each room to memory as she closed her eyes and then moved to the next and she thought of the cold wind rushing across the fields in winter and how the farmer would go out with hay for the sheep, she thought of what

Christmas would be like at such a place, paper garlands strung across from corner to corner against the ceiling and holly gathered from their own hedges for decoration in the windows.

She thanked the woman and left and John had to get back to the pub so she thanked him too and then she took the train back to Durham. She wanted badly to cry for the happiness which her parents had not known and for how even after death they were not together. How lonely her father must have been before he died, longing for his wife and child, and her mother had disgraced herself and her name for the love of her life, so short-lived. Were people punished for such things in such a way? She hoped not.

Her first inclination when she got off the train was to hurry down to Aidan's office. Somebody was just leaving and Mrs Manners said he had no other appointments that afternoon so she could go in and once she got there she found herself spilling out the story and then bursting into tears.

He was sitting on the front of the desk, having cleared away papers, and now he took hold of her hands and spoke calmly to her.

'At least they found one another and however disgraceful it seemed to their families they lived together and had a child so they must have had some happiness.'

'So little, though.'

'I don't think you can measure happiness like that,' Aidan said. 'Most people never find the one true person who completes them.'

'Do you think there's only one person for each of us?'

'I don't know and the only happy marriage I know of is Ned and Annabel.'

'I suppose if you put it like that then at least my parents had one another.' She thought of Ralph waiting for her at home and was not eager to leave the comfort of Aidan's office but she had to go. She could not help turning back to him and saying, 'I wish things had been better.'

And for the first time ever he put a hand up to her hair and smoothed it.

'It'll be all right,' he said.

It was a terrible lie, she thought.

*　　*　　*

When she got home Ralph was waiting for her, as though he had been waiting to talk to her all day.

'I called the cook because I could see that the house maid's expecting and she said you said the girl could stay here. I never heard anything like it.'

'Didn't you?' she said. 'Why shouldn't she stay here, what is she meant to do?'

'That's not our problem.'

'Isn't it?' She took a deep breath and then she said, 'Have you or have you not – lain with Tessa?'

To her surprise he grinned. 'That's an interesting way of describing it. Everybody's had her. Even Henry. You're so naive, you think you know everything.'

'That is not the point,' Lorna said, ignoring the aspersion cast upon Tessa. 'She has nowhere to go.'

'There's a place for girls like that.'

'Yes, there is, and it's here.'

'She should be sent back to her family.'

'She's not going,' Lorna said.

Ralph looked at her. 'And if I insist?'

She had never thought she would manage to stand up to Ralph in difficult circumstances like these but she had had such a hard day.

'Are you going to insist? What does it matter to you?' Lorna said.

Ralph looked at her and she thought his handsome face was beginning to show signs of dissipation, there were deep grooves in his cheeks such as middle-aged men had and shadows under his eyes.

'What have you been doing today?'

'I've been clearing the shop.'

'You will sell the shop, there'll be money from that.'

'I'm hoping so.'

She thought that Ralph had turned into the kind of man who was ceasing to care where the money came from as long as he had it for his debts and so that he could go on with the lifestyle he cared for so much, a way of living which had enveloped him. Indeed she thought, looking at his pale face, it had suffocated him as no doubt it had done with his father.

She went to the kitchen and told Mrs Routledge, the cook, that she wanted a word with her and the woman followed her into the cold of the little pantry, a room Lorna would never have taken anybody to talk to if she had thought about it properly. She wasn't thinking beyond how angry she was.

'How dare you talk to Mr Ralph behind my back about Tessa?' she said. 'I make the decisions here, I decide who goes and who stays.'

Mrs Routledge looked horrified and afraid and that was a surprise.

'I meant nothing, Missus Carlyle, but she had told me and I thought you and Mr Ralph wouldn't want it to happen here.'

Lorna took several deep breaths and wished she had not said so much.

'I'm sorry, Mrs Routledge, I didn't mean to shout at you, I should have told you that I have said to Tessa she will stay here and have her child.'

Mrs Routledge stared. 'You're really not going to put her out?'

'Certainly not.'

'Well,' Mrs Routledge said.

'You will help?' Lorna appealed.

Faced with this Mrs Routledge seemed to relax for the first time ever in Lorna's presence and said, 'You're nothing like the first Mrs Ralph.' This by the look on the woman's face was a good thing. 'Mind you, when he found her after she died he was taken something fierce.'

'Ralph found her? I thought he was away from home at the time?'

Mrs Routledge looked puzzled. 'Aye, he was. When he got back he found her outside, laying there on the ground.'

'Had nobody realized?'

'It was January and dark days.'

'So he came back early?'

'He'd spent the night in town. He often did that.'

'I see.'

Lorna hesitated.

'Will there be anything else, madam?'

'No, thank you, Mrs Routledge.'

When the cook had gone Lorna went into the little sitting

room and huddled over the fire and tried to remember what Aidan had said. He had said that Ralph was away from home at the time and she had taken that to mean that he was in some other town or some place far away from which he would not be able to return so promptly.

She wondered whether that was what Aidan had believed or whether it was just something he said so that she would not worry. Ralph could have come back early, he could have not left at all. How would anybody know?

There must have been people who knew at the time or would his word be taken as the truth because his family was so important or was it just that the law did not care so very much about women and in any case how would it be proved that a woman had had an accident like that, had done it herself or had been pushed off the edge of the building or even hurt or murdered inside and then thrown off the building?

Lorna felt very sick now. She remembered Ralph telling her that he had only married the woman for her money and now he had done that a second time. The baby had died. Would he have learned to care for Sylvia had it lived?

# Twenty

It was August already, Aidan thought, looking through his office window. How had it happened so quickly? Summer had been a series of days so windy and wet that all the leaves were coming off the trees. The pavements were slithery with leaves which had lost their form and colour.

Things had changed at his house. He felt guilty about not being happy for Bea that she had made a kind of life for herself though he did not think it was what she wanted in the first place. She had ceased to think of a husband and children as her future. He only hoped she had ceased to regret what she could not have and now when he went home she was very often not there.

If she was she stayed in her room, writing, and if she was out he knew that she was at the magazine offices where Annabel Fleming had made a place for her. She looked younger and she dressed differently and his mother complained that she was 'gallivanting'.

'Girls shouldn't be gallivanting all the time, especially at her age, old maids. She should learn to stay at home and put up with her lot. What am I supposed to do?' she complained when he finally reached home that Monday evening.

Monday was always the hardest day in spite of the fact that very often he worked Saturdays and Sundays. Somehow there was nothing else to do now that Bea was not at home or so caught up with her new friends that her working or social life took her away.

He missed her but he missed also the way that she deflected his mother from him. Now there was nothing to save him from the conflict. His mother would listen for him coming home and stomp downstairs and berate him for the lateness of the hour and bemoan the fact that he had missed dinner and tell him he was just like his father and neglected her and talk about Bea disparagingly.

He was so tired of it. He didn't argue, much as his father had not argued. When you spent your days as a lawyer the very last thing you wanted to do when you came home was enter in any kind of dispute and since she was his mother rather than his wife he had little to lose.

Her company or lack of it meant nothing to him. He would listen to her shouting and wait until she had gone and then he knew that he could retreat to his study and Heather would bring him dinner if he was not too late or sandwiches if he was and she had also taken to bringing him a glass of whisky on the tray. After a decent interval when he had finished his sandwiches and the whisky she would bring him another larger glass of whisky.

Really, he thought, Heather was good, and then he thought how good all the people who helped him were and he determined to give them a big increase in wages at Christmas and a special bonus. His father had done that every year and he had carried it on but he would make it extra-special this year.

Unfortunately his mother had not gone to bed and as he was sitting by the study fire instead of working, drinking his whisky and thinking reasonably happy thoughts about Christmas, his mother barged in.

'So that's what you do when I go upstairs?' she said.

Aidan was jolted out of his good mood and he turned on her as his father had never done and said, 'Is there something the matter?' in such a sharp voice that she took a step backwards.

'Your father would not speak to me like that and you are my son. You are supposed to be grateful to me.'

'For what?' Aidan demanded and really, he was amazed at himself because it had been a very difficult day. He had been in court and things had gone badly and he didn't want to get himself into further complications and it was already too late.

'I brought you into this world and I suffered,' she said, 'you have no idea how women suffer over such things and this is the thanks I get for all the nights I stayed up with you—'

'Mother, is there something you want?'

That silenced her. And then she recovered herself and he thought she was looking much better these days, it was a pity he couldn't be pleased about it.

'I want us to move from here,' she said, 'this house is far too small and we have been here all these years. It was your father's choice, I've never liked it and we're due something better. You seem to have plenty of money, you should find us a much better home.'

He didn't like to remind her that he had suggested more than once that they should move after his father died but she said she wouldn't because St Cuthbert's Church was so near. It was strange, he thought, for all his mother and Bea were nothing alike Bea had come to him the previous evening, in a much better mood than his mother was now, and she had said, 'I'm thinking that I might move out, rent a little house for myself.'

He wanted to say to her, half joking, 'Oh hell, Bea, you can't leave me with this harridan,' but it was unfair, he knew it was. There was no reason why Bea shouldn't have a house of her own. She wasn't going to get it through marriage, she wasn't going to have the usual domestic situation, but he knew exactly how she felt, she wanted peace to write in and little rooms to call hers and the arranging of them and perhaps even buying a special chair, curtains, a writing desk – he made a mental note to himself that he was to go with her and buy her a special writing desk and it would be his parting gift to her – and time to choose what she would do and enough space so that she could invite her friends to dinner and he was so glad for her.

'I could rent somewhere on what I'm making.'

'Bea, find a place to buy and I will gladly pay for it.'

'No, I can't let you.'

'It's owed to you for putting up with everything and the way that things have been. Please, find somewhere you want, no matter what it is, and I will make sure you have everything you need.'

She kissed him. She only did that very occasionally and he found that he was pleased he could bring the colour and warmth and pleasure to her face and he knew that she had half believed he would say, 'Please don't go,' but he thought she knew in her heart that he would not stop her.

'I have seen a little house and it looks perfect,' she said, 'but I haven't gone there, just in case.'

'Go and see it.'

'Will you come with me?'

'Of course, if you want me to.'

'I haven't told Mother.'

'I'll tell her.' He wished he wouldn't do that, he wished that he had cared more for his own ease of mind that hers in a way and yet he could not. She had been a good sister, she had put up with their mother for so long and now she was entitled to her freedom.

That Monday lunchtime she had burst into the office, she had the key and so he had gone with her to see the house and it was charming, it was just right for her and he told her so and he tried not to think what it would be like when he was left alone with their mother.

It was a little Georgian house in Old Elvet, terraced with neat rooms and a garden which had herbs, sage and rosemary, lavender and thyme. There were chrysanthemums in cream and red, and pinks with their tall pale-green stalks. The grass in the garden was slightly unkempt and held on to it still the remnants of a heavy dew like a million diamonds. Each room had a pretty tiled fireplace and stained-glass windows and from there you could hear the cathedral bells and clock striking and there was the sound of students' footsteps passing by and the happy voices of young people.

He hoped it would not make Bea think of all that she had not had, he didn't think it would. She had so much now, she had made it herself and he wanted to help her as much as he could. He had not seen her look so happy and straight away he had said he would arrange it for her and she had laughed and he had left her there to her thoughts, to the way that she was planning each room, and no doubt picturing herself there.

'We won't need a bigger house,' he said now to his mother. 'Bea is leaving home.'

His mother reacted as though she hadn't heard him, as though she had suddenly gone deaf and finally when he didn't repeat himself she said, 'What?'

'Bea has found a house she likes.'

She stared at him. She almost smiled at the apparent jest and then her eyes hardened.

'Bea has chosen a house for us?'

'No, for her.'

'But she cannot do that.'

'Why not?'

It was the wrong thing to say, of course, he should not have invited his mother to think of reasons why Bea should not and he did not have to listen to them to know, she was unmarried, she was not safe on her own, she was needed here. He took another sip of whisky and sadly realized it was the last and he wished that Heather would bring him another though there was no chance of that while his mother held court in his study.

'She has not sufficient money to rent a house of her own.'

'I am buying it for her.'

She stared so hard he thought her eyes would drop out.

'You have? Why was I not told?'

'Because we knew what your reaction would be, that you would try to stop her.'

'I will go and live with her.'

'You will not,' he said and his mother gasped with shock. 'You will stay here with me. You will go nowhere. Bea is entitled to her life. You had yours,' and he said it so teeth-grittingly low and determined that his mother stood for a few seconds and then she walked out of the room without a word and he could not remember the last time she had lost an argument and that was when Heather brought him another drink and to his pleased astonishment it was even larger than the last and he could not help saying to her,

'Heather, you have a rare gift for measuring whisky,' and she smiled and she said,

'Aye, I know, sir. My father was from Jura,' and she smiled back at him and went out and she shut the door with a little click and left him to the warmth of the smell of the peat of the whisky and to the rest of his evening.

It was several days later when he had a visit from Lorna. He had thought his feelings for her might alter when he could see that she was pregnant with Ralph's child, he had heard that many men lost their desire for a woman who was about to become a mother and the feeling should have increased when she was having another man's child and that man her husband but unfortunately, he felt, it was not so. He wished that he did not feel like this about her because he was sure now that in time he would marry and have a child of his own and shake off the old feelings of childhood and learn to forgive his parents for being nothing more than people.

But when Lorna turned up that day, having written and made an appointment, it filled his morning with joy. It was a bright day, not far off September. The leaves upon the trees were golden with the sun and the branches were softly dark behind them. The sun glinted on the windows of the buildings across the street and the fire in his office burned sweetly, a red-blue glow giving off a hint of applewood as she walked into his office.

He thought she had never looked more lovely, her body big with the child, her hair shone and her face was cream and roses and he had a terrible desire to take her into his arms and hold her against the world. He sat her down and she told him what Mrs Routledge had said about Ralph and he let her tell the story to its end without interruption and then he said slowly, 'If this is so then why didn't it come out at the time?'

'I don't know, perhaps she was afraid of Ralph.'

'Are you afraid of him now?'

She hesitated.

'He isn't the man now that he was then. He's—' She stopped, as though even at this point she would not do the Carlyle family a disservice by speaking badly of her husband. 'He's always drunk and he's got past the stage where he would fight or shout or cause any kind of problem. All he does now is drink and sleep, eat his meals and occasionally go riding—' She stopped again.

'And then he asks you for money?' Aidan guessed.

'Sometimes he does, yes.'

'And you give it to him.'

'If I have it.'

'Or if you say you have it.'

She got up, obviously uncomfortable.

'It was a long time ago that Sylvia died. Perhaps Mrs Routledge didn't see the relevance of Ralph's coming back like that even then.'

'It was all gone into very thoroughly at the time,' Aidan said.

'Haven't you said to me that men get a better deal in the law? The Carlyles were seen as important people – perhaps they were afraid of him.'

'I can't see it.'

'I feel mean to even imagine such a thing when Ralph is little better now than—'

'He forced you to marry him,' Aidan pointed out.

She looked at him.

'What must it be like to care so very much for a building? What must it be like to have such pride in one's name, in one's ancestry.' She stopped there and Aidan, aware of the tension in the room, said lightly,

'Do you know what they say about people who care too much for their ancestry – that they are like root vegetables, most of their importance lies underground.'

That made her smile. 'You think I'm a pregnant woman making too much of this.'

'I think you're absolutely delightful and I adore you.' It wasn't what he had meant to say, he felt sure.

She laughed and then she blushed and then she said, 'Aidan Hedley. You've never said such a thing to me before or I dare say to any woman.'

'And my timing is atrocious and Ned would say that I feel safe here in my feelings because not only do you belong to another man but you're having his child, that I dare not love a woman who is available to me.'

'This is going to sound very vain but I rather thought you had always cared for me, at least a little.'

'I have always been your lawyer.'

'There are worse things for a man to be. You cannot imagine how comforting it is to have someone to run to.'

When she had gone he remembered that more than anything and as the day wore on and he worked it played in his head like a lovely melody.

Lorna was going to the magazine offices and she loved being there best of all and everybody was there. Camille had come into town with her and gone straight there, Eliza was at her desk typing as usual, Bea was making tea and Annabel was reading some new article and they all looked up when she walked in and they greeted her with enthusiasm and Bea gave her tea and she thought how wonderful it was that they should have found a place here together, every woman should have a place of work to go to that she cared for and friends like these.

They had a discussion about the next issue and spent the afternoon deciding on the layout and what else they needed to do but long before the afternoon was over Annabel took her aside and said, 'I've got something to tell you, something exciting that nobody else knows,' and they donned their coats and went out into the busy street.

'What is it?'

Annabel said, 'Ned's father has bought us a house.'

'Really?'

'I have mixed feelings about it. We've been so happy in that little house in Sutton Street and this one is rather grand and on its own so that Tom will have nobody to play with.' She blushed and faltered and then said bravely, 'Ned says we can solve that problem with another child and I think I may be pregnant but it's too soon to say, so I haven't told anybody yet. I daren't risk losing it.'

'You didn't lose Tom.'

'I know but it happens so often, I don't want to jinx anything.'

'I'm so happy for you. Where is the house?'

'That's another thing. I don't know how you'll feel about it, it's Black Well Tower. It's been empty since you moved out and his father just – just went ahead and bought it. He does things like that and Ned was inclined to be angry but I'm so grateful to him because all our money goes into the business and it would be nice to have a lovely house like that for ours. You don't mind?'

'Of course I don't mind. I'm so very pleased that you should have it beyond anybody. I was happy there and I do hope things go well with the baby. You do feel well?'

'Very well. Our children will play together, you aren't so far away and we'll be able to visit, we'll be families.'

Lorna couldn't imagine such a thing, she thought Ralph was beyond it and that somehow they had not had a chance in the first instance. She envied Annabel her life and it was no place to be friends from so she shook off the feelings and they went to the cafe and after that Annabel hesitated and then she said, 'Would you like to go and see it?'

Lorna didn't really want to go and would have given a lot to have got out of it but she couldn't take from Annabel's animated face the joy she felt and besides, Ned and Annabel had made her life bearable in so many ways.

'You have a key?'

'I just got it from Aidan this morning. Did he say anything?'

'Not a word. Always the solicitor.'

'Too much the solicitor,' Annabel said. 'And taking on himself so much responsibility,' and she told her about Bea moving and how generous Aidan had been and Lorna thought how like him that was and she winced, thinking of him living alone with his mother. Would he end up living with his mother for the next twenty years? It was enough to make a brave person shudder.

She did not like to tell Annabel that the very last thing she wanted was to go back to Black Well. Her good memories of it were tainted by what had happened since the night she had gone back to it and found it empty and though she said nothing she thought about Sylvia and Ralph.

Ned went with them and on the way he asked her about the business premises which had been the millinery shop and she thought Annabel was right, he wanted an office in every small town and it would bring to life some of the places and it would mean every scrap of news would go into the newspaper belonging to that place. He explained how it would work.

'The majority of the newspapers would be the same but local events would go on the front page and the different news from different places would go throughout, like the meetings of all the small societies and the football matches would be covered and the sales of work, and births, deaths and marriages of course and there would be local advertising as well as county—' He stopped there because he had run out of breath and she finished,

'So that everybody would buy it in each town because it would be relevant to them. That's very clever.'

'Why, thank you,' Ned said modestly. 'We would keep either one or two members of staff in the office there, local people who knew everybody and they would gather up the news each week and take in the advertising and they would cover local matches and wedding reports and leek shows and whatever else happened.'

He chatted freely until they got to the house and she knew that he had done it deliberately because he was not sure she wanted to be there, whereas Annabel was so very taken with the idea of having this house for hers that she had gone into the kind of reverie which is concerned with furniture and kitchen gardens.

They stopped in front of it. Lorna's heart pounded and he turned to her as Annabel went through the front door and said, 'Are you sure you want to go in?'

She nodded. Somebody had been in and cleaned the place. There was nothing left of the Carlyles, not a piece of furniture, not a smell of game, not a hair of spaniel. It smelled of lavender polish and it had been refurbished to a great extent so that it seemed to her that Tranter Fleming had bought this house as soon as it was unoccupied and had it altered with Ned and Annabel in mind and she wished, as she had never wished before, that she had a father or an uncle, somebody slightly interfering and caring so much as Ned's father did. Ned often grumbled about him but she could tell that they was a huge bond between the two men which would not be broken and she thought how wonderful it must be for Ned's father to have a grandchild.

The floors were new and were oak, the doors also, the rooms were replastered and redecorated and the kitchen was completely new and bang up to date. Annabel crooned over the stove and the new sinks and the kitchen cupboards to hold precious pans.

There were new large fireplaces in each room and there were even new curtains, expensive and swathing the windows, but Ned assured his wife that his father had said she could change anything she wished, this was temporary. Annabel, after an initial little frown that someone else's taste might impinge upon her new kingdom, relaxed and looked at the curtains with favour, which Lorna had to admit were elegant and generous and in beautiful colours according to the rooms, and said she liked them very much though she would of course have to consider the furniture and then she heard herself and laughed.

'Oh dear,' she said, 'I sound like one of these matrons who has nothing else to think about. Do hit me round the head, I'm getting carried away. The house is beautiful, Ned, and your father is more than generous.'

Ned, being a man, insisted on seeing the attics and would have gone alone but Annabel was determined to see all of her realm and wanted to follow so they went up there and it was a different story.

The place was clean but there were boxes and chests which were so obviously not new but someone had not seen fit to get rid of them or even to open them. Tranter Fleming had very discreet help, Lorna decided. Annabel, however, had no such scruples now that the house was hers and opened up boxes and was disappointed to find nothing more exciting in them than extra light fittings and replacements for her new bathrooms should something fail but in the corner in the shadows there was a particularly large chest. Annabel stopped there.

'Oh dear, you don't think it's a body,' she said with a little quiver of laughter in her voice.

Ned opened it and there were all kinds of things which had belonged to the Carlyle family, though nothing they would have wanted to take with them, if they had been of any worth they would surely have gone, Lorna could not help saying, old ledgers with regard to expenditure when someone had been of mind to worry about what was spent and several very dull books on horse-rearing and pig-keeping.

Delving to the bottom Annabel complained about the dust on her gloves and then came up with another book but it was the kind that somebody wrote in and after she had opened it she handed it to Lorna and said, 'I think it's some kind of diary, one of your family no doubt,' and it was of very boring things about the weather and which tradesman had delivered what and there was another much smaller book inside it, blue-leather-covered, the ink faint and that was a real diary though there was not sufficient light to study it.

'May I take it?'

'Oh heavens, yes, anything you like. Would you want this book on poultry-keeping too?' and Annabel giggled.

They went back downstairs and through each room again and Annabel talked of moving in for Christmas and where they would stand the Christmas tree and Ned said he was far too busy to move before then and so was she and eventually they left the house, still talking about this and walked back to town and Lorna slipped the little blue-leather diary into her pocket.

# Twenty-One

Lorna half forgot about the diary, it was such an uninspiring thing, slim and most of it blank, and she merely rifled through it and saw several entries and they were mostly about the weather and how cold it was and she longed for something that had headings day after day and secrets and indiscretions. There was, however, a name at the beginning and it was Sylvia Hope.

She had not known that Sylvia had had such a delightful surname, though of course it was quite common in this area and her house had been Hope House, as though her family owned it and as though they were the kind of people who were optimistic. Hope House, Westgate.

Westgate was miles away in Weardale and she perused more of the diary and discovered that this was nothing to do with anything other than perhaps Sylvia's desire to think back to her childhood. Perhaps she had been very happy there. Lorna certainly wished this so, since she had died young and apparently unhappy.

There were several entries about living at Black Tower and they were good, rather, Lorna thought uncomfortably, like her own first days had been, full of small tales of rides with Ralph and the riding habit she had had specially made – thankfully not the one which Lorna had worn – blue and so fitted and pretty and then stories of parties and dresses and a ball which he had taken her to and how pleased she had been but it was the kind of diary which Sylvia neglected. Months went by with no entry and Lorna found herself rather cross that Sylvia cared so little for noting things down that she would let six months go by and not a single entry and then it was very short, she got up, she dressed, she went for a walk in the garden and what she ate and what she read, if anything.

Three-quarters of the way through the book it all changed.

> I begin to think that Ralph cares nothing for me now that
> I am expecting his child. I thought he would care more, I
> thought he wanted a son. He spends my money.

Lorna's insides gripped at this.

> It is his money, he reminds me, it is rather our money but
> he takes it for his and I would deny him nothing because
> my parents wanted me married so very badly, I thought I
> would not marry, being thirty.

Thirty, Lorna thought, how very old to be married and how very
much older than Ralph she had been and what a difference it
would make.

> I miss them though it seems they do not miss me, they talk
> of how pleased they are that I am living in Durham and
> mistress of my own house and how they will come to visit
> when the child is born as though I were a hundred miles
> away. They seem not to want to come here nor do they
> invite us and I miss it, I miss the little town I love so much
> and my friends.
>     Nobody ventures near but I know now that the Carlyles
> have a certain reputation and people are afraid. I did not
> know this, I was so naive and I thought my parents were
> but I can see now that they wanted rid of me, I was nothing
> more than a burden, an unmarried daughter, now they can
> speak of me with relief to their friends, for I have a husband
> and a home and I am gone away.

Lorna felt such sympathy for Ralph's first wife that she stopped
reading at that point. It was true, she thought, of many families,
they were ashamed when their daughters did not invite eligible
suitors, would rather have them married to men like Ralph than
be left at home, unwanted and a burden on their families. Perhaps
they did not know what he was like, or rather they turned a
blind eye and were grateful and Sylvia would see Ralph as handsome and careless and passionate and he was all those things.
    The next entry was months later.

I am so very unhappy, I long for my room which looks out over the little street of the village and from where I can see how the houses go up at the sides of the valley and I long to lie in my bed and be young again and listen to the sheep and the wind and feel safe at home with my parents. I cannot believe I ever lived so freely.

The house that I have now is large and has so many rooms and I am indeed mistress of it except that no one heeds me. Ralph is master here and he no longer wants me, I do not think he ever really wanted me and why should he? I was never pretty and Ralph is young and handsome and black-haired and I did worry from the beginning that it was my money and not me though he reassured me.

He does not do that now, he goes to town and when he comes back, late and drunk, I can smell other women on him, not just perfume but baser smells, the very scent of their sex and I wish to God that I could go home again and hear the wind on the tops and be wanted there. Now I am wanted nowhere and I am having his child and I am already fat and he dislikes it. It did not occur to me that a man could dislike a woman who was having his child, I thought it would please him.

How wrong I was. Some men, I have discovered, do not like mothers or motherhood, they wish for women to be slim and virginal and for it to be forever the first time so motherhood does not fit, will not do. I think these men would like boys if they could have them, they want someone slim and tall and not showing any signs of womanhood like plumpness or having breasts or hips. If it is boys they wish it is cruel in them, both to boys and to women.

How can men hate women, and yet they seem to? What do we do which is so offensive? My cousin, Amy, has gone to be a nun. I begin to think she has the right of it. To give oneself to God seems so clean and so easy and a cell could not be worse than this.

The next entry was dated much further on and Sylvia had given birth.

Oh God, Ralph has his son but I fear he will not live and I do not think I will be long after him. No one comes to me, nobody cares. Camille has tried to be good but the men, I think they keep her from me, they do not wish for us to see one another as anything other than rivals and she is beautiful. Her beauty has kept us apart and they have been glad of it.

Last night I thought my son would take his final breaths, I listened and listened for each one and they were strained. The doctor came but what does he know? He is not a woman, he does not understand what it is to give birth and he mutters the things which he thinks Ralph wants him to say so that he will be paid. He keeps saying that all will be well.

I think he fears Ralph, he does not like to say there is anything wrong with my son's strength and it is almost gone from him and mine is nearly there too. I think of nothing but of being home again, of being in the hills, in the dales, of being a child and running through the village and people calling my name with joy. I wish so much that I could go back there, I can feel the wind on my face and the sweet breath of the horses as they stand by the gate in the field and wait for me to bring them apples from the orchard behind the house.

The next entry was several days later.

The worst has happened. My son is dead. Ralph blames me. Of course it would be my fault. His part in this was nothing. He wants a Carlyle, he wants an heir but he does not own this place and he does not own the place he cares for so very much. I fear that Snow Hall will never be his. Was this all our son meant to him? He rants and raves and always it is 'your son' and indeed the child was all mine because he must have known how short would be the child's life upon this earth and he does not care. I begin to think he cares for nothing but himself. I have never felt so alone. Ralph did not love me from the beginning and though I hoped, I did not love him either.

I was very taken with him because he was young and he knew so much about women – how stupid was I, to think that was a natural thing when it was not, he knew so many women and I have no doubt that he will know so many more in this way while knowing nothing of importance about them, their hopes and dreams, their needs and desires, it is all nothing beside his own self and he is like many other men thinking that women are not real creatures but beneath them so that they are not to be thought of at all except for breeding. How can he know how cruel it is? God must be male or how could he have designed a world in which one sex has all the advantages and the other all the trials?'

The last entry ran,

I want to live. I want to go back to the dale and to the house where I was born even though my parents seem not to wish me there. Perhaps a little cottage of my own, somewhere they cannot see me. I might find a place for myself in another town but I know where my heart lies, it is the house up the lane, with the waterfall, with the garden beneath, the water-fall hidden in a dark shadowed place around a bend and the garden under it and the house nobody's but mine, so that no one can find me, no one would know that I have failed, that I have not done what my parents and my husband wished me to do. I will think of it tonight, go to sleep with it in my head so that my dreams may bring me release.

When I sleep from my torment my dreams are sweet such as they never were. It is strange but when I was happy my dreams were frightening but now that I have nothing left my dreams urge me on. My window is beautiful with ice patterns. When I go over to it I can trace them with my fingers, they are so exquisite and none of them is ever alike. How can God have fashioned such things and yet done nothing for women? He leaves us here, bereft and so alone.

No clue then as to what happened, Lorna thought, yet enough for her to worry, enough for her to want to go to Weardale, enough for her to worry about her own safety and yet Ralph came to bed and he was not a man who would harm anybody, he was not even a man any more, he merely existed, he smiled and pulled off his clothes, he got into bed and slept and he snored and he snuffled and he turned over once or twice and she thought that in some ways it had been just as hard for him as it had been for Sylvia.

He had so much to lose and although he did not know it was already gone. She felt responsible and then she thought down through the years and it was so hurtful. Sylvia and Ralph had no son, he had died and Sylvia had died too. Was it grief? Was it murder? Was it Ralph's grief?

# Twenty-Two

The weather turned stormy with perpetual sideways wind and lashing rain so that the roads were awash and both Lorna and Ralph were stuck at home a good deal. She was too tired now with the weight of the unborn child to trudge to the office and Ralph sat by the fire and drank brandy and slept for a long time in the afternoons.

She still had the running of the household but she had put so much time and energy into it that there was not much to do. The house was weather-tight and warm, big fires blazed in every room.

One night when Lorna had gone thankfully to bed there was a knocking on the bedroom door. She had not realized that she had been asleep but she stirred, felt Ralph sleeping on beside her and got out of bed, clutching a wrap around her as she went to the door. It was Mrs Routledge in her nightclothes.

'Tessa is taken bad, I think the baby is coming,' she said and Lorna put on a robe and went to Tessa's room and the girl was crying and clutching at her insides.

Luckily the rain had stopped, the night was fine so she sent one of the men on horseback to the town to get Dr Menzies. It seemed a very long time before the doctor arrived but when he came she felt the responsibility slide from her.

'You must go back to bed, this is not the place for you or we'll be having two births and yours is a little longer yet.'

She would not go and abandon Tessa, who had such a hold on her hand that she doubted she could leave, but it was not reassuring to go through the birth of Tessa's baby. It was so very painful and lasted so very long. The sun rose clear and yellow in a pink sky which Mrs Routledge said she was sure meant more bad weather and Tessa suffered. The doctor was calm and gave advice and reassured Tessa in his soft Scottish tones and yet the baby did not arrive. He said first births always took a long time, there was nothing to worry about, it was all perfectly normal.

Camille brought them food and cups of tea and bustled about since she could do little to help and even this was comforting but it was mid-afternoon before Tessa's baby made its way into the world. By then they were all very tired and Lorna had wiped Tessa's sweaty brow so very often that it had become automatic.

The baby was a cross red slippery little thing which Lorna thought horrid for the first few minutes but later when it was all finished, when Tessa had become much calmer and the doctor wiped his own freely perspiring face for the umpteenth time and pronounced that all was well, the baby looked more human although crying in a way Lorna found ear-splitting and it was a little boy.

At that point Lorna envied Tessa. She had come through the birth, hard though it had been, and her baby was perfect. She took the small creature into her arms and Lorna realized that once you had had a child your life was never the same again. The other good thing about it was that Dr Menzies was calm and competent and since he was her own doctor it made her feel better about the ordeal that was to come. He even turned to her and smiled and said, 'You did very well for Tessa, she's lucky to have you as a mistress. Many a woman would have thrown her out to fend for herself in such circumstances.' He sighed and then he said, 'Men would ever blame women for these things as though it were nothing to do with them and their wretched worse selves,' and she thought if he had not been so tired he probably would not have said such a thing but she liked him even better for it and thanked him and told him his bill would be paid straight away and he laughed and said, 'Perhaps you should wait until we see the next bairn into the world,' and he nodded at her rounded front.

Camille insisted on Lorna going back to bed. Lorna felt that somebody should inform Ralph that he had a son. It was not a task she relished but she went to lie down and slept and mid-evening he came yawning into the bedroom, smiling the smile she had grown used to, he was already drunk but he was harmless that way. He did not mention the child and she wondered whether that might be from some kind of delicacy and then laughed at herself, Ralph had no delicacy.

She bathed and dressed to go down to dinner and still he had said nothing, just sat about the room, going from the window from time to time as the night was still, the stars were out and there was a crescent moon.

'I can never remember whether it is a new moon when it points that way or whether it is the end of the old moon.'

'Did you see the baby?' Lorna managed.

'Look at it, Lorna, it's the prettiest moon we've had in days.'

She went to him.

'Have you seen the child?'

She had his attention now.

'Camille told me.'

'You haven't seen him?'

'Women's work,' Ralph said. 'I did hear him. Dear God, what a noise.'

'That is your son,' she said.

Ralph looked at her.

'So you keep telling me.' He looked at her, said nothing for a moment and then smiled a smile she didn't like but she had become used to. There was no such thing as a proper smile from Ralph any more, the drink had seen to that. 'It could be anybody's. That girl has seen a great many ceilings,' and he laughed at his joke.

'She says it isn't so.'

'Well, she would, wouldn't she?' and Ralph changed for dinner and then they went downstairs.

The weather softened. Lorna had tried to talk herself out of going to Westgate. She didn't know why she wanted to go so much, she told herself that it was curiosity and such was always idle and she tried not to peruse the diary, looking for clues. As to what she was looking for she pretended to herself that she didn't know and she knew also that she ought to have gone to the office when she was able but she didn't, she made sure that she caught the train mid-morning out of Durham station and it took her on to Bishop Auckland and after that she found herself heading towards the dale.

The rain lingered there but it was only on the tops and in the shadows beside the hedges and everywhere in the country she enjoyed seeing the animals. Sometimes there was the flash of brown and gold when a pheasant strode across a field. Horses were standing looking over gates as though something more interesting might be occurring elsewhere and people walked their Labradors and spaniels on the country roads not far beyond the railway line. Sheep littered the fields and stone walls broke up the landscape and she wanted the train to go on and on and never to stop, she liked the rhythm of it, she liked how she was getting further and further from Durham and away from Ralph and from the responsibilities which she seemed to have to shoulder alone.

Westgate was a place she had not been to before and when she got there she realized how tiny it was. She thought back to what Sylvia had said of the house where she was born and when she asked a woman in the street about the house with the waterfall she pointed just out of town.

'Do they still live there?'

'Mr Hope, he lives there. They took his wife off,' and having thought she had said too much by her look, the woman hurried past and was gone before Lorna could think of anything more to ask.

She took the winding lane that had been indicated. It was tiny with stone walls on either side and fields beyond and it went on and on for so long that she began to think she must have the wrong way though there had been no turnings off. Eventually the lane twisted to the right as well as straight on and there was a sign, a good solid sign which read 'Hope House' and she continued.

It was a pretty house, in the local grey stone, and stood apart from the village as though the people who owned it were a cut above and lived beyond the rest of the village. It was neat and square and had gardens all around it. She took the path to the front and knocked tentatively upon the door and after a short while a young woman came to the door and Lorna enquired for Mr Hope. She gave her name and then the young woman went to ask and after another short while she came back and ushered Lorna inside.

It was dark, the walls and the floors, and she was taken into a room which was large, the walls were covered in books and before a big fire sat a middle-aged man. He got to his feet.

'Mrs Carlyle. I am Mr Hope. I trust I can be of service.'

It was a polite enquiry and Lorna barely knew what to say.

'Do sit down,' he said, seeing the state of her.

'I don't want to disturb you, sir, but I am Ralph Carlyle's second wife and I – I found Sylvia's diary and I thought that perhaps you would wish to have it. We moved – a while ago and some friends bought the house where Sylvia and Ralph had lived when they were married and we found this in the attic.'

He looked at the little blue book as though it could bite him and she felt guilty for having offered it to him when if he read it it would show how unhappy his daughter was and how she felt her parents had wished her into the marriage. He did not take it.

'I don't think it would help me to own such a thing,' he said.

Lorna sat down reluctantly and wished for the first time that she had asked Aidan to go with her because she did not know how to conduct this and he would have known.

'Did you see her much after she married Ralph?'

He looked hard at her.

'If I may be frank, Mrs Carlyle, I did not see much of anyone in those days. My wife was taken ill and the nature of it was such that I wanted to go to Durham and see how Sylvia did but I had no time.' He looked down and so sorrowfully that Lorna wished she had not come. 'She went mad, you see. I tried to keep the knowledge from Sylvia. People here, they would cross the road to get away from us. It was not a gentle thing, it plagued her, it made her weep, she could not see any way up, she could not get beyond the melancholy state of herself and she was so ill, so very very ill.'

He said nothing but Lorna waited and when she heard the fire crackle he said, 'People do not understand, they think when they have a bad day, when they have low humours, that it is the same thing, they do not know what it is like. I had to lift her out of bed, I had to feed her. It was as if the storm clouds had come inside the house and settled upon us.' He paused there and then he looked directly at her, it seemed to her for the first time and he said softly, 'Sylvia had it too, the melancholia. They may call it what they will. All I know is that it is a curse and some people would die rather than endure it.'

Lorna felt an icy blast in the room despite the fire and she knew it for despair.

'We hoped that if Sylvia married she would reach beyond such things. We wanted her to be happy, we wanted to get her beyond the dale, beyond the fields and spaces and to the town where there were so many things going on that she might be distracted by the happenings in her new life.

'I should have known better but my wife insisted. Sylvia did not want to leave and I very much regretted sending her away. I did not think Ralph Carlyle a suitable husband for one of her disposition but there are few suitors in such a place and Sylvia's grandmother had left her enough money to make her attractive to such men.

'I have shuddered since at the course I took. What else might I have done? We both wanted her to get away, we tried so hard. I do not think that she was happy. I do not deceive myself. We did the best we could and my wife, knowing what misery was hers, she did not want it for her daughter. She wanted so many other things. When Sylvia died she gave up and now—'

He stopped there.

'Nobody understands and now my wife has nothing to live for, you see, and she has gone down into the black depths and she does not come back again and I am left. I try to understand but I do not. I want her to be the woman I married, I want to shake her, shout at her, redeem her somehow but it will not do.

'I am left here with the house which has been mine for many years and which my wife loved so very dearly. She loved the waterfall, she loved the sound of its splashing day and night and the darkening of the stones over which it flowed. It was as if the very water kept her sane. Now it feels like a torment, yet I cannot leave it, we were so happy here once. I miss Sylvia. She was my only child and so dear and I loved her. They are both gone from me now.'

He was silent after that and in time made polite enquiries as to when she would become a mother and seemed so pleased for her.

'Parenthood, no matter what comes after, is the best joy,' he said, 'I trust you will find it so.'

She thanked him and brushing off his enquiries of whether she had eaten and if she would like tea and cake, she left him there and as she did so she heard the waterfall gushing with the recent heavy rain and the ground absorbing it and she thought of Sylvia tracing the icy pattern on the windows at Black Well and she could not resist following the narrow path with stones laid through the dark shadows of the trees and bushes until she came at last to the waterfall and it was a shock because it was so high and it was a curtain of water, she could see inside it and it splashed and fell and small birds flew at this side as though they owned it, almost dancing within its light.

She thought they were kingfishers, their wings were peacock-blue and their necks red, and their colours smudged and shimmered and created light and movement beyond the gleam when the sun suddenly came out and made a rainbow. There was a wooden bridge at either side of the waterfall and there they seemed at home and there the water was contained and went into the land, above it caves, formed over centuries, water from the fall dripping and dripping, slowly for years and years, beyond men's time, beyond a dozen generations.

Lorna went home, chastened, guilty, thinking of the man by his fireside. What did he have to look forward to? She did not notice the views on the way back and fittingly somehow it rained and the rain with a wind behind it fell upon the train windows in a kind of slanted tear which ran and ran beyond the edge of the train window. She did not know where it went from there, she did not much care. The little farms, the tiny towns, the fields and stone walls and the river swirling its way toward Durham could no longer be seen and did not interest her. She reached Durham station and all she could think of was to get to Aidan.

It was early evening by then, she did not realize until she bolted into his office to find that Mr Gray and Mrs Manners were about to go home. She apologized and Aidan came out of his office, no doubt hearing her voice, and urged his staff to leave and when they had gone he sat her down by his fire and he said, in ever-patient tones, 'What on earth have you been up to now? You should be at home, resting.'

She told him about Tessa's child, she told him about her visit to Weardale and her meeting with Mr Hope and he sat and he looked pensive before the fire, his young face full of concern, and when the tale was finished he glanced at her and then he said, 'I suspected it.'

'Why didn't you tell me?'

'There was no evidence. How do people know such things?'

'Poor Mr Hope. His wife and his child.'

'It's very sad.'

'You believed, then, that Sylvia killed herself?'

'I thought it was possible but—'

'But with Ralph as a husband—'

'Lorna, Ralph has never knowingly hurt anybody physically. The worst that could be said of him is that he is dissolute.'

'He made me marry him.'

'He frightened you into it, yes.'

'But he meant me no harm, is that what you mean?'

'I believe Ralph would do whatever was necessary to gain what he wanted.'

'Then perhaps he did kill Sylvia?'

'I think you shouldn't go back to him.'

'Because he's dangerous?'

'Because he drinks, because he has no care of you. Please, stay here, put up with the monotony of my mother and me, just for a little while, in case we are right.'

'I cannot leave. I cannot go because of Tessa, because of Camille, even because of Mrs Routledge. It is my duty to be there.'

'Then I will come with you.'

'No.' She looked him oh so steadily in the eyes. 'I have to do this my own way.'

'Lorna, I cannot guarantee your safety.'

'When did you ever have to? It is my house – I know, I know, you own it but it is mine and Ralph's and the home of all the Carlyles for so long that it could never be anything else. I'm sorry, I know that you feel differently but it is mine and my ancestors' and for hundred and hundreds of years it has been ours and in some way, no matter who owns it, it will always be and I will not abandon it, no matter what.'

He sighed. He put her in mind of Mr Hope and yet not, because he was so young and she was so thankful.

'Very well then but I will take you there and the minute you feel that it is not safe you will come to me. Promise me.'

She promised because she knew that it was the only way that she could get from him but she needed to go back.

He saw her as far as he could and as far as she would let him and then she turned around and she was aware of Snow Hall and she knew that it was all to do with what had gone and what was yet to be and it was, yes, it was to do with the Carlyles, all the Carlyles that had been before her were somehow urging her on and all those yet to be born and Tessa's child, so newly born under the roof that it felt good. Tessa's son was a Carlyle, whatever the circumstances of his conception.

It didn't matter what Ralph said, it didn't matter whether it was his son, or his brother's son or indeed any man's, it was the woman who mattered, it was the fact that Tessa had borne her child at Snow Hall, that she had grown with it, borne it, suffered for it and taken it to her breast there and that was what mattered. The women made what was and what would be.

When she went back to Snow Hall everything was as normal and she and Camille sat in the room she loved best with the Delft wall tiles and she told Camille about what she had done.

Camille thought back to what had happened.

'The child was damaged, well beyond help and she could not bear it and neither could I somehow. I had wanted a child so very much and neither of us seemed able to have one.'

'And Ralph?'

'He came back, he made such a noise. He was never an easy drunk, you know him well. The child was dead and he was easing the hurt with brandy. He came back and found her.'

'Were you there?'

'No.'

'So you don't know how long he had been there?'

'No, I heard his cries. I went to him and she was lying there on the ground and it was icy, bitter and cold. She had gone to her death, whether or not she meant it, whether or not they had argued and he had pushed her or somehow lost his temper and thrown her out there. I wish I could tell you more. In a way the information you found makes it worse, makes it so much more difficult. How can anybody ever know what happened?'

They sat there over the fire in silence for a little while and then quite suddenly Lorna felt different and then her waters broke. Camille took her upstairs to bed and sent for the doctor.

He came but he told her that it could be some hours before

anything more happened and it was, there was nothing to do but wait and in time, but oh God, when the pain began it was so awful. Was childbirth always like this? she wondered. If it was then women would cleave to men no more. My God, it went on and on. She was hot, the sweat ran, the pains had stopped being something at intervals and ran into one another like colours. Somebody was screaming. Camille was placing a wet cloth upon her forehead and the doctor in his Fife voice was proclaiming that all would be well and she told him that he was in jest, that he did not know what this was like. And then, after several black eternities, she heard a cry and it was her child.

Oh God, a child. It was not hers, it was nothing to do with her, yet they cast it upon her and said it was and then she looked clearly and thought, my God it is.

The warmth, the skin, the peachy smell, the wonder. It really is mine and then they took it away and she was at once bereft and she knew in those seconds that when that child was from her in any way for any reason for the rest of time that she would feel less. It was nature's way and how cruel. Never to be free, never to know a quiet mind. No mother has ever had such, she thought. And yet it was the magic of devotion. Could you call it love? It was slavery, gibbering stupidity, the urge always to be there. You could not better it, you could not make it worse.

Her child. Her beautiful, beautiful child, smelling of ripe peaches, the orchard, the long summer grass, the warm wind over the wheat, the beginning and the end. Her wonderful, wonderful daughter.

Camille was first to come back in when the doctor had gone. She had been there throughout and such a good help. Lorna apologized for squeezing her hand so much that it hurt but Camille only laughed and said it was of no consequence. Camille was now bright-eyed with envy and admiration.

'We'll share her,' Lorna said and Camille nodded and took the baby from her.

'Will you send Ralph up to me?'

Camille hesitated.

'Has he been told that the baby is a girl?' It was hard to ask the question but it had to be said.

'I think the doctor would tell him on the way out. Mrs Routledge wants to know if you are hungry. You must be, and exhausted.'

'I can't eat or sleep until I've seen Ralph.' It was only midday, surely he was there and could not be drunk already.

Camille hesitated again. She tried to hide the concern by looking down at the baby but when Lorna said her name she turned to Lorna with dismay

'He left the house after the doctor.'

Lorna had been afraid of this, that Ralph would not even pretend that the baby was what he had wanted, that everyone in the household would be aware of his disappointment and she felt sure they would be disappointed for him because he had no legitimate son for the second time.

Lorna managed to drink a cup of tea, Camille took the baby downstairs to show her to everybody. Lorna turned into towards her pillows and tried not to cry. It was not fair to the baby to come into this world and feel that she had already failed yet many women had to face such prejudice. In the silence Lorna fell asleep. When she awoke she heard the door.

'Ralph?'

'No, it's me.' Aidan came into view, strode to the bed. 'I heard in town. How are you and how is your little girl?'

He sat down, took hold of her hands, and she was so relieved that he was there she began to cry. She assured him that all was well. Camille brought the baby in to be admired and gave the child into his arms and for the first time since she had gone into labour Lorna felt safe. This man would shield her child as he had shielded her.

He had been there a few minutes when the thing Lorna had begun to dread happened. Ralph came in just as it began to rain outside and the day darkened.

'Hedley. What are you doing here?'

'Visiting,' Aidan said levelly, as he gave the child back to Camille. He got up and offered a hand which Ralph looked at. 'How are you, Ralph? Congratulations. You have a lovely child.'

Ralph glanced over at Camille.

'Take the brat away,' he said.

He had not even looked at the baby. Lorna knew how weak she was when the tears welled up in her eyes straight away.

Camille didn't go but he said, 'Get it out of my sight,' and then she went. Lorna heard the door and when she had gone he said, 'Even Tessa has bettered you. If we aren't careful a little bastard will be heir to this place.'

Lorna swallowed the tears and very quickly brought a hand across her eyes as Aidan said, 'I don't think that will happen.'

'What do you know about it?'

'Nothing,' Lorna said hastily. 'There is plenty of time, Ralph, we are young.'

Ralph shook his head.

'That's what Sylvia said when our son died, that we had lots of time and then – do you know what I did, I prayed to God that he would take her and leave me with my son.'

It was as this point that Lorna realized how very drunk her husband was, he would never have said such a thing in front of Aidan had he been even remotely sober. Ralph smiled bitterly. 'He thought I was too bad a man to have either. Perhaps it is a curse on me and now all I have is a legitimate female child. Like the world needed more women. Why don't you take it away, Hedley, give it to your sister? It's the only way she's ever going to get one.'

'Aidan, no!' Lorna tried to get hold of his arm but he was too quick for her.

'I will,' he said, 'I will take the child and Lorna too since you don't appear to want to look after either.'

'You always wanted her right from the beginning, didn't you?' Ralph said. 'Lorna could never have married a milksop like you. She's a Carlyle through and through. She would have grown bored very quickly. She hated being in your house even for a short time, how could she ever go back to living with you and that harridan of a mother in that awful little hencree which was all your father could ever afford? You have no breeding. You could never say that your family had lived on their own land for a thousand years. You have nothing, you're just a little tin-pot lawyer, like hundreds of others.'

'Aidan.' Lorna could hear her voice, quivering and watched the restraint as he stood there. It was as though she drew him back with speech.

'Go on,' Ralph urged him, 'ask her to go with you. She won't do it.'

At that moment Camille came back with the baby, who was screaming.

'She's hungry,' she announced. 'Why don't you gentlemen go downstairs to the sitting room?'

'Oh no, we're not having that,' and as she passed him Ralph took the child from her.

Lorna got out of bed more quickly than she had moved in her life. She didn't know if he even knew how to hold a baby. Had he ever held his son and would that make things worse?

'Give her to me.' The weakness made her legs wobble, she was not sure whether it was fear for the child or because she had given birth only a few hours since. She felt herself sway.

'Why?'

The baby screamed louder than ever in Ralph's careless arms. In seconds he crossed to the window and pushed the top window down. Lorna didn't know what to do. She was so afraid of what might happen now. She wanted to scream with terror.

'You're just drunk,' she said, 'you would never hurt a child.'

'Is she mine?'

'Of course she's yours.'

'What about him? Did you sleep with the tin-pot lawyer?'

'Of course I didn't. Give her to me, Ralph. If anything happens to her I will go from here.'

'It doesn't matter. Tessa has my child, he's really mine. You're just to keep, you and your daughter.'

As he eyed her Aidan made a grab for the child and because Ralph had no good hold on her he took her.

Ralph stared. 'Give me the child.'

Aidan didn't speak but as Ralph watched him he began to move slowly back further into the room.

Ralph eyed him. 'Give it to me or I swear I will kill you.'

Aidan moved further back and then stopped in the centre of the room and that was when Ralph took a small silver pistol from his inside jacket pocket. It didn't look as though it was real and in fact for a few moments Lorna thought it must be some kind of joke, it was a toy, a very short barrel to it, and then she realized that Ralph meant it because he was so drunk and angry, he was beyond control.

Aidan gave the child to her as she moved instinctively forward but he made sure that she was behind him before he delivered the child into her arms.

'That's typical of you, Hedley,' Ralph said.

She gave the baby to Camille and tried to move back in front of him but he pushed her hard, he hurt her in doing it so that she cried out at the grip and then fell to the ground, which was what he had intended all along, she knew. She was so very weak.

'Oh please don't,' she begged but her plea was lost when the gun was fired. One moment Aidan was on his feet and the next he was on the floor and in the report Ralph lost his balance and crashed into the window. There was a terrible splintering of glass and wood as the window fractured and broke and he fell, with barely a cry, on to the hard paving beneath as the gun went off again. There was a stone statue below the window which broke his fall.

Lorna was reduced to whimpers, she could not believe what had happened. She crawled over towards Aidan as the blood began to flow. She said his name over and over, touching him very delicately as though he could be hurt further.

Camille, with the child in her arms, ran out on to the landing, shouting for help and for somebody to call a doctor. Suddenly there were other people in the room and just as fast somehow down below, she could hear the noise and feel the cold air rushing the room and the floor around him became sticky and she was dabbing at his shirt with the sleeves of her nightgown. She kept calling his name but nothing happened and her voice became croaky and then she was crying and the baby began to howl.

Amid the noise and confusion Aidan opened his eyes.

'Lorna?'

She started kissing him as though it would help and crying and putting her fingers into his hair and then he closed his eyes and lost consciousness.

She insisted they didn't move him until the doctor arrived and Camille assured her that the baby was not hurt in any way and she went on sitting on the floor while Mrs Routledge, who seemed well versed in these matters, staunched the flow of blood somehow.

'You need to go downstairs,' Camille said at her elbow.

'I do not.'

'You have to. Henry says Ralph is in a bad way.'

'No.'

'Go on,' her housekeeper said, 'you're not doing anything here. Go.'

Lorna went out into the rain as somebody put a coat around her shoulders and shoes on her feet. It was still raining, just as though nothing had happened, she thought.

Outside Henry was kneeling. Ralph was still and silent, lying in a heap, the statue had toppled to one side and was broken almost in half. All around her husband the stone had turned crimson in the lamplight. She remembered the second shot but she didn't think that Ralph had been hurt before he fell. The other men moved back when they saw her.

'Ralph?'

There was no answer.

'He's breathing,' Henry said.

She got down beside Ralph.

'Ralph?'

He didn't stir.

'What on earth were you doing?' she said.

And then very slowly he opened his eyes. They were dull as though he couldn't focus.

'Just drunk,' he said. 'Didn't mean it.' After a few moments he said, 'Are you still there?'

'Yes.'

'I can't see you. Hold me.' When she hesitated he said, 'Please, Lorna,' so she did. Henry helped her to lift the top of Ralph's body into her arms.

'I killed her,' he said in a low voice.

'No, no, you didn't do anything of the kind, she's fine. Camille has her.'

'I was so tired of her. She was mad, you know. I just couldn't bear it.'

He stopped there. She waited for him to go on but nothing happened. She said his name again and then again and then Henry said very gently, 'Let me hold him, he's my brother. Let me.' She let go as best she could, her arms ached and were on the verge of going numb and her clothes were covered in bloody patches and her hands were slippery with it.

Henry took Ralph. And then Camille was with her, somehow, with the baby and she urged her back inside.

'It's too cold for you. Come back in.'

'Ralph—'

'Henry will see to Ralph.'

Lorna began to cry. 'Oh God, this is all my fault.'

It was almost spring in Castle Bank Colliery which meant that it was freezing. Icicles hung from the buildings in great spiky lines and the snow was hard-packed on the street and made walking almost impossible. Ned had only that day sent the carpenters to fit up the shop back and front for selling and advertising with a little office at the back where she had once sewn hats but it was well lit now and there were fires in the both rooms, not least because both back and front doors had been open all the day as the men went in and out, carrying and sorting, and the place stank of sawdust and varnish and the floor was covered in various pieces of wood of different shapes and sizes and the men whistled while they worked so that she was afraid the baby would wake up but she didn't, she slept on during the day. She was hell at night and Lorna was exhausted but she was glad at the progress.

The shop already bore the inscription 'Castle Bank Chronicle' across its front outside in big bold black letters with a white background and the carpentry had to be finished that day because the following day Ned had promised desks and chairs and files and rugs and everything the newspaper office would need because he wanted to open it at the end of the week in line with all the other offices, they would open together and his 'newspaper empire' as his wife called it would be complete.

Lorna had the feeling that it would never be complete, that Ned was not the kind of man who would be satisfied with anything. It made her feel rather tired and then she reminded herself that all she had to do was to run this small office here with the help of a junior reporter and together they would make sales and take in the news and it would be something she could do while the baby was still so little without having to have help.

When the men at last left as the darkness fell she was only glad of the respite and locked the place up and went upstairs and had a little time before the baby awoke once again, hungry, but eventually she lay down by the fire upstairs and fell asleep and she was comfortable there, almost happy, did not think beyond what would happen the next day when the furniture arrived and all the small business of the newspaper would begin.

The next morning she swept the floors once again because the wood shavings had got everywhere and mid-morning the men appeared with the furniture and when it was installed Ned appeared too, kissing her and glancing around, taking in everything without saying a good deal.

'How's Annabel?'

His wife had just had their second child, another boy. Lorna remembered that they had dreamed of spending time together with their babies and regretted now that it would not happen.

'Complaining,' he said.

'She has too much to do.'

'She wanted Black Well,' he said. 'Big houses take so much organizing.'

'And you are never there,' she guessed.

'I can't be everywhere,' he said. And then he stopped looking around, he went into the back and then returned and he looked at her. 'When are you coming back to the city?'

'I'm not.'

'I can get somebody in to look after this place.'

'So you keep saying.' She turned her back, walked about and in the silence which went on and on she felt obliged to offer, 'I wrote to Aidan.'

'Did you? Well, hell, I'm sure he's really grateful.'

'I don't want to see him.'

'I think he has understood that for some time now. You needn't be afraid to come back to town because of him, I don't suppose he particularly wants to see you either. It isn't every day you get shot and then ignored.'

'Ralph's dead,' she said and that put an end to the conversation.

She went into the back room again because the baby had begun to cry and Ned stayed in the front, counting the damned files or whatever he was so intent on. Some time later he came through.

'I should be going.'

'Do by all means.'

He hesitated and then after a moment or two he wished her goodbye and went. There was no reason whatsoever for her to want to cry. She took the baby upstairs and sang her to sleep and then some time later when it was almost dusk she heard a banging on the front door. She wasn't going to go downstairs at all, the notice said closed so it couldn't be anybody wanting anything important to do with the newspaper but the banging on the glass of the door went on and on so in the end she cursed under her breath, afraid that the baby would wake up, and she hurried downstairs.

She couldn't see who it was, a tall man wearing a hat and heavy coat against the weather and then he looked at her and she unlocked and opened the door.

'What on earth are you doing here?' she said.

'I can't damned well imagine,' Aidan said as he stepped inside.

Nobody spoke. She wanted to tell him that he couldn't come in but it was too late for that. It wasn't too late to stand there with arms folded and more or less bar the way.

'Ned said you got my letter,' she felt obliged to say.

'Yes, it was lovely. I'm thinking of having it framed. I especi-ally liked the part that told me you were ready to pay me back most of the money so that you could own Snow Hall again when in fact I have most of it anyway and there's no way you can afford to pay me the rest.'

'I will in time.'

He hesitated.

'Are you going to ask me in? I would love to see the baby.'

'She's asleep and I'm very tired, I've had a long day.'

'I'm sure you can spare me half an hour while we talk about Snow Hall.'

'There's nothing to be said. I will pay you what I owe you in time. Henry and Camille deserve to stay there.'

'Did you think I was going to put the rest of the Carlyle family on to the street because one of them shot me? Hardly a good enough reason.'

'Sarcasm doesn't suit you,' she said. She folded her arms more tightly and looked down at the floor because she didn't want to notice how thin and pale he was. This man had almost died to save her child and the debt was so enormous that she couldn't bear the sight of him.

'I'm not here because of that,' she said.

'Aren't you? What are you going to do, turn into Felicity and bring your child up in this godforsaken place like you were?'

'It won't be the same at all.'

'Let's hope to God not. Ralph would turn in his grave.'

'Don't talk about him.' She would have turned away but he got hold of her and not content with that he shook her until she protested, pushing both fists at him.

'He tried to kill me,' Aidan said. 'He might have killed his child and I believe, though you have said nothing, that you know only too damned well that he killed Sylvia.'

'How do you know that?' she said, wrenching away.

'Because it's my bloody job to know it. I can see by the look on your face even now. You were so horrified by it all that you ran away to this godforsaken hole. You tried to run back to something you had hated in the first place.'

'There was nowhere else to go.'

'There was me and my mother and my dreadful little house.'

'Oh stop it,' she said, almost sobbing and she turned from him and put both hands up to her face and one cupped over her mouth in case a sob should escape and once in the room would be the first of so many that she broke down. He didn't say anything, he just waited until she had better command of herself, until she managed, 'This place felt like all I had.'

'You know that's nonsense.'

She could feel the sobs coming up from the back of her throat again and this time they didn't stop and she moved back into the shadows to get away from him but the sobbing got worse and worse and the thing she had told herself she would never say to him found its way past her lips.

'You were almost killed because of me.'

'So I went through all that for nothing? You prefer this?'

She didn't answer.

'You really thought we would live with my mother, that's what put you off. I tell you, my mother wouldn't lower herself to your level. She hates the Carlyles even more since they tried to kill me.

I wouldn't be surprised if she never spoke to you again. I can afford a house, you know, perhaps not like Snow Hall and not even like Black Well but I probably could manage an up-and-down in Waddington Street.'

She shook her head and the sobs were beginning to subside, even though she could see nothing and her face was soaking and her cheeks burned with the fury of the storm.

'Now you're being silly,' she said.

He fidgeted for a few moments.

'You might have come to the hospital to see me. Even my mother managed that.'

'I was burying Ralph.'

'What, for four weeks?'

She said nothing for a few moments, and then she said, 'I feel so humiliated and you—' She managed to look at him.

'I'm better,' he said. 'I love you, Lorna. I want us to be married. It's not going to be very exciting, of course, not like being married to Ralph.'

'Oh, be quiet,' she said.

In the silence which followed the baby began to cry and Lorna sighed and listened as the cries, which were nothing much at first, grew and grew as they were ignored. The baby knew that she was gone.

'What did you call her?' he asked.

'Sylvia.'

She walked slowly through into the back and then she turned in the doorway because he was still standing beside the door. She looked at him and just for another few seconds she ignored the way the cries from upstairs were turning into screams. 'All right then, I'll marry you, but only if you let Henry and Camille and the old people live at Snow Hall. It is the Carlyle inheritance after all.'

'For God's sake,' he said, and when she didn't move he capitulated. 'Oh all right,' he said, 'I will.'

'You will make sure the door is locked before you come through, won't you?' she said and after he nodded and began to take off his coat and hat she went hurriedly up the stairs to her complaining child.